Belville S. Penley

The Bath Stage

a history of dramatic representations in Bath

Belville S. Penley

The Bath Stage
a history of dramatic representations in Bath

ISBN/EAN: 9783337303402

Printed in Europe, USA, Canada, Australia, Japan

Cover: Foto ©Andreas Hilbeck / pixelio.de

More available books at **www.hansebooks.com**

THE

BATH STAGE:

A HISTORY OF

DRAMATIC REPRESENTATIONS
IN BATH.

By BELVILLE S. PENLEY.

ILLUSTRATED.

LONDON : WILLIAM LEWIS & SON,
BATH HERALD OFFICE, 74, FLEET STREET.
BATH : 12, NORTH GATE.
1892.

DEDICATED

BY PERMISSION

TO

HENRY IRVING, ESQ.

PREFACE.

The history of the Bath stage is more than a matter of local interest, for bound up with it are many of the greatest names, and many of the most notable incidents of the English stage. It may, indeed, almost be said to be a history of the English stage in miniature; at least, many of its vicissitudes are here represented, most of the greatest actors of which England can boast have received the applause of its audiences, and it has in its time been the recruiting ground of both the greater and lesser lights of the London stage.

But while it has thus played its part in a larger sphere, its purely local interest is no mean one ; yet no attempt has hitherto been made to place its story upon record, except in a very fragmentary and incomplete fashion, and it is with the purpose and desire that this omission should be supplied, and that the darkness which surrounds one of the brightest chapters in the history of the city should be dispelled, that this work was undertaken, and originally published in the *Bath Herald*.

In consequence of the difficulty in obtaining the necessary material for a complete history of the Bath stage, the author fears that inaccuracies may have crept in, for which he craves the indulgence of his readers.

It has, of course, been in the early part of the last and preceding centuries that difficulties have principally been experienced, and here the valuable assistance of several gentlemen must be acknowledged, particularly that of Major C. E. Davis, who has

been at great pains to supply material for the work, and to whom
the writer is indebted for the extracts from the city rolls which
will be found to form so important a part of the early chapters.
These extracts are now placed before the public for the first time,
and cannot fail to prove of great interest, while they will also be a
valuable addition to local lore. The kind assistance of the late
Dr. Plumptre, Dean of Wells, must also be acknowledged, and
researches made by Mr. W. B. Penley supplied much valuable
information upon several points involved in some obscurity.

Finally, the writer desires to tender his thanks to Mr. Henry
Irving, who so readily and kindly accepted the dedication of the
history of, to borrow his words, "the theatre of my native
county."

B. S. P.

Bath; September 5th, 1892.

CONTENTS.

\

LIST OF ILLUSTRATIONS.

THE BATH STAGE.

CHAPTER I.

EARLY HISTORY.

EARLIEST PERFORMANCES IN THE CITY—MIRACLES, MYSTERIES
AND MORALITIES—STROLLING PLAYERS—PRIMITIVE PLAY-
HOUSES—SECRET OF THE PRE-EMINENCE OF THE ENGLISH
STAGE—NOBLEMEN'S COMPANIES—MODE OF PAYMENT—
VARIOUS RECORDS.

 HISTORY of the Bath stage could not pretend to
completeness without some attempt to trace the
earliest known dramatic representations in the city.
This, however, is by no means an easy task, since
until we reach those years when a building existed
specially used for the purposes of a Theatre, there
is little material from which facts may be gleaned.
One thing is certain, that the earliest performances are only to be
discovered very far back in the history of the city. It is asserted,
and there seems no reason to doubt the accuracy of the statement, that dramatic representations were given as early as the
reign of Edward III., in the form of "miracles, mysteries, or
moralities," that is to say, representations of scripture history, and
that they took place in St. Michael's Without the Walls. The
Reformation proved almost, if not quite, a death blow to performances
of this character, at any rate, they were no longer performed within
sacred walls. Whatever may have been the exact manner of the
dramatic representations which immediately followed, they took place
upon temporary stages erected in the open air, and in course of time
began to assume the nature and proportions of the legitimate drama,
being performed by mimes or strolling players, who, upon certain
particular occasions, such as fairs and festivals, visited some of the
larger cities and towns in the country. Bath was undoubtedly one of
the places so visited, and, according to a writer in an old guide-book,
the company paid the Corporation a stipulated fee for permission to
act their plays within the limits of the Mayors jurisdiction. When,

B

however, the Guildhall (of which the celebrated Inigo Jones was the architect) was built in the year 1626, the players who visited the city obtained permission to give their performances within that building. This was about a century before the erection, or adoption, of any building solely for the purpose of dramatic representations, and during that period no doubt the Guildhall continued to be the principal scene of those performances, though rooms in public inns, barns, and even cart-sheds, were utilised in that respect, and served as the forerunners of the recognised Theatre. Of course there was no attempt at stage effects, scenery, or anything of that description. The surroundings of the actors were of the most primitive kind, and as unrealistic as they could possibly be. Even when theatres were first erected in London (the first public theatre in Blackfriars was opened in 1576) there was no pretence at scenery, nothing but the plain platform, as unlike our modern idea of a stage as it would be possible for two things to be. Curtains were stretched across the back of the stage, through which the entrances and exits were made, and they sometimes bore the name of the scene, but not always even that. What then must have been the surroundings of the actors at the time of which we are speaking, when they held their plays in barns and inns?

There is abundant evidence that even as early as the sixteenth and seventeenth centuries the taste for dramatic performances had greatly developed in Bath, and that the city bore a good reputation in this respect. Nor is this surprising. Bath was already becoming a place of fashionable resort, patronised by royalty, famous for its waters, and, therefore, providing audiences calculated to appreciate and reward the efforts of the performers. The rapid developement of the drama into vigorous life during the Elizabethan era is one of the most remarkable events in the literary history of our country. This has been ascribed to various causes, and particularly to continental influences, but Mr. J. R. Green is probably not far from the truth when he asserts that the real origin of the English drama "lay not in any influence from without, but in the influence of England itself. The temper of the nation was dramatic." There we undoubtedly have not only the secret of the rise of the Elizabethan drama, but of the pre-eminence of the English stage ; "it was," writes Green again, "the people itself that created its stage," and throughout its history it has been curiously influenced by the temper of the nation, and that the public maintains that influence even in the present day, can scarcely be denied. This is one of the reasons why the history of the English stage is so full of interest and affords so wide a scope for the student, both of our history and our literature. To it may also be ascribed the position occupied by Bath with regard to the drama in the sixteenth and seventeenth centuries, during the period when Shakespeare was contributing his enduring works to dramatic literature, and building up for himself a never-dying fame.

In addition to strolling players, against whom, by the bye, a clause in the Vagrant Act was directed,* it had become the fashion for the leaders of society in that day to keep their own companies of actors, who performed under their protection, and travelled in the provinces, visiting certain favoured cities. Naturally, Bath was one of these, and the city records show us that noblemen often brought their companies here to display their talents before the fashionable, and no doubt critical, audience which assembled at the Guildhall to witness the performances. What the plays were which were presented by these actors, what were the merits of the performers, or what the surroundings and circumstances of the stage, there is no actual record, but it is pretty certain that Bath was visited by some of the best players of the time, as is shown by the fact that the visiting companies included the more important of that day. It is alleged, and the subject has recently attracted some attention, that Shakespeare himself was among the players who appeared here, but that is a point which we shall presently consider. The memorable era of the Bath stage is generally said to have been during the latter part of the last century and the commencement of this, but it seems very probable, bearing in mind the difference between the two periods, that Bath occupied very nearly, if not quite, as distinctive a position in the Elizabethan period as in more recent years. The city rolls show that a certain sum was paid to these companies of players, varying in amount, and giving the impression that this payment was made in addition to what they might be able to collect from the audience. To speak vulgarly, no doubt the hat was always sent round, and, indeed, in one or two instances it is expressly stated, where the item occurs in the accounts, that the sum paid out of the city treasury was to make up what "was gathered at the benche," or, besides "that which was given by the companie," to a certain amount, which must have been previously stipulated. As it is, however, uncertain what proportion the payments mentioned in the accounts actually bear to the total sum received by the players it is difficult to ascertain what was the average amount received by each actor. The only instance we can find in which the amount actually received is distinctly stated was on the occasion of a visit of the Queen's players in 1587, when we read that nineteen shillings and fourpence was given "to make it up twenty six shillings and eightpence that was gathered at the benche." Sup-

* Messrs. King and Watts in their valuable work on "The Municipal Records of Bath," make a reference to, and quote this act as follows :—"The Act 39, Eliz., c. 4., forbids 'all fencers, berewards, common players of interludes, and minstrells wandering abroad, other than players of interludes belonging to anie Baron of this realm, or anie other honourable person of greater degree to bee authorised to play under the hand and seal of such baron or personage.' The punishment is, to 'be stripped naked from the middle upwards, and be openly whipped till his or her bodie be bloudie.'"

posing, then, that the company comprised twelve players, it would amount to a fraction more than two shillings and twopence each, but that was probably rather an unusual payment. The largest sum which we find entered as paid to a company of players is thirty shillings, given to the King's players according to the roll of 1604, but as they probably came upon some holiday in connection with the celebration of King James's accession, the amount was, no doubt, exceptional. Next to this the largest payment is about twenty three shillings—paid on two occasions, namely, to Lord Leicester's players in 1587 (23s. 8d.), and to the Queen's players in July, 1589 (23s.)—and the lowest is the small sum of tenpence given to the Lord Admiral's players in 1604. Elevenpence was all that was paid to the Earl of Worcester's players in 1594, and Lord Sheffield's players in 1585 received only two shillings from the city purse, and it does not appear that they repeated their visit.

We must presume that the performances of these companies consisted of the representation of interludes and such dramas as then obtained, and probably the works of the earlier Elizabethan dramatists, such as Nash, Peele, Kyd, Greene, and Marlowe, found a place among them, and later, perhaps, even the far grander works of Shakespeare. Occasionally, we find items in the city rolls of entertainments and performances of a different character. For instance, in 1588, there is a sum of six shillings and eightpence paid to the "Lord of Warwicke's tumblers," and in the following year the Mayor is credited with a sum of ten shillings paid by him "to the quene's men that were tumblers." Two and sixpence is the sum paid to a fencer that performed at the celebration of the proclamation of James I., twice that amount being paid to musicians on the same occasion, and in an earlier roll (1569), there is an entry of cloth to the value of eight shillings and sixpence having been given to "the bage pype players." That there were local aspirants to histrionic fame seems also proved by the payment of ten shillings to "the younge men of our men that plaid at Cristmas," (1601), and again in the following year, of lesser sums to "the younge men of our cittie that played att Christmas," and also to "the children that played at Candellmas." There is also a record of payments to a local playwright, a Mr. Long, a preacher, who in 1583 received 6s. for one play, and 3s. 4d. for another.*

* Municipal Records of Bath.

CHAPTER II.

SHAKESPEARE IN BATH.

DID SHAKESPEARE VISIT BATH?—A DIFFICULT QUESTION—
REASONS FOR INFERRING THAT HE DID — COMPANIES OF
WHICH SHAKESPEARE WAS A MEMBER—THEIR APPEARANCES
IN BATH — PROBABLE DATE OF SHAKESPEARE'S VISIT — AS
PLAYER OR PATIENT?—HIS SONNETS—SUPPOSED REFERENCES
TO THE BATH WATERS—"A MIDSUMMER NIGHT'S DREAM"
AND SOMERSET FOLK-LORE—SHAKESPEARE'S CONTEMPORARIES.

 HERE is no direct or actual evidence that Shake-
speare ever was in Bath, but from the fact that
companies with which he was known to be associated
were from time to time in the city, it is inferred that
he may have accompanied them and have made the
acquaintance of the city in the capacity both of
strolling actor and dramatic author. It would be
indeed interesting and valuable could we establish as a fact what is
now only an inference, but we fear that is impossible. The mystery
which surrounds Shakespeare's life has been pierced only with
difficulty, and there are many points which it is almost hopeless to
suppose will ever be satisfactorily cleared up, and among them must
be reckoned the question of whether Shakespeare ever was in Bath.
If, as is supposed, he journeyed with the companies to which we shall
presently show that he belonged, when they toured in the western
counties, then, taking into consideration the probable attractions of
the city to such a man, and also the fact that among the visitors there
would probably be some with whom Shakespeare could claim friendship or acquaintance, there is good reason to presume, even without
actual evidence, that the greatest of dramatists was familiar with the
Bath of that day. This inference has recently been dealt with by
Messrs. King and Watts, in their local work to which allusion has
already been made, and also by the late Dr. Plumptre, Dean of
Wells, in an article which appeared in the *Contemporary Review*, the
former speaking of the general inference to be drawn from the fact
that the companies with which Shakespeare was connected played
here, and the latter assigning a particular year as the date of a visit
which he considers is supported by outside evidence. He says :—

"I find that in the summer of 1593, the London theatres were closed on account of the prevalence of the plague, and that Shakespeare's friend, Edward Alleyne, afterwards memorable as the founder of Dulwich College, was at Bath in the August of that year. With him were travelling other members of Lord Strange's company of actors—Kempe, Pope, Hemmings, Philips and Brian, with a license from the Privy Council authorising them to play 'where the infection was not.' This was the company to which Shakespeare belonged, and the absence of his name and those of others from the license is naturally explained by the fact that he was not as yet a shareholder in the company. We trace the movements of that company in the course of the year to Chelmsford, in May; Bath and Bristol, in July; and afterwards to Shrewsbury, Chester and York . . . . Shakespeare was hardly likely at that stage of his progress, and with his mind bent on professional success, to have separated himself from his comrades."

Before going further, it would be well to state to what companies Shakespeare belonged. He is believed to have gone to London about the year 1585, or 1586, having joined the Earl of Leicester's players during, or immediately after, their visit to his native town. In September, 1588, the Earl of Leicester died, and his players soon after found a new patron in Lord Strange, and on the death of that nobleman in 1594, they were absorbed into Lord Hunsdon's company, who took the title of the Lord Chamberlain's servants, a title which they retained till the accession of King James, in 1603, when they became the King's servants.* In 1592 and 1593, we have evidence

WILLIAM SHAKESPEARE.

* F. G. Fleay's "Shakespeare's Manual," and "Life of Shakespeare."

that Lord Strange's company were obliged to leave the metropolis in consequence of "a malignant fever, called the plague," having broken out there, which "put a stop to all dramatic performances, which, from the congregation of persons in theatres, were thought to promote and spread the infection."* They then took to a strolling life, visiting certain places—where, however, they are said to have been frequently little welcome to the inhabitants, under the fear that they might convey the pestilence which was devastating the metropolis—and the city rolls show that they visited Bath in both of the years mentioned, as there are entries of payments made to "my Lord Strange's players." Reference is found in Alleyn's correspondence of the visit to Bristol in the August of 1593, which must have either preceded or followed the stay in Bath, but no mention is made of Shakespeare as having been among them. The precept issued by the Privy Council authorised "Ed. Allen, Wm. Kempe, Thomas Pope, Jno. Hemminges, Augustine Philipes and George Brian" to play "where the infection is not, so it be not within seven miles of London or of the Court, that they may be in the better readiness hereafter for her Majesty's service." This list of names, although not by any means comprising the whole of the members of the company, is thought to probably include all who were shareholders therein, and that Shakespeare had not then become a shareholder. Acting upon this assumption, Dean Plumptre considers that he was still with the company in their travels, and, therefore, argues the possibility of his having visited Bath in 1593. This may have been so, but, as Mr. Fleay points out, it was not usual for a whole company to travel together, it being found more profitable to separate them into companies of half-a-dozen, and Shakespeare may have been in company with the other members of the troupe, including probably Burbage, Sly, Condell, Holland and Cowley. There is no documentary evidence either one way or the other. and, therefore, no reason why the Dean may not be correct. Supposing that Shakespeare travelled at all, it seems more likely that he would have been with Alleyn's section of the company than the other, and if so, why then it is perfectly permissible to infer that he was in Bath with his colleagues. Dean Plumptre goes on to argue, with no little ingenuity, the probability that Shakespeare at the same time paid a visit to Wells. That is a point somewhat foreign to our subject except that it may be interesting to notice a fact which the Dean mentions in the course of his argument. The Bishop of Bath and Wells at that date was no other than John Still, famous for his song in praise of "Jolly good ale and old," found in the popular comedy of "Gammer Gurton's Needle," which was played at Cambridge in 1566, "amid a world of laughter."

* Memoirs of E. Alleyn, by J. Payne Collier.

It may have been that Shakespeare neither travelled with Alleyn nor with Burbage, but that he remained in the metropolis for the purpose of quietly perusing his literary studies, and proceeding with his sonnets and poems. His "Venus and Adonis" was published in 1593, and Mr. Halliwell-Phillipps thinks it very likely "that Shakespeare was in town when his manuscript was at the printers, and not impossible that he glanced over the proof sheets, besides superintending the general arrangements of the work." But, even supposing that the theory of Shakespeare having been in Bath in 1593 is not sustained, there are still grounds for believing that the city was honoured by his presence; or, if he did visit Bath in that year, there are also strong grounds for believing him to have done so in 1597. Mr. Halliwell-Phillipps, a recognised authority on Shakespearian questions, has stated that the company in which Shakespeare was, was at Bath some time between October, 1596, and October, 1597, and in his "Outlines of the Life of Shakespeare,"* he says :—

"Early in the year 1597, on New Year's Day, Twelfth night, Shrove Sunday, and Shrove Tuesday, Shakespare's company again performed before the Queen at Whitehall. In the summer they made a tour through Sussex and Kent, visiting Rye in August, and acting at Dover on the 3rd of September. In their progress to the latter town, he, who was hereafter to be the author of "Lear," might have witnessed, and been impressed with the samphire gatherers on the celebrated rock that was to be regarded the type of Edgar's imaginary precipice. By the end of the same month they had quitted the southern counties, and travelled westward as far as Bristol."

The company to which Mr. Halliwell-Phillipps is referring is the Lord Chamberlain's, with which, as we have already shown, the company under the patronage of Lord Strange was amalgamated in 1594. The Lord Chamberlain died in 1596, and his players passed to his son, and were called Lord Hunsdon's players, as they had been previous to 1585, until the second Lord Hunsdon was made Chamberlain, in 1597, when they again resumed the title of the Chamberlain's servants, and continued to be so called until 1603, when, on the accession of King James, the title of " King's servants " was conferred upon them, and Shakespeare was expressly mentioned in the patent. Mr. Halliwell-Phillipps traces this company to Bristol in 1597, and the city rolls confirm his supposition that they may have visited Bath, for in the accounts made up in October of that year, there appears the entry, ' Gave unto the Lord Chamberlain's players, xxs." The same company again visited Bath in 1603, during the celebration of King James's accession to the throne by the local authorities. If Shakespeare did visit Bath, we are inclined to fix either 1597 or 1603 (perhaps both) as the date of that visit, and, although it is unsupported by documentary or direct evidence, it may be fairly inferred that such a visit was made.

* Vol. I., p p 118-119.

Additional reasons for believing Shakespeare was acquainted with the city are to be found in his works, the last two of his sonnets being considered to have a direct allusion to the City of the Waters. In sonnet 153 he says—

> Cupid laid by his brand, and fell asleep :
> A maid of Dian's this advantage found,
> And his love-kindling fire did quickly steep
> In a cold valley-fountain of that ground ;
> Which borrow'd from this holy fire of Love
> A dateless lively heat, still to endure,
> And grew a seething bath, which yet men prove
> Against strange maladies as sovereign cure.
> But at my mistress' eye Love's brand new-fired,
> The boy for trial needs would touch my breast ;
> I, sick withal, the help of bath desir'd,
> And hither hied, a sad distemper'd guest,
>   But found no cure : the bath for my help lies
>   Where Cupid got new fire,—my mistress' eyes.

These lines are so peculiarly applicable to Bath that it is pardonable to infer that the city may have been in the poet's mind when he penned them. As Dean Plumptre says, though doubtless allegorical, it seems to be an allegory resting upon fact, and it bears too close a resemblance to a description of something actually within the poet's knowledge, to be considered a mere coincidence. As we have already remarked, Bath was coming to be a place of considerable repute. Visitors of rank and quality came for the benefit of the waters. It had been alluded to by Spencer in his " Faerie Queen ; " treatises had been written upon its springs, and Queen Elizabeth visited it in 1574 and again in 1590, facts which naturally increased its popularity and prosperity. What more likely then that Shakespeare should have accompanied his fellow-players to a city so interesting, and so much thought of. Again in the following and last sonnet we read—

> The little Love-god lying once asleep
> Laid by his side his heart-inflaming brand,
> Whilst many nymphs that vow'd chaste life to keep
> Came tripping by ; but in her maiden hand
> The fairest votary took up that fire
> Which many legions of true hearts had warm'd ;
> And so the general of hot desire
> Was, sleeping, by a virgin hand disarm'd.
> This brand she quenched in a cool well by,
> Which from Love's fire took heat perpetual,
> Growing a bath and healthful remedy
> For men diseased ; but I, my mistress' thrall,
>   Came there for cure, and this by that I prove,
>   Love's fire heats water, water cools not love.

In each sonnet we have the statement that the writer tried the
"healthful remedy," though without deriving benefit therefrom, whatever his ailment may have been, from which we may infer, assuming
that the mineral waters of Bath are referred to, that his visit, or visits,
to the city were not altogether in connection with the drama, but that
he also came hither to test the efficacy of the spa, and to seek relief
through its reputed medicinal qualities. Dean Plumptre points out
that the sonnets "are more or less pervaded with medical imagery
such as would be natural in one who, with the poetic temperament
which finds parables in all things, had recently been passing through
the experience of illness." We take it, then, that there are very strong
reasons for inferring that Shakespeare did visit Bath, though whether
as a player or a patient, it is impossible to say. The probability,
however, is that it was in the former capacity, and that being perhaps
at the time in poor health, he was induced by the fame of the waters
to try what they could do for him. His visits would probably be but
brief, extending at the most over only two or three days, and, therefore,
it is not surprising that he "found no cure."

In the year which has been suggested as the date of Shakespeare's
visit, 1593, or in the following year, appeared that charming comedy,
"A Midsummer Night's Dream," and Dean Plumptre suggests, as a
matter for inquiry, "whether its fairy scenes may not have been based
on the folk-lore of Somerset, whether the picture of the altered seasons
and disastrous rains, and the sea-born 'contagious fogs,' may not have
been drawn from the scenes which met the poet's eye in the valley of
the Avon in 1593 (a year almost as disastrous as 1594), whether the
prototypes of Bottom and his friends may not have been found in the
provincial performers with whom the travels of Lord Strange's company brought him into contact."

The same difficulty which is experienced with regard to Shakespeare
exists also in the case of his contemporaries ; while it is possible to
infer that many of them must have been in Bath at one time or
another, it is almost impossible to speak with any certainty. We have
already alluded to the visits of Alleyn, and other members of Lord
Strange's company, and another actor whom we may suppose to have
visited Bath is Richard Tarlton (1530-1588), the most popular comedian of his day, and for some years the star of the Queen's company,
a company that paid frequent visits to the city. He was one of those
naturally humorous men whose very appearance was sufficient to create
laughter. It is said of him that "for the clown's part he never had
his equal."

CHAPTER III.

MUNICIPAL RECORDS.

Interesting Extracts—Players and their Payments—The
Civil War and the Commonwealth — State of the
Drama—Bath and Charles II—Commencement of Pros-
perity—Proposals for Building a Theatre.

EFERENCE has already been made to the fact that the
records of the city contain a large number of interest-
ing entries, from which much of the information contained in the preceding chapters has been gleaned.
As we are not aware that these important links in
the history of the Bath Stage have ever been given
to the public in a complete form, their publication
cannot fail to be of great interest and value. They have been collected from the city rolls with great care, and are reproduced as faith-
fully as possible. It may be said by way of explanation that the
financial year extended over portions of two years, consequently it is
difficult, if not impossible, to fix the precise date of the visit of any
company of players. The year and date given in each instance is
that on which the accounts were made up ; the year of the reign is
inscribed upon each roll :—

1577   (Said to be 1567, 5 June, 9th of Elizabeth, but really 1577, 19th Eliz.)
       I My Lords Chamberlaine's players, xiijs. iiijd.
       given to the Erle of Bathe's players, viijs. iijd.
1569   June 8,   11 Elizabeth.
       Clothe for the bage pype players, viijs. vjd.
       to the erle of Worsyter's players, iijs.
1573   May 20,   15 Elizabeth.
       To my Lorde of Worcesester's players. vjs. ixd.
       To my Lorde of Sussex players, iiijs. ijd.
       Given to my lorde of Essex players, xs.
1575   (Roll retained by Churchwardens of St. Michael's).
       Given to the Queresters of Wells, att the Queen's Matie, being
       heare, xs.
1576   June 22,   18 Elizabeth.
       Given to my Lorde Stafford's players, iijs. xd.
       Given to Sir James Fitziame's plaiers, iiijs. ijd.
1577   June 1,   19 Elizabeth.
       Given to the Erle of Worcester's plaiers, ijs. vjd.

1578   June 30,   20 Elizabeth.
to my Lords of Sussex players, vs.
to my Lords of Lesiter's players, xiiijs. iijd.
to my Lords Montegue's players, ixs.
to my Lords Mungeye's (?) players, xijs.
geven to Sir Rugard Boyoe's (?) players, vjs.

1579   June 9,   21 Elizabeth.
given to my Lord Barklei's plaiers the 11th of July, iiijs. iijd.
to my L Charles Hayward's plaiers, iiijs. vjd.
to my L of Darby, his plaiers, iiiis.
to my L Chamberlaine's plaiers, xs. vjd.
to my L Strange's plaiers, vs. ijd.
to my L Barklei's players, vijs. ijd.

1581   June 10,   23 Elizabeth.
given to my lord Sheffyld's players, vs. vd.
given to the lord Strange his players, vijs. ixd.
given to the lord of Darby, his players, xs.
given to the lord Cartleye's (?) players, vijs. iiijd.

1583   June 15,   22 Elizabeth.
to my lord Sheffyld's players, vs. vd.
to the lord Strange, his players, viis. ixd.
to the lord of Darby, his players, xis.
to the lord Cartleye's (?) players, viis. iijd.

1584   June 16,   26 Elizabeth.
to the lorde of Hunsdon's players in June, vijs. viijd.
to the Kuene's (Queen's) players, xxs. vijd.
to the lorde Cartleye's players, xs.
to the Mr. of the Revells players, vs.
to the lord Shandey's players, vs.

1585   June 16,   27 Elizabeth.
To the lord of Oxeford's players, vijs. ixd.
To the lord Dudley's players, xiijs. iiijd.
To the lord of Essex players, vijs. iiijd.
To the lord of Oxeford's players, xs.
To the lord Shiffyld's players, ijs.

1586   June 14,   28 Elizabeth.
Givin to my Lord of Sussex plaiers the xxii of Julye, vijs. viijd.
Givin to my Lord of Lecester's players in August, xiiijs.
Givin to my Lord of Sussex players in Maye, 1586, vjs. ixd.

1587   June 14,   29 Elizabeth.
Givin to the Queen's plaiers, xixs. iiijd., and was to make it up
    xxvjs. viijd. that was gathered at the benche.
givin to Ld Harry Barkle ffe players, viiijs. xd.
gave to my Lord Amerald's players, xs.
givin to the waites of Brystoll for playinge at my lords (Warwick)
    comynge, vjs. viijd.
given to my Lord of Lecester's plaiers, xxiijs. viijd.

1588   June 18,   30 Elizabeth.
To the quenes mties. plaiers the xiijth of Julye, xvs., beside the
    gatheringe.

1588   .To the L of Sussex plaiers, xs. xd.
given to the L of Warwicke's tumblers, vjs. viijd.
To the L of Lecester's plaiers, xxs.

1589   June 20,   31 Elizabeth.
given to the Quene's mte. plaiers the xix daie of Julie, xxiijs.
givin to my lord of Essex plaiers, xs. ixd.
givin to the Quene's plaiers the xiiijth daie of August, xvijs.
more given by Mr. Mayor to the quene's men that were tumblers, xs.

1590   June 20,   32 Elizabeth.
givin to the quene's mate. plaiers in November, 1589, xvs.

1592   June 10,   34 Elizabeth.
givin to my Lord Durnd's (?) players, ixs. vjd.
paid to the quene's players, xvs. vjd., besides that which was given
by the companie.
paid to my Lord Admirall's players, xvjs. iijd.
paid to the quene's plaiers, xs.
paid to the Earl of Harford's plaiers, xxs.
paid to my L Strange's plaiers, xvijs.

1593   Sept. 10,   35 Elizabeth.
paid to the quene's plaiers the 22 of August, xiiijs. ixd.
paid to my L of Montegue's plaiers, xs.
paid to my L Pembroke plaiers, xijs.
paid to my L Strange's plaiers, xijs. iijd.

1594   36 Elizabeth.
paid and givin unto the Lord Admirall's, the L Norris players, xvjs.
paid and givin more to the same players, vijs. ixd.
paid and givin unto the L of Woster's players, xjd.
paid and givin more to the same players, vjs. xd.
paid unto the Quene's players, xxijs. vjd.

1595   Oct. 10,   37 Elizabeth.
paid unto the Quene's plaiers, xviijs. iiijd.
paid unto my Lord Admirall's plaiers, xiijs. xd.

1596   Oct. 14,   38 Elizabeth.
paid unto my Lord Admiralls plaiers, xiiiis. ijd.
paid unto my Ld Darby, his plaiers, xiiiis. vjd.
paid unto Ld Worsester's plaiers, viiis. xd.

1597   Oct. 14,   39 Elizabeth.
gave to the Queene's players at two sundrie times, xxxjs. xd.
gave unto the Lord of Pembroke's players, xxs.
gave unto the Lord Chamberlain's players, xxs.
gave unto the Lord of Darbie's players, xiijs. iiijd.
paid unto the Lord Shandon's plaiers, xxs.

1598   Oct. 30,   40 Elizabeth.
gave unto the Lord Shandos' players, xjs. ixd.
gave to the Queene's players, xs.

1599   Oct. 13,   41 Elizabeth.
gave unto the Lord of Pembroke's plaiers, xivs. ijd.

1600   Oct. 13,   42 Elizabeth.
gave unto the Lord Heywarde's players xs.

1601   Oct. 27,   43 Elizabeth.

1601   gave to the younge men of our men that plaid at Cristmas, xs.
        given to the Queen's players, xxs.
1602   Oct. 15th,   44 Elizabeth.
        gave unto the Earle of Hertford's players, xxs.
        given unto the younge men of our cyttie that played att Christmas,
        vjs. viijd.
        given unto the Children that played att Candellmas, vs.
1604   Oct. 14,   1 James I.
        item givin to a fensor that did plaie before the Shott with the Sword
            att the proclayminge of our Dreade and Sovereign Kinge, ijs. vjd.
        item given to the musicins att the same tyme, iijs. iiijd.
        item paied for fyve gallons of clarrett wyne given the Shote uppon
            the Kinge's hollidaie, xiiijs. iiijd.
        item paid for a pounde and halfe of Suger at the same time, ijs. iijd.
        item givin to the musicins att the same tyme, vs.
        item givin to the Kinge's players, xxxs.
        item paid for two gallons of Beare givin to the Shott uppon the
            Kinge's hollidaie, viijd.
        item paid for a glasse that was loste att the same tyme, ijd.
        paid more for cake givin to the Shott att the same tyme, vs.
        item given to the Ld Admirall's players, xs.
1606   Oct. 10,   4 Jas. I.
        given to the players at Christmas, vs.
        given to the Prince's players, xxiiis. viiid.
        given to the Queene's players, xxs.
1608   Oct. 16,   5 Jas. I.
        given to the Queen's players, xs.
        given more to the Queen's players, xxs.
        given to the Prince players, xxs.
1609   Oct. 16,   7 Jas. I.
        Given to the Duke's players, xs.
        Given to the King's trumpiters, xs.
1612   Oct. 12,   9 Jas. I.
        to the ladye Elizabeth, her players, xxs.

After 1612 there comes a break in these entries, though, as during the
reign of James I. and the early portion of the reign of Charles I., there
was no great falling away in the love for the drama which sprang into
such vigorous life during the Elizabethan era, nor did Bath drift into
an obscure city, it is only fair to assume that the visits of the travelling
companies did not cease, and that the drama continued to occupy
that position in the city which it had maintained for so many years.
Of course, a change soon came. When the Civil War broke out, the
" poore player " found his occupation gone, and changing his stage
sword for one of a more serviceable character, joined in that greater
drama which was being played with the whole country for a stage.
It is stated that with one exception no noted actor is known to have
joined the Parliamentary party, but all exposed their lives for the king
who had been their patron. The people, too, must have been little

in the mood for such recreation as play-acting, and the position occupied by Bath during that civil conflict must have put dramatic representations entirely out of the question for the time being, although,
according to Wood, the City Fathers, in the year 1650, were not
unmindful of the prosperity of the city, for in October of that year
certain by-laws were made for the removal of great nuisances which
then existed, after which "people began to flock to Bath for recreation
as well as for the benefit of the waters." By the Puritans theatrical
representations were prohibited ; all amusements were attacked by
them, theatrical performances in particular being looked upon with
feelings of horror and contempt, while dramatists were classed with
the enemies of morality and religion.   "Much that is objectionable,"
writes Macaulay, "may be found in the writers whom they reprobated ;
but whether they took the best measures for stopping the evil appears
to us very doubtful, and must, we think, have appeared doubtful
to themselves, when, after a lapse of a few years, they saw the unclean
spirit whom they had sent out return to his old haunts, with seven
others fouler than himself." But although playhouses were ordered
to be dismantled, and actors and spectators alike rendered liable to
punishment—the former to be whipped and the latter fined—Cromwell
was not so bigoted, and was willing to connive at performances which
his followers would not sanction.

Where extreme methods are adopted, there is almost sure to be a
reaction, and the reaction which followed the bigotry of the Puritans
placed the English drama on a far lower level than it has occupied at
any time in its history.   After the austerity and the cant of the
Roundheads, came the ribaldry and licentiousness of the Restoration.
Every department of literature was affected, and, perhaps, the drama
more than any other ; no sooner was restraint removed than the playhouses became scenes of dissoluteness and vice.   Their attractions
were increased, and the plays were produced with greater completeness and attention to detail and effect than had been the case in the
days before the Commonwealth, but this, by making them more
popular, only tended to drag them down and make them hotbeds of
vice.   Macaulay, writing of this time, says* :—

"The spirit of the Antipuritan reaction pervades almost the whole polite
literature of the reign of Charles the Second.   But the very quintessence of
that spirit will be found in the comic drama.   The playhouses, shut by the
meddling fanatic in the day of his power, were again crowded.   To their old
attractions new and more powerful attractions had been added.   Scenery,
dresses, and decorations, such as would now be thought mean or absurd, but
such as would have been esteemed incredibly magnificent by those who, early
in the seventeenth century, sate on the filthy benches of the Hope, or under
the thatched roof of the Rose, dazzled the eyes of the multitude.   The fascina-

* Macaulay's " History of England."

tion of sex was called in to aid the fascination of art : and the young spectator saw, with emotions unknown to the contemporaries of Shakespeare and Jonson, tender and sprightly heroines personated by lovely women.   From the day on which the theatres were reopened they became seminaries of vice ; and the evil propagated itself.   The profligacy of the representations soon drove away sober people.   The frivolous and dissolute who remained required every year stronger stimulants.   Thus the artists corrupted the spectators, and the spectators the artists, till the turpitude of the drama became such as must astonish all who are not aware that extreme relaxation is the natural effect of extreme restraint, and that an age of hypocrisy is, in the regular course of things, followed by an age of impudence."

Such was the state of the drama at an important period in the history of Bath, for, according to Wood, the prosperity of the city dates from this reign.   In September, 1663, the King brought his Royal consort to Bath, and from this period, writes Wood, "the drinking of the hot waters of Bath may be very justly said to have been established ; and from the same period the trade of the city began to turn from the woollen manufacture to that of entertaining the strangers that came to it for the use of the hot waters."   It is much to be regretted that there is a lack of accurate information respecting the condition of the Bath Stage at this time.   It stands to reason that if visitors were flocking to the city amusements must have been provided for them, and the drama, no doubt, occupied a prominent place among them.   It is stated by one writer that during this reign a company of comedians became permanent in Bath, but inasmuch as that statement is coupled with another which we know to be incorrect, doubt is thrown upon its accurateness.   It certainly was not the case that these players "performed regular plays in a theatre which occupied the site of the General Hospital," for no such theatre at that time existed.   In 1694 Mr. Joseph Gilmore, of Bristol, published plans for proposed buildings in the city, somewhat after the manner of those subsequently drawn by Wood, and in these "a stable by the Abbey gate" was appropriated for a theatre, but that was a proposal never carried out, and the first building actually erected for the purposes of dramatic performances dates from the commencement of the following century.   The Guildhall, therefore, most probably continued to be the scene of such dramas as were enacted within the city (with, perhaps, occasional performances in inn yards, and rooms in various hostelries), and, as a proof of this, there is record of a payment of 1s. "to the players at the Towne Hall," in the year 1673.

CHAPTER IV.

THE FIRST BATH THEATRE.

A RECOGNISED HOME FOR THE DRAMA—ITS SITE AND DATE
OF ERECTION—INDIFFERENT ENCOURAGEMENT—ACTORS' EM-
BARRASSMENTS — THE "ENEMY"—PERFORMANCES AT THE
ROOMS—KINGSMEAD THEATRE—BATH COMPANY OF COMEDIANS
—A DISTINGUISHED AUDIENCE.

E now come to a point in the history of the Bath Stage which marks a distinct departure from what has gone before, and may be taken as a starting point from which its story gradually becomes less a matter of doubt and uncertainty, until we arrive at that period when Bath rose to such an eminence in the theatrical world that the greatest luminaries of the English stage were proud to court the applause and good graces of its audiences. The erection of a recognised home of the drama within the city, a building intended for, and devoted to, dramatic performances, must naturally have given zest to the love for the drama which many of its citizens no doubt possessed, while it provided suitable entertainment for the visitors and fashionables who, probably, found time hang somewhat heavily upon their hands. The days of Richard Nash had not yet arrived, when the amusements of those who crowded the Pump Room, and met at the Baths, were liberally catered for, but the building of a theatre may be taken as the first step in that direction. The date of the erection of this theatre is given as 1705, and its position, the site of the Royal Mineral Water Hospital, is indicated in a map of the city published in 1723, where it is to be seen adjoining the top of Vicarage lane, now better known as Parsonage Lane. This theatre was erected by Mr. George Trim, a member of the Corporation, who also built Trim street, named after him, and the first street built without the city walls, upon land of which he was the proprietor. The cost of building this theatre was about £1,300, which was raised by subscriptions, the subscribers being mostly persons of high rank, whose armorial bearings were painted on the interior walls as testimonies of their liberality towards it.* Although so much money was spent on its erection it must have been

* Wood's Description of Bath.

C

a very primitive affair, small and incommodious, indeed, it is spoken
of as merely "a play-room." There is no description of it extant,
except what is contained in the following extract from Mainwaring's
Annals of Bath :—

"The first regularly built Theatre in Bath was erected in 1730 *(sic)* on the
ground where the General Hospital now stands. It was the property of
Widow Poore, and under the management of Hornby, a comedian. But as
gaming was the prevailing rage at the time, the Theatre met with very indifferent encouragement, and the performers were hardly able to support themselves. Lady Hawley afterwards became the purchaser of the property, but
that did not mend the condition of the actors. .The Theatre was under her
Ladyship's ballroom, and the seats were placed one above the other, until they
reached within four feet of the ceiling ; there was only one box, placed above
the door, which held four persons, and the price of admittance was half-a-crown
to every part of the house. Thirty pounds was the receipt of the fullest house,
and her Ladyship was entitled to a third share of the profits, and one-fourth
for the use of scenes and dresses. The standing expense was £2 10s. per
night, which included music, attendants, bills, and *tallow candles* ; the
remainder was divided among twelve performers."

Tallow candles ! What a picture does this conjure up, and what a
revelation of the difficulties under which the followers of the histrionic
art had to struggle. There was nothing in those days to take the
attention of the audience from the actor, no artistic scenery or
realistic effects, simply his own art with which to win the applause of
his audience, and there is reason to believe often a tolerably critical
audience too. Under difficulties such as these, or at least not far
removed from these, some of the earliest of the great names which
adorn the history of the English stage won their laurels and gained
an evergreen reputation.

The very year of the building of this house a Rev. Mr. Bedford,
vicar of Temple, published an advertisement concerning the profane-
ness of playhouses, and in the following year inveighed against "the
actual building of a playhouse " at Bristol, and wrote that "frequent
actings" had from time to time occurred near Bristol "as well as at
Bath." "These emissaries," he says, "travel from place to place.
. . . . The enemy lay sometime without our gates, and is now
come into the city." The "enemy" apparently was more tolerated at
Bath than in the sister city, for on the 10th August, 1706, the following presentment was made by the Grand Jury at Bristol :—"We
present Mr. Power and his company for acting of plays within the
liberties of this city, without your Worship's Leave and Consent."
Beyond the fact that in 1706 his Grace the Duke of Grafton's servants
were acting in a play entitled "Love at a Venture," at "the new
Theatre, Bath," we have been unable to discover anything about
either the performers at this Theatre, the plays they presented, or the
audiences who witnessed them, but Defoe, in his "Tour through

HENRY IRVING.

Great Britain," 1725, makes the following somewhat uncomplimentary reference to the city. " In the afternoon there is generally a play—though the decorations are mean, and the performance accordingly—but it answers, for the Company (presumably the visitors) here make the play to say no more." But, then, Mainwaring has told us that the profits arising from the performances, especially that portion of them which found its way into the pockets of the wearers of the sock and buskin, were exceedingly small, so that it cannot be supposed they would support any company of comedians of anything like repute and position.

The time had not yet arrived when Bath was looked upon with covetous and eager eyes by aspirants to the stage, and when veteran histrions displayed their talents to audiences, the most critical and discerning in the country. But the time had almost arrived when a change in this direction was to take place. Already rival claimants for the patronage of the public were springing up, with the ultimate result that the theatre of 1705 fell into disuse, and playgoers were invited to transfer their favours to other quarters. The old theatre, as we know, subsequently gave place to the Mineral Water Hospital, the building of which commenced upon the same site in the year 1738. Dramatic performances were then transferred to the Assembly Rooms, better known as the Lower Rooms or Simpson's Rooms, and were also given in a theatre in Kingsmead street, which, in the playbills of that time, was termed "The New Theatre." As a matter of fact, it was nothing more than a room about 25 feet wide and 50 feet long, with a gallery at the end opposite the stage. It was probably built about the year 1723, and was, we believe, situated at the rear of premises now occupied by Messrs. Fuller, in Kingsmead street. When it was no longer used for theatrical purposes, it became the Jews' Synagogue for a number of years, and was ultimately pulled down about twenty years ago. The Assembly Rooms occupied the site of the present Royal Institution, and were kept by a Mr. Simpson, while on the other side of the road, where Terrace walk now stands, was another place for public amusement, kept by a Mr. Wiltshire. In addition to these we again find that performances were given at public inns. Here is an extract from the *Bath Journal*, under date Feb. 17, 1747 :—

" We hear that the Bath Company of Comedians have taken the great room at the Globe, without West-gate, which is making very commodious ; and that they intend to perform on Monday next the tragedy of THEODOSIUS, or, *The Force of Love ;* with the entertainment *Miss in her Teens*, or, *The Medley of Lovers*, as it is now acted at the Theatre Royal, Covent Garden, in London."

Several such notices as this are to be found in this year, and others having reference to performances and benefits at the George, where the same company apparently played in the following year, at prices which could scarcely have proved very remunerative. The following is found in the same journal for 15 Feb., 1748 :—

" This evening the Bath Company of Comedians will play the Tragedy of *Cato*, with an entertainment called the *Contrivances*, in a large room at the George, near the Cross Bath, prices 2s. 6d. and 1s. 6d."

But the prices charged at the Kingsmead Theatre were even less, the pit being only one shilling and sixpence and the gallery one shilling. Performances were constantly given at this theatre as late as 1750, in which year it was honoured by the presence of Royalty.

"July 16th, 1750.—Thursday in the evening their Royal Highnesses (the prince and princess of Wales) drank Tea at Ralph Allen's, Esq. ; and afterwards went to the play, and saw the Tragedy of *Tamerlane* performed, by Mr. Sinnett's Company, at the command of Lady Augusta."

The new theatre in Orchard street had not been opened in July, 1750, and Mr. Simpson's Rooms were also not opened till the season had commenced, therefore this extract must refer to the Kingsmead street playhouse, at which performances were given at various times during the summer. Probably the building of the Orchard street theatre and the fierce competition for the favours of the playgoing public which followed proved the death blow of this venture, at any rate we lose sight of it after about August, 1751, in which month we read that "a company of comedians " were at the theatre, and they were announced on a particular date to appear in " Richard the Third," when the part of King Richard was " to be attempted by Mr. Cartwright."

CHAPTER V.

THE ORCHARD STREET THEATRE.

THE DRAMA IN A CELLAR—PROPOSALS FOR A NEW THEATRE—
DEATH OF THE PROMOTER — FRESH PROPOSALS — RIVALS—
DISTINGUISHED VISITORS—JOHN PALMER'S LUCKY VENTURE.

S we have seen, the principal scene of dramatic performances after the dissolution of the old theatre of 1705, was Simpson's Rooms. As a matter of fact, the performances were given in an apartment under the ballroom, which must at best have been a small and inconvenient place for the purposes to which it was applied, and yet it was largely patronised, and continued for many years, even after the erection of the Orchard Street Theatre, to be a recognised resort for playgoers. Wood goes so far as even to describe the place as "a cellar," but it rejoiced at the time in the high sounding title of "Mr. Simpson's Theatre," and secured the patronage of visitors of rank, and even Beau Nash himself. But, notwithstanding this support, the drama could not be said to be in a flourishing condition in the city, and in 1747 Mr. John Hippisley, a London actor of some repute, and who was connected with the theatre at Jacob's Wells, Bristol, conceived a scheme to raise the Bath stage from its languid and impoverished condition by providing it with a new home which should be well suited to its requirements and be more acceptable to the company which regularly assembled in Bath during the season. Accordingly he submitted a proposal to the public in November, 1747, in the following words :—

To the

NOBILITY AND GENTRY AT BATH.

" PLAYS *are like mirrors made, for Men to see*
" *How* BAD *they are, how* GOOD *they ought to be.*"

IN all Ages, and in all Countries, where Liberty and Learning flourish'd, the STAGE never fail'd of receiving *Sanction* and *Protection* from the Great and Noble.

Theatrical Performances, when conducted with Decency and Regularity, have been always esteem'd the most rational Amusements, by the Polite and Thinking Part of Mankind :—Strangers, therefore, must be greatly surpris'd to find at BATH Entertainments of this Sort in no better Perfection than they are, as it is a Place. during its Seasons, honour'd with so great a Number of Persons, eminent for *Politeness, Judgment* and *Taste;* and where might reasonably be expected (next to *London*) the best Theatre in *England.*

The present *Play-House*, or rather *Play* room is so small and incommodious, that 'tis almost impossible to have Things better done in it than they are. The Profits arising from the Performance, as now conducted, will not support a larger, or better, Company of Actors. And nothing can be more disagreeable, than for Persons of the *first Quality*, and those of the *lowest Rank*, to be seated on the same Bench together, which must be the Case here, if the Former will Honour and the Latter have an Inclination, to see a Play.

To remedy this, and for the better Entertainment of the Quality it is humbly proposed to erect a Regular, Commodious THEATRE, on the most convenient Spot of Ground that can be got ; to be managed by Mr. *Hippisley* (who for many Years has been a Performer in *London*) and Others ; and to add such a sufficient Number of Good Performers to the present Company, as will (it is hoped) never fail of giving Pleasure and Satisfaction to the most judicious Audience, and greatly contribute towards rendering BATH the most *agreeable Place* in the Kingdom.

The house, we are told by Wood—who was apparently much interested in the scheme, if it did not originate with him—was planned to be " sixty feet long and forty feet broad in the clear ; it was to front westward to Orchard street, and the front was to have consisted of a rustic basement, supporting the Doric order." It was estimated that the expense of erecting such a building would be £1,000, £300 less than the old Theatre un the Borough walls cost, although the new house was to be considerably larger. It was naturally to be expected that such a scheme as this would meet with opposition from those interested in the existing play-room, who, of course, did all in their power to obstruct the introduction to the city of so formidable a competitor, for they must have felt that a building so much larger, more commodious and better appointed, as the new Theatre promised to be, would be a serious rival, and would, even if at first old associations sufficed to draw audiences to the Rooms, ultimately secure a monopoly in the drama. Vigorous, however, as the opposition was, it did not prevent Mr. Hippisley, with whom was associated a Mr. Watts, in persevering with his scheme, and he received considerable encouragement from persons of rank and distinction who were interested in the city. The same liberality which had been bestowed upon the Theatre of 1705, says Wood, " seemed to me to have been upon its dawn in favour of Mr. Hippisley's intended house ; and if he had lived but a few months longer, I am well satisfied as many fifty pound tickets, for the privilege of the Theatre, would have been subscribed for as would have paid for the whole expense of building it." The death of the principal agent in the scheme does not seem, however, to have proved much check to its progress, for the matter was taken up by Mr. John Palmer, an enterprising and well-to-do citizen, a brewer and tallow-chandler by trade, jointly with nine other inhabitants, who, in March, 1748, issued the following advertisement :—

PROPOSALS *for* Building *by* SUBSCRIPTION, A Regular, Commodious

THEATRE,

To be situated near the Grand Parade, in the City of Bath.

On the following CONDITIONS :—

I. THAT the propos'd Undertaking shall be divided into *Twenty Shares.*

II. That the *Subscribers* shall pay down *Fifty Pounds* for each Share, into the Hands of the *Undertaker,* or to his Order, at Two equal Payments, the First on the 25th of *April,* and the other on the 25th of *July* next.

III. That the Building shall be begun as soon as *Fifteen Shares are subscribed for.*

IV. That the *Subscribers* shall have a proper legal Title to the Shares they severally subscribe for, which shall be granted to them by the *Undertaker,* as soon as the *Building is finished.*

V. That the *Subscribers* shall receive Yearly, for each Share, *One Shilling per Night* for *Seventy Nights,* or *Three Pounds Ten Shillings per Annum,* certain. And if the House shall be play'd in *more than Seventy Nights in a Year,* they shall receive, for each Share, *One Shilling* for every Night of such Playing ; the Whole not to exceed *One Hundred Shillings,* or *Five Pounds per annum.*

VI. That the *Subscribers* shall, for every Share, have a *Silver* Ticket, which shall admit the *Bearer into any Part of the House,* every Night of Performing, except on *Benefit nights.*

VII. That the House shall be *compleatly finished,* in a *Substantial, Workman-like, Ornamental, Theatrical Manner ;* and opened with a *good Company of Performers, new Cloaths, Scenes,* &c on, or before the Eleventh Day of *October,* next, 1748.

Subscriptions are taken in by Mr. James Leake's *Bookseller, in whose Hands a proper instrument, Signed by the Undertaker is lodg'd for each Subscriber to set his Hand to.*

The promise that the Theatre should be completed and opened by October of that year was not fulfilled, probably because the necessary funds were not forthcoming with sufficient alacrity. The house was, however, built, and some arrangement was entered into with the proprietor of the old playroom, that it should not be used for the purposes of dramatic performances after the new building was completed. The prospects of the new Theatre were, therefore, tolerably rosy, but, unfortunately for those connected with it, the agreement was not kept, and when the Theatre was ultimately opened about the commencement of the season of 1750, instead of having the monopoly which was expected, the old playroom, which had been improved and renovated, was reopened and a determined opposition offered. The reason for this does not transpire ; evidently there must have been some serious misunderstanding, and one is inclined to think there must have been faults on both sides to account for so strange a rupture. Bath could not support two theatres, and give to each a sufficient measure of patronage to enable them to carry on so fierce and expensive a competition, although we read that the previous season had been a particularly successful one, there appearing among the names of visitors in December, 1749, ten peers, nine peeresses, five earls' daughters, fifteen baronets and knights, and altogether a greater number of visitors than had previously been known at that time of year, and there is reason to believe that the season of 1750 was equally brilliant. As a matter of fact, we know that the competition was too severe, much loss was sustained by both parties, and, of course, the shares in the Orchard Street Theatre were greatly depreciated in value. Most of the proprietors of the New Theatre were unwilling to incur further expense, and it then appears to have occurred to Mr. Palmer to secure the interests of both houses himself. Accordingly he bought up—no doubt at a very moderate price—the shares of his co-proprietors, and also obtained the interest of the old house by an annuity, and so placed the Orchard Street Theatre in that position which it was intended from the first it should occupy, and started it upon a career which was destined to be more brilliant and successful than Palmer probably anticipated even in his most sanguine moments.

CHAPTER VI.

RIVALRY.

THE ROOMS AND THE THEATRE—COMPETING FOR PATRONAGE—
INTERESTING PROLOGUES — TAKINGS — BEAU NASH — AN
OBJECTIONABLE CUSTOM — AN UNSEEMLY DISPUTE — PLAYS
AND PLAYERS—THE TRAINING GROUND FOR LONDON.

T is not until after the building of the Orchard
Street Theatre that we begin to learn particulars
about the performances which took place in Bath ;
even then it is possible only to glean superficial
facts, and some years must still elapse before contemporary journalism and other means of reference
to what was going on in the city provide us with
interesting and entertaining details both of the performances themselves and those who took part in them.   In this chapter we propose
to deal with the period during which the managers of the old Rooms
and the new Theatre competed so keenly for the patronage of the
playgoing public.   It must be borne in mind that during this time
Beau Nash was exercising his drastic sway over the conduct of
the city, and of course it was only the large number of wealthy
visitors who resorted to the city during the season that rendered
it at all possible for these two places of entertainment to be run
together.   Had they to depend upon the city itself, probably not even
one of the two would have been able to make both ends meet.

The season commenced in September, about which time the
arrival of Beau Nash and various persons of title is annually recorded.
In 1750—the year which saw the opening of the Orchard Street
Theatre—theatrical performances were commenced in October,
though the Kingsmead Theatre appears to have been open all the
summer, or, at any rate, performances were given at various dates
during the months of June, July, and August, perhaps by travelling
companies, since on one occasion the play was announced to be given
"by a Company just arrived."   "The Theatre at Mr. Simpson's," as
it was sometimes described, opened first, on October 22nd, the first
performance at the new Theatre being given on the following Saturday,
when the first part of "King Henry the Fifth" was presented.   On
both occasions a prologue was delivered, which it will be interesting
to reproduce.   That at the Rooms was spoken by a Mr. Hallam, and
was addressed to "The Worshipful Mayor and Corporation of Bath,"

from which it may be assumed that the performance was given under their patronage, whereas there is no mention or indication of such patronage, or, indeed, of any at all, at the opening of the new Theatre. It was as follows :—

> Since 'tis the Intent, and Business of the Stage,
> To Copy out the Follies of the Age ;
> To hold the Mirror full in each Man's Sight,
> And shew the Passions in the strongest Light :
> Our Stage, tho' humble, still has this in View,
> Not only to divert, but to improve you too.
>   Rome that subdu'd the World in ancient Days,
> Cherish'd our Art, and sung their Roscius' Praise :
> ATHENS, and GREECE, renown'd for sagest Laws,
> Esteem'd their Actors, and maintain'd their Cause.
>   This ancient City, oft' the pleading Seat,
> Of Patriots, Heroes. of the Good and Great ;
> O may it rise, like ROME, in Splendor and in State.
>   And tho' no ROSCIUS on our Stage appears,
> To fire to Glory, or to charm your Ears ;
> Yet You, like ancient ROMANS, Good and Just,
> With Honour fill your Offices and Trust :
> With ROMAN Justice execute our Laws,
> And stand the foremost in your Country's Cause.
> Like them too,—smile upon the Poet's Lays,
> Protect us, and guard Us, for our Wish to please.
> So may the Guardian Pow'rs with You combine,
> To make BATH flourish, and Her STAGE to shine.

The prologue at the new Theatre was spoken by Mr. Watts, who was associated with Mr. Hippisley in the original scheme for the erection of the building, and was afterwards probably manager for the proprietors. The following were the lines delivered by him :—

> As some young Shoot, which by the Planter's Hand
> Is gently mov'd into a kinder Land ;
> If the warm *Sunshine* spread its genial Rays,
> Soon a fair *Tree* its verdant Leaves displays,
> And rears with *Blossoms* its luxuriant Head,
> Whilst all the *Warblers'* wonton in the Shade.
> 'Tis Steadiness alone can fix the *Root*,
> And rip'ning *Autumn* gives the *Golden Fruit*,
> But if the nipping Blast, or dead'ning Frost
> Too fierce advance, the hopeful product's lost.
>   So will it he with Us, whose Art and Care
> Have raised this *Structure*, to what we call fair ;
> With ev'ry varied Art have strove to charm,
> If *Painting* please, or *Harmony* can warm.
> Shine forth auspicious,—our Endeavours crown,
> And fire Us, by Success, to gain *Renown*.

A *British* Audience shou'd assert Good Sense,
Nor shou'd the Muse e'er give the least Offence ;
Cautious she treads the Stage in humble State,
And from the *Ladies'* Eyes expects her Fate :
If they propitious *beam* her into Life,
Just Emulation is her only Strife.
SHAKESPEAR with Energy shall warm the Heart,
And JOHNSON the true *Comic Force* impart :
LEE in high pompous Verse shall nobly Swell ;
And ADDISON in *Patriot Thoughts* excel ;
Ev'n laurel'd DRYDEN with the rest shall vie ;
And OTWAY'S Lines imperil the melting Eye.
When plaintive ROWE shall paint the Nymph's Distress,
Each heaving bosom shall her grief express :
Nor shall we fail to add the Changeful Scene
With hum'rous Farce and motley Harlequin.
Here let your leisure Hours with Mirth and Joy,
That hateful enemy the *Spleen* destroy.
Small faults excuse, with Cordial Smiles attend,
Encouragement will urge us on to *mend.*

The players at the Rooms styled themselves the "Bath Company of Comedians," and Mr. Hallam, who spoke the above prologue, is subsequently spoken of as "Mr. Hallam of London." It is very probable that he was the Mr. Hallam who for a period was manager of Goodman's Field's Theatre, and was the father of the accomplished actress, Mrs. Mattocks, and who lost his life from a wound in the eye, the result of a blow with a walkingstick struck by Macklin, the celebrated Shylock, during a dispute at a rehearsal.

Some idea of what the takings at these places of amusement were is supplied by the notices of performances which appear to have been annually given about this time on behalf of the General Hospital, as it was then called, Royal Mineral Water Hospital as we know it now. In 1750 these performances were given in November, and resulted in £108 12s. 6d. being handed over to the institution as the receipts of both entertainments, though it would seem that this was unusually large, as in the following year a similar performance at the new Theatre produced £44 19s., which sum was handed over without any deduction, and in 1753 a performance at the Rooms in November enabled the proprietor to add £40 4s. 6d. to the funds of the Hospital. Ordinary performances would probably yield less than these sums, although they were frequently given under the patronage, or in the phrase of that time, "by command of" persons of rank and title. Thus we find among the names of such personages, the Marchioness of Carnarvon, the Duchess of Somerset, the Duchess of Queensbury, Countess of Suffolk, Countess of Clanrickard, Countess of Northumberland, Lady Fortescue, and various others, while, naturally, the name of Richard Nash frequently figures in this connection. His favours were distributed, sometimes appearing at one house and sometimes at the other, more often, perhaps, at the Rooms than at the Theatre. The prices of admission at this time were :—At Orchard Street— Boxes 3s., pit 2s., first gallery 1s. 6d., upper gallery 1s. ; and at the Rooms—Boxes 3s., pit 2s., front gallery, 1s. 6d., side gallery, 1s. The performances commenced at half-past six in 1753, but as " complaints of not beginning in ti·ne were very general," the time of the rising of the curtain was changed at both places of amusement to six o'clock. Occasionally we come across such notices as these :—

N. B.—As the play is an extreme full one, 'tis hoped no gentlemen will take it amiss if they are not admitted behind the scenes.

N.B.—Nothing under FULL PRICE will be TAKEN.

BEAU NASH.

It was a custom at this time for places at the theatre to be taken by servants of persons of position during the after-noon, who occupied them until the arrival of their master or mistress. The play bills fre-quently contained the announcement that "Ladies and gentlemen are desired to send their servants to keep places by half an hour after four o'clock," but accord-ing to a writer in the *Weekly Register* the practice was a very undesirable one, as these foot-men frequently be-haved themselves very badly, laughing and talking aloud even after the performanance had commenced, and holding conversations with their acquaintances from one side of the house to the other.

During the season of 1751-2 the management of the playroom at Mr. Simpson's was undertaken by a Mr. Brown, and the house went,

during that time by the name of " Mr. Brown's Theatre." A violent
dispute occurred during this gentleman's management between those
connected with the two theatres—by which, no doubt, the bitter feeling
of jealousy already existing was largely increased—in consequence of
Mr. Brown publicly stating that his head carpenter and mechanist
was for several days made drunk and inveigled away from the Rooms
by the company belonging to the new Theatre. The charge was
indignantly denied by those accused, who asserted that Smith, the
carpenter, had of his own free will entered into a six months' engagement with the Orchard Street management, at a wage of one guinea
a week, after having publicly complained at the Three Crowns public-
house of the illusage he had received at the hands of Mr. Brown's
Company, and stated that they wanted their entertainments out before
he could get them ready, and "expected things to be done for forty
or fifty shillings that would come to many pounds." This unseemly
dispute was publicly carried on, long affidavits being published in the
papers, serving only to show how bitter the rivalry was. Mr. Brown's
name does not appear in connection with the management after this
season, the playroom afterwards being advertised by the old title of
" Mr. Simpson's Theatre." It is last mentioned in March, 1754, but
after that performances were advertised at the "concert room, near
the parade," both in that year and the following. Mr. Simpson died in
May, 1755, and, no doubt, it was his death that enabled Mr. Palmer
to secure for the Orchard Street Theatre the monopoly of dramatic
performances. The Rooms, however, were still carried on in the
same name, probably by a son, as we find an announcement that the
Rooms were given up by Mr. Simpson in 1771.

Of the performers and performances during this period, as we have
already intimated, little can be learnt. Most of the pieces played we
are still familiar with, in some cases by actual performances on the
stage of to-day. There was, for instance, " The Beggar's Opera "—
a great favourite, apparently—" The Miser," " The Tender Husband,"
" The Gamester," " Every Man in his Humour," " The Beaux Strate-
gem," " The Rehearsal" (produced with considerable success in 1753),
" George Barnwell," " Miss in her Teens," " The Devil to Pay," and
certain of Shakespeare's dramas. Among the artists appearing at the
Theatres we find Mr. Dancer, Mr. Palmer, Mr. Morgan, Mr Castle,
Mr. Furnival, Mr. Brown, Mr. Brookes, Mr. Barrington, Mr. Fitz-
maurice, Mr. Martin, Mr. Green and Mr. Falkner ; Mrs. Green, Mrs.
Clayton, Mrs. Mozeen, Mrs. Cowper, Mrs. Bishop ; Miss Ibbott,
Miss Lowe, Miss Hippisley, Miss Roche, Miss Young, and Miss
Helme. These histrions did not always appear at the same Theatre,
for names which were at one time associated with the Rooms are
afterwards found in the cast at Orchard Street, and vice versa.
Performances of " The Gamester " were given at both theatres in one
week in February, 1753, with the following casts :—

Mr. Simpson's Theatre Feb. 27.			Orchard Street Theatre Feb. 29.		
Beverly	...	... Mr. Falkner	Beverly	...	... Mr. Dancer
Stukely	...	... Mr. Cooke	Lewson	...	... Mr. Cox
Jarvis	...	... Mr. Philips	Stukely	...	... Mr. Castle
Charlotte	...	Miss Helme	Jarvis	...	... Mr. Furnival
Mrs. Beverly	...	Mrs. Mozeen	Bates	...	... Mr. Brookes
			Dawson	...	... Mr. Richardson
			Charlotte	...	... Miss Kennedy
			Lucy	...	...Mrs. Cartwright
			Mrs. Beverly	...	Miss Ibbott

Few of these names call for special notice. Mr. Dancer may have been the first husband of the well-known actress, Mrs. Crawford, who was the daughter of an apothecary at Bath. Having been jilted by some one in her seventeenth year, she sought to forget her troubles by going to the theatre, where she fell in love with an actor of the name of Dancer, whom she married in spite of her relations, who looked upon the connection as a disgrace. That Mr. Dancer was privately married in Bath in 1754 there is evidence, for the following advertisement is to be found in the *Bath Journal* :—

Bath 18, 1754.
Whereas it has been wickedly and maliciously reported, that Mr. Richard Stephens and wife were privy and accessory to our late private wedding : In justice therefore, we think it our indispensable duty to certify their innocence, they being in no way concern'd or acquainted with it. Of the truth of which, we whose names are underwritten now make affidavits.

Sworn before   William Dancer
      Thomas Attwood, Mayor.   Ann Dancer

Mrs. Dancer became the star of Dublin Theatre, and soon after the death of her first husband, married "the handsomest man on the stage," Spranger Barry, and at his death gave her hand to a man who afterwards greatly illused her. She was at no time a great actress, though capable of producing startling and thrilling effects. Mr. and Mrs. Green were well known on the London stage, Mrs. Green being an actress of considerable humour. Bath, it should be mentioned, had already given at least two stars to the London stage, from the old theatre on the Borough walls—Henry Giffard, who subsequently appeared at Lincoln's-inn-fields and Drury lane, first appeared in public at the Bath Theatre in 1719, and William Mynitt, who, after a preliminary trial in London, was "solicited to add a promising member to the company at Bath, where there is a regular theatre, and an audience as difficult to be pleased as that in London, being generally persons of the higher rank that frequent those diversions in the capital. He had the good fortune to give satisfaction there, insomuch that several persons of distinction and taste promised to recommend him to one of the established theatres in London."*

* Chetwood's " History of the Stage."

CHAPTER VII

THE PALMERS.

FATHER AND SON — ALTERATIONS AND IMPROVEMENTS — THE
FIRST THEATRE ROYAL — THE YOUNGER PALMER — HIS
ENERGY AND TACK—RECRUITING FOR THE STAGE--BRISTOL
AND BATH — MAIL COACHES — A GREAT AND SUCCESSFUL
UNDERTAKING.

O no one so much as to the Palmers, father and son,
is Bath indebted for the brilliant position which its
Theatre has occupied in the history of the English
stage. But for the energy and perseverance which
John Palmer showed in the early days of the
Orchard Street Theatre, and his persistance in
resisting until he finally overcame the ruinous
opposition with which it had to contend, it is most probable the Bath
Theatre would never have taken the position it did. The vigorous
contest between the rival managements would no doubt have ultimately
collapsed without Palmer's interference, but when that time came there
might have been no one of sufficient ability ready at hand to carry on
the surviving institution and raise it to any degree of eminence. It
is not likely that Bath would have remained long without a Theatre
under any circumstances, for the character of the city, as the resort of
persons of fashion, would have necessitated the provision of such a
place of entertainment, and would have induced someone to undertake
it. We have not, however, to do with what might have been, but
with what actually occurred, and subsequent events have shown how
fortunate it was that the destinies of the Bath Theatre fell into the
hands of men of such resource and determination, of so much enterprise and public spirit, as John Palmer and his son.

When Palmer succeeded in establishing the Orchard Street Theatre as
the only house in the city having any claims on the playgoing public,
he immediately set about making it as attractive as possible, and
various alterations and improvements were carried out before the
commencement of the season in 1755. The new buildings which were
springing up in Bath about this time, outside the old city, and what is

D

now called the upper part of the city, were at such a distance from the
Orchard Street house, that the building of a theatre in their vicinity
was contemplated. This roused Palmer to renewed and successful
efforts. He set about further improvements, re·constructed the house,
and re-opened it in March, 1767; the "most brilliant and polite
audience" which assembled on that occasion expressing "their approbation with universal applause." The New Theatre, as it was again
called, was described as being something similar to the theatre then
existing at Bristol, but larger, more lofty, and more ornamental, the
ceiling rising into a dome, in which were placed, in alto·relievo, Apollo
and the Muses.   The building thus furnished was "esteemed, in
fancy, elegance, and construction, inferior to none in Europe," but, as
a matter of fact, these alterations proved neither so convenient or so
appropriate as was at the time supposed. They were planned by Mr.
Arthur, who at that time was manager, and were adopted in preference
to plans submitted by Mr. Palmer, architect and builder.

Time and experience, however, proved that the requirements of the
theatre had not been met, and its increasing popularity necessitated
further alterations being made. This time—either in the year 1774 or
1775—the plans previously rejected were accepted, and the work was
entrusted to Mr. Palmer, the architect, who very successfully carried
out the new improvements. The Theatre was enlarged by extending
the building at the back, which provided greater accommodation, increased the auditorium, and rendered it more airy and agreeable. One
of the great drawbacks of the house previously had been the difficulty
to keep it cool ; the heat was a constant source of complaint, and this
was now relieved by providing a suitable ventilator at the top of the
building, which, an old playgoer wrote, supplied a quantity of fresh
air, equally diffused over the whole house, and prevented "its rushing
in streams or currants which are so apt to give colds." The dome,
which was so prominent a part of Mr. Arthur's plan, and was
at first considered so elegant and ornamental, had been condemned
as injurious both to sight and hearing, and Apollo and the Muses, so
proudly alluded to at the opening of the theatre, had been ridiculed as
" preposterously mixed with the Gothic architecture." This was now
all removed, the proscenium was adorned with pillars of the Ionic
and Doric orders, its ornaments, according to an admiring writer, being
"expressive of, and bore analogy to the ornaments of the place."
The pit was raised, greater space was given between the seats, and a
new and handsome lobby, or crush room, and retiring rooms provided.
The stage, too, was improved and enlarged, and the theatre altogether
transformed into a more convenient and tasteful structure than the
city had before possessed, and such as was worthy of the stage that
was second only to the Metropolis. Mr. Palmer evidently made a
great mistake in not adopting these plans in the first place ; they
could have been executed even at less cost (whereas their subsequent

adoption caused an additional expense of at least £1,000) and would have rendered the building more profitable than it had been by reason of the increased accommodation and greater attractions. Perhaps, however, in consequence of the threatened opposition to which allusion has been made, the decision to adopt the manager's plans was arrived at hurriedly, and without mature consideration.

Another and more important step taken by Palmer to defeat opposition was to petition Parliament for an Act to enable the King to grant him a patent. The only patent houses in existence at that time were Drury Lane and Covent Garden, and no new letters patent could be granted by the King without the sanction of Parliament. To the younger Palmer was entrusted the task of securing the necessary Act, which was warmly supported by the Mayor and Corporation of the city. Surmounting the many difficulties which lay in the way of this undertaking, he succeeded in getting it passed, and in 1768 his Majesty George III. granted letters patent, under which the Bath Theatre obtained the title of " Theatre Royal." This was the first Act ever passed in this country for the protection of theatrical property, and the Bath Theatre was the first Theatre Royal of the provinces. No doubt the prominence thus given to it had greatly to do with its increased popularity, at any rate the part which young Palmer took in procuring the Act of Parliament brought him into contact and gained him the friendship of many persons of influence connected with the stage, besides enabling him to make the acquaintance of many distinguished politicians, whose recognition of his untiring energy and perseverance proved of considerable service to him in after life.

It will not be out of place here briefly to sketch the life of the younger Palmer, especially as his success as the first projector of mail coaches arose out of his work in providing entertainment for the city. He was educated for the church, but objected to that, and, as his father would not listen to his preference for the army, he entered the counting-house of his father's brewery, and subsequently, having a violent quarrel with his relatives, he worked in the brewery as a common workman, until his health succumbed to the strain put upon it and he was forced to recruit his strength by change of air.* Returning to Bath he devoted himself to the theatrical business, and showed his ability to grapple with difficulties by obtaining the Act of Parliament just referred to. No sooner was that accomplished than obstacles had to be encountered at home, which also required great energy and tack to overcome. When he returned from London he found the company at the theatre on strike, for some reason, perhaps through the unpopularity of the manager ; at any rate they refused to act, and the only thing to be done was to get together a new company. To this end Palmer mounted his horse and proceeded on a tour of

* "Historic Houses of Bath," by R. E. Peach.

several hundred miles in search of fresh comedians. In a fortnight he returned, having been successful in engaging artists of repute at various towns, and it was the success of this journey that induced him to adopt a method of securing the best available actors for his company, which was undoubtly an element in the success of the Bath stage. His plan was to make an annual journey through the country, travelling from place to place and visiting all the principal theatres, in order that he might become acquainted with all that was being done in theatrical matters, and, while thus keeping well abreast of the times, strengthen or maintain the efficiency of his company by offering engagements to rising performers. Palmer had a very quick eye for merit in an actor or actress, a quality which many of the managers who succeeded him fortunately possessed, and it is greatly due to this discernment and acuteness of judgment that Bath has been so fertile in histrionic talent. Not content with the responsibilities and cares of the Bath Theatre, which now entirely devolved upon him, he undertook similar responsibilities at Bristol, having also acquired an interest in the theatre there, for which he likewise obtained a patent, subsequently working the two theatres together,* adding thereby to the prosperty of both houses, though appearing at both theatres during the week entailed an amount of work of which the actor of the present day has little or no conception.

It was while thus engaged in travelling from town to town that he first conceived the idea of mail coaches. We can well understand how a man of such energy and activity must have chafed at the intolerable slowness of the existing locomotion. The mails were at that time conveyed in a mail-cart, drawn by one horse, which took nearly two days to cover the distance between Bath and London, and, being in charge of only one man, were frequently the prey of highwaymen, by whom they were robbed and the driver not unfrequently murdered. He no doubt heard at Bath continual complaints from the visitors of the slowness of the carriages, and, at the same time, he noticed that the journey between Bath and Bristol was accomplished in far better time by the conveyance he had supplied for the purpose of taking his company from one theatre to the other, than by the ordinary conveyances then in vogue. Consequently he thought out and matured a plan for transmitting mails by coaches with guards, arranging stages over the whole kingdom, and, in spite of the manifold difficulties with which he had to contend from existing interests, he finally succeeded in persuading the Government of the utility of his scheme, and in 1789 he was appointed Surveyor and Comptroller-General of the Post-office, with a salary of £1,500 a year. In consequence of some disputes with the Postmaster-General, however, he lost the post in 1792 ; and though he was afterwards, through petitions to the Houses of Parliament, re-

* "John Palmer," a paper by J. Murch, D.L.

imbursed, the compensation was very inadequate to the percentage he was to have received in case his plans succeeded. That his merits were recognised by his native city is shown by the fact that he was elected Mayor in 1796, and that he twice represented it in Parliament. Notwithstanding his arduous labours, he continued to take the greatest interest in theatrical matters, and we shall have occasion to frequently allude to him in connection with the history of the theatre which owed so much to his perseverance and abilities.

CHAPTER VIII.

UNDER PALMER'S MANAGEMENT.

INTRODUCTION OF STALLS—AN UNPOPULAR MANAGER—FIRE—
JOHN HENDERSON—HIS FIRST APPEARANCE—HIS SUCCESS—
FROM BATH TO LONDON—FOOTE'S "DISH OF TEA"—CON-
FLICTING INTERESTS—QUIN AND GARRICK.

ALMER continued his management of the theatre
until the year 1785, when he was succeeded by
Messrs. Keasberry and Dimond. Engaged as he
was in other laborious work, he could not of course
give his undivided attention to the theatrical business, and the actual work of the management
devolved upon managers who occupied the position
of stage and acting managers rolled into one, though their labours
were considerably lightened by the prompter and box-office keeper,
whose duties were in those days much more extensive and responsible
than is now the case. Mr. Floor was prompter at the Bath Theatre
for many years, and it was partly due to him, as we shall presently see,
that Mrs. Siddons became connected with the Bath stage and there
laid the foundations of her unrivalled career. Of the managers
whom Mr. Palmer employed, there is little to be learnt ; one of
the first was a Mr. Brown, but whether he was the Mr. Brown
already alluded to, who for a time was manager at the Rooms, we
cannot discover. The probability, however, is that he was, since
others who were in the company at the Rooms, subsequently were
enrolled at the Theatre. He appears to have been an energetic
and enterprising man, besides being an actor who always played
prominent characters, and from what we know of Palmer we can well
imagine that he would not entrust his interests to anyone but those
who he was confident could be depended upon to carry out his ideas
with energy and ability. The introduction of stalls to the pit of the
Theatre—a plan which has not since been adopted in Bath, and both
for and against which there is much to be said—is not so modern an
innovation as some may think, for as far back as the year 1755 the
plan now adopted at the Haymarket Theatre was introduced at the
Orchard Street Theatre, namely, doing away entirely with the pit and
devoting one of the galleries to the pittites. The management was

induced to make the change owing to the practice of having seats upon the stage, which, it is not surprising to read, was found to impede the performance, not to speak of other objections. It is not recorded with what success the alteration was effected, though, as the old prices were subsequently returned to, we may infer that the pittites resented, as they would to-day, being turned out of what they look upon as theirs by right. The following is the announcement that was issued in the *Bath Journal* of January 27th, 1755 :—

The great demand for box places having obliged Mr. Brown to lay the pit and boxes together, rather than crowd the stage, and impede the performance —He flatters himself the Town will so far indulge him, as to accept the first gallery as pit, which shall be kept entirely for that purpose, and the upper gallery at eighteen-pence.

Although the advertisement does not indicate it, it is just possible that the announcement may have been intended only for the production of " Hamlet," which was advertised at the same time, when Mr. Brown made his first appearance as the Prince of Denmark. At any rate only two months later we find a notice similar to one quoted in a previous chapter, hoping that no persons will be offended at not being admitted on the stage in consequence of all the space being required for a production of " The Rehearsal."

A manager under the elder Palmer, Mr. Arthur, calls for some notice, if only on account of his unpopularity in the city. We have already made allusion to the acceptance of his plans for the first alterations in the Theatre, and he was the unpopular manager whom young Palmer had to replace on his return from London, after securing the patent for the Theatre. He was accused of treating the public with contempt, of taking the best parts in pieces whether they suited him or not, of presenting only old plays, or if he introduced new ones they were said to be got up in such a manner " as would disgrace a barn." Articles appeared in the Press so strongly worded that no editor of the present day would think of inserting them, unless he wished to run the risk of heavy damages for libel, and unless the complaints of the writers were well founded they were scurrilous indeed. Arthur had formerly been manager of the Bristol Theatre, but, to quote from a contemporary print, " his insolence and tyranny" met with such resentment that he was discharged, "to the great pleasure of all the company, and the satisfaction of the whole city." Fault was found with him only as a manager, for even his detractors admitted his histrionic abilities, especially when he appeared in characters which were suited to him. It seems that the idea of building another theatre in the upper part of the city was partly suggested by the unpopularity of this manager.

In May, 1758, a very unfortunate accident occurred, by which a quantity of scenery and properties belonging to the Theatre and to the members of the company was lost by fire. The fire, however, was not at the Theatre—for the Orchard street building escaped the fire fiend—but on Salisbury plain, and the loss was occasioned by the wheel of a wagon, on which the property was being conveyed to the Isle of Wight, taking fire. The following paragraph concerning the occurrence appeared in the *Bath Journal* :—

> Saturday evening the waggon that was conveying the scenes, cloaths, &c., belonging to the comedians of this city (intended for the Isle of Wight), took fire by accident going over Salisbury plain, and we hear the greatest part is entirely consumed.

This item of news found its way into the *Gentlemen's Magazine*, where a more detailed account of the accident appeared, from which we learn that the wagon was laden with "the whole rich wardrobe, scenery, and apparatus of the Bath Theatre ; besides the entire property of each performer belonging to it." It appears that an employé at the Theatre, who was travelling with the wagon, noticed the danger which threatened the property and pointed it out to the driver, entreating him to stop and unload. This he refused to do, saying that he had "driven twelve miles with his wheels smoking," but the result of his obstinacy was that when about three miles from Salisbury flames burst out and everything was destroyed, with the exception of a few boxes which the attendants were able to secure. The amount of the damage was estimated at £2,000. In March of the following year a performance was given "by desire of Richard Nash, Esq.," for the benefit of Mr. Stephens, who, it was stated, was the principal sufferer by this fire.

Among those who were connected with the Theatre during Palmer's management, the foremost names are those of Mrs. Siddons and Richard Brinsley Sheridan, but these are of sufficient importance to be dealt with in separate chapters, and, therefore, we shall not further allude to them here. Another well-known name is that of John Henderson, who was one of those noted actors which Bath has given to the English stage. The fact that he made his *début* in Bath is due to Garrick, who obtained for him the engagement. Henderson was the son of an Irish factor, and is spoken of by Doran, in his work entitled "Their Majesties' Servants," as the sole celebrity of the street in which he was born in March, 1747—Goldsmith street, Cheapside. He was descended from Scottish Presbyterians and English Quakers, and his ambition to shine upon the stage is attributed, in some measure, to his mother (who was left a widow when Henderson and his brother were very young) encouraging him in the study of Shakespeare, and making him familiar with the great dramatist's choicest works. He had some taste for art in another form, being very ready with his pencil, but the desire to tread the stage consumed him, and after much difficulty he contrived to gain an audience with

JOHN PHILIP KEMBLE
(*From the Picture by Sir Thomas Lawrence, R.A.*)

Garrick. Neither his personal appearance, for he was apparently a weakly lad, nor his voice, which was not striking, were able to produce any great impression on the Roscius of his time, but Garrick obtained for him an engagement at Bath at a very modest salary. He made his first appearance in Oct., 1772, under the assumed name of Courtney and in the character of Hamlet, the playbill announcing that the part would be performed " by a young gentleman." The following notice of the performance appeared in the *Bath Chronicle* :—

Last night a young gentleman, whose name is *Courtney*, made his first appearance on our stage in the character of *Hamlet*, which he supported throughout with so much ease, judgment and propriety in action as well as expression, as gained him the warmest plaudits of the whole audience.—And we cannot help congratulating the admirers of the tragic muse on so valuable an acquisition to our Theatre.

The impersonation was such a success that a few days later came the announcement that " Richard III." would be played by " Mr. Courtney, the young gentleman who acted Hamlet " Still adopting this *nom de théâtre* he subsequently appeared in Benedict, Macbeth, Bobadil, Bayes, Essex, and other important characters, until, having satisfied himself that he had abilities which warranted his adoption of the stage as a profession, he threw off disguise and in the following December appeared as Hotspur in " Henry IV." under his own name. The occasion was considered of sufficient interest and moment to permit of the young actor's reciting an address to the audience. From this address, which was written by Mr. John Taylor, of the Circus, Bath, we take the following lines :—

Ye candid Fair, while wav'ring here I stand
In sad suspense,—O lend a helping hand !
May I, protected by your fostering care,
When Critics murmur, to your Court repair ;
I have alas ! on this wide sea of Fame
Launch'd my poor bark, under a feigned name ;
That if your frowns foretold a boist'rous gale,
I might in time have low'r'd my shiv'ring sail :
Have soon retreated from the stormy Main,
And hopeless shrunk into my port again.
May your kind Favour still to me be shewn ;
My merit pleads not,—make the act your own :
And since you've deigned t' approve my weak essays ;
From princely Hamlet, down to puzzling Bayes,
I now, with trembling hand, the mask resign,
And hence appear before this beauteous shrine,
    COURTNEY no more !
O name ! so flattering, to my fame-sick heart,
I bid farewell—we now, though friends must part.
To thee ! thy borrower, grateful tribute pays,

With thee, he hopes, not now to lose your praise :
Shine still propitious ! still your smile renew !
And COURTNEY'S pains in HENDERSON review ;
Perfect the work, that's now but rudely form'd,
And save the fruit which in bud you warm'd.

He continued to play principal parts, and became a great favourite
with Bath audiences for five seasons, gaining the title of "The Roscius
of the Bath Theatre." According to Doran, although the news of
his success reached London, no manager offered him an engagement,
but that statement may safely be contradicted, for in December, 1774,
there appeared in a Bath paper a notice to the effect that, although
Mr. Henderson's engagement at the Bath Theatre terminated in the
following spring, he had determined not to leave the city for some
time longer, notwithstanding he had received "the most pressing
invitations and advantageous offers to engage himself in London.'
In 1777 Colman, being in want of some novelty, invited him to the
Haymarket, though, it is stated, without anticipating much benefit
therefrom.   But Henderson speedily became a favourite ; the applause
of the Bath audience was re-echoed in the London house, and in little
over a month his manager had reaped £4,500 by the engagement.
Writing in 1775 Garrick said : "I have seen the great Henderson,
who has something, and is nothing—he might be made to figure
among the puppets of these times.   His Don John is a comic Cato,
and his Hamlet a mixture of tragedy, comedy, pastoral, farce, and .
nonsense.   However, though my wife is outrageous, I am in the
secret ; and see sparks of fire which must be blown to warm even a
London audience at Christmas—he is a dramatic phenomenon, and
his friends, but more particularly Cumberland, has (have) ruined him ;
he has a manner of paving when he would be emphatic, that is
ridiculous, and must be changed, or he would not be suffered at the
Bedford Coffeehouse."   In a letter from Bath, Garrick wrote, "'The
Inflexible Captain' has been played here with success ; Henderson
played Regulus, and you would have wished him bunged up with his
nails before the end of the third act."*   Notwithstanding these uncomplimentary criticisms there is sufficient evidence that he was really
a great actor.   One well known writer speaks of Garrick's contempt
for him, and yet the following paragraph is found in the *Bath Journal*
of August 30th, 1773 :—

The frequent paragraphs in the London papers of Mr. Henderson's being
engaged at Dury Lane Theatre, we suppose to have arisen from his being often
with Mr. Garrick rehearsing there this summer, and from that gentleman
speaking very highly of his merits.

In 1778 Henderson again played in Bath, and the following notice

* "Representative Actors," by W. Clark Russell.

of the performance, taken from the *Bath Chronicle*, Jan 7th, 1778, will be read with interest :—

Mr. Henderson made his appearance last night, at our Theatre, in the character of *Shylock*, before a very elegant and crowded audience, and never was received with more applause. It is needless to remark on his perform-ance of a character in which his merits are so universally allowed, but it was with singular pleasure we observed the warm approbation he received from persons of the first distinction and judgment in this kingdom, at a time, that he is loaded with the most impudent and frontless abuse in the very paper, where, last summer, while he tilled Mr. Colman's Theatre he received the most extravagant commendation. We believe it to be the general opinion of every person of dramatic taste and judgment, that this gentleman, though very inferior to Mr. Garrick, is at this time by far the best performer on the English stage.

Crowded audiences bestowed their plaudits on the favourite, and his every appearance was a scene of great enthusiasm. He appears to have played frequently in Bath during the early months of 1778, but during a part of the time he was laid up with so severe an attack of rheumatism that he was deprived of the use of his hands and feet, and it was feared he would not be able to perform again during the season.

Among others whom the quick eye of Palmer singled out and engaged for the Bath Theatre, and who justified his selection by acquiring such proficiency in their art as to induce London managers to transplant them to the London stage, were Mr. Edwin, Mr. Brett, Mr. Didier, Mr. Bonnor, Miss Kemble, and Miss Scrace. Of these Mr. Edwin became a well-known actor ; he was a low comedian of extraordinary ability, though he took unwarrantable liberties with his parts. He was naturally humorous, had great powers of facial ex-pression, and had a style of singing, which, while it created roars of laughter, was yet melodious and true. Henderson said of him that he had never seen him equalled in dumb action ; without uttering a word he would keep the house in roars of laughter for several minutes together. His career was a very short one, for he died at forty years of age, a victim to drink, but he remained a favourite to the last. Mr. Didier was a member of the Bath Company for some years before he was summoned to London, and he made his first appearance in the Metropolis at Covent Garden Theatre, in December, 1786, in the character of Dashwood, in the Comedy called "Know Your Own Mind." He was received with marks of approbation, but neither he nor the others we have mentioned, gained popularity anything approaching that of Henderson and Edwin. Miss Kemble was a member of that great family who played such an important part in the history of the English stage, and consequently sister to Mrs. Siddons, with whom she appeared in Bath.

Although they did not graduate in Bath, mention must be made of

two noted actors who appeared at the Theatre during the period with
which we are dealing—they are Samuel Foote and James Dodd.
Foote was a rare mimic, and the greatest theatrical caricaturist of his
age ; he was no actor, except in those parts of his own writing, but
entertained his audiences with remarkable imitations of the peculiarities and weaknesses of his contemporaries. He called his entertainment "Giving Tea." and the following is the advertisement of his
appearance which appeared in the *Bath Journal*, 28th January,
1760 :—

> One Day this Week (perhaps on Saturday) after the usual Concert will be
> presented (Gratis) a Play of some kind, for the Benefit of M—r L—e. After
> which, the Town will be entertain'd with a dish of Mr. Foote's Tea, artfully
> imbued after only *one Infusion* by the Original.
>
> > " And for the Taste of every Guest to hit,
> > "To please at once the Gallery, Box, and Pit,"
>
> There will be provided a large Mess of HIS OWN WATER GRUEL, made it is
> presum'd, in his late Indisposition ; being chiefly designed for those who have
> *queasy Stomachs*, and may not perhaps relish the Tea.
>
> N.B.   This Gruel will be cramm'd thick with the *Bread* of discharg'd
> Actors, and Forfeit-Cake ; but those who love *Seasoning*, are requested to
> bring it with them, for there will be neither Sugar nor *Salt in it.

Foote had previously appeared in Bath at the Rooms. One of the
most remarkable things about him was that for ten years of his life
upon the stage he was obliged to play with a cork leg, having met
with an accident while accompanying the Duke of York on a party of
pleasure, which necessitated amputation of the limb.   The Duke of
York, in consequence of this accident, obtained for him the patent of
the Haymarket Theatre for life.   Dr. Johnson had a poor opinion of
Foote, but there seems no doubt that he was endowed with great wit
and humour, although his mimicry bordered on, if it did not
occasionally overstep the borders of vulgarity.   Garrick spoke of him
as the most entertaining companion he ever knew, but no one was
safe with him, for he ridiculed his dearest friend the moment his back
was turned.   James Dodd, "the most perfect fopling ever placed upon
the stage," was an excellent actor of the old school and an admirable representative of such characters as Sir Andrew Aguecheek and
Bob Acres.   In him the stage had one of its most ardent supporters,
for he was excessive'y proud of his profession, of which he considered
himself no mean ornament.   Charles Lamb in his delightful essay
" On Some of the Old Actors," speaks in laudatory terms of Dodd, but
other writers are not so complimentary.†

* Attic Salt.

† It is told of Dodd, who was fond of a long story, that being in company
one night, he began at 12 o'clock to relate a journey he had taken to Bath ;

Three other names of note which are found in the play bill during this period are those of Reddish, Wewitzer and Mansell. Miss Wewitzer, who was in the company in 1782, was the sister of Ralph Wewitzer, a member of the Covent Garden and Drury Lane Compⲁnies. She also played at Covent Garden, and acquired some notoriety both as an actress and a singer. Mr. Reddish fulfilled an engagement at the Bath Theatre in 1767, and coming from Dublin with good recommendations was well received. Reddish married Mrs. Canning, mother of George Canning, the statesman and orator. He died in York Asylum, a confirmed maniac. Miss Mansell first appeared at Drury Lane in 1772, and in the season of 1776-7 she was engaged to play the principal parts in tragedy and serious comedy at Bath. As Mrs. Farren she again played in Bath in 1783-4, but does not appear to have acted here after that, though she died in the city in February, 1820.

Of those who formed the company at the Bath Theatre under Palmer's management, but who do not call for any special mention here, were Mr. Keasberry, Mr. Dimond (afterwards joint proprietors of the Theatre), Mrs. Keasberry, Mr. and Mrs. Didier, Mr. Brookes, Mr. Blissett, Mr. Egan, Mr. Furnival, Mr. and Mrs. Lee,* Mr. and Mrs. Sheriffe, Mr. Death, Mr. Brunsdon, Mr. Rowswell, Mr. Rowbotham, Mr. Haughton, Mr. Jackson, Mr. and Mrs. Barnett, Mr. Bonnor, Mr. Castle ; Mrs. Quelch, Mrs. Arthur, Mrs. Mozeen, Mrs. Bishop, Mrs. Martin ; Miss Ibbott, Miss Lowe, Miss Wheeler and Miss Summers. Many of these appeared for a number of consecutive years, and some had been members of the companies at the Rooms and at the Theatre before it came into Palmer's hand's—Mr. Furnival, for instance, who died in Bath in 1773, at an advanced age. We may judge from the critical audiences before whom they had so frequently to appear, that they were all possessed of considerable histrionic talents, although they were not so fortunate as some of their fellows in gaining advancement to the Metropolis.

Occasionally, but not often, and probably only in the off-season, dramatic performances were varied by variety entertainments, such as the following advertisement indicates :—

and at six o'clock in the morning he had proceeded no further than *Devizes!* The company then rose to separate, when Dodd, who could not bear to be curtailed in his narrative, cried, "Don't go yet ; stay and hear it out, and upon my soul I'll make it entertaining."—W. Clark Russell.

* The *Bath Chronicle*, February 21, 1781, in speaking of the death of Mr. Lee, at the age of 56, says :—He was long contemporary with Mr. Garrick and extremely admired for the propriety, force and justness of his delivery. In a variety of parts he was excellent, in a few, perhaps, unequalled ; and in the course of his theatrical progress has distinguished himself on many occasions as a capital performer and worthy man.

48 THE BATH STAGE.

At the Theatre in Orchard Street.
To-morrow being Tuesday, June 21, will be
performed several surprising
EQUILIBRES ON THE WIRE,
By MR. MATTHEWS, from the Theatre Royal,
Covent Garden, who has had the Honour
To perform before their Majesties.

He puts the Wire in full Swing, and turns himself round ; sits on a Chair on the Wire in full Swing, and carries a balance on his Nose at the same Time. He walks upon a Deal Board on the Wire, turns himself round on the Wire as swift as the fly of a Jack, and carries a Balance while in full Swing. He stands upon his Head in full Swing, and quits his hold at the same Time ; and performs a Variety of other curious Equilibres, all without a Pole. He will balance a half-pound weight on The top of a Straw, and stand on his Head on the Foot of a Drinking Glass. With many other curious Perform- ances never attempted by Mr. Maddox. Likewise his Equilibres on the Ladder, not performed before these 17 years.

The celebrated Sig. FRANCISCO, who performed at the Theatre Royal in Covent Garden in the Entertainment of Harlequin Sorcerer, will ring eight Bells, namely, two on his Head, two in each Hand, and one on each Foot, rising, changing and falling them with unparallelled Dexterity. He also plays several Tunes on them with the greatest Exactness, and is allowed the greatest Curiosity of the kind in the world.—TUMBLING by Mr. Matthews who will fly over ten Men's heads. The Clown by Mr. Franklin.—Tickets to be had at the Pine Apple opposite the Theatre, and at the Wheat Sheaf in Stall Street. Boxes 2s., Pit 1s. 6d., First Gall. 1s., Second Gall. 6d. The Doors to be open at Seven and the Performance to begin at Eight.

It must not be forgotten that during the greater part of this time Palmer was running the theatre at Bristol as well as the Bath Theatre, and that the same company appeared at each. Certain nights were set apart for performances in each city, and an alteration of these nights in 1780 caused some disagreement between the proprietor and the promoters of the weekly concerts which were held on Wednesday nights. Formerly one of the play nights for Bath had been Thursday, but on account of the Cotillon balls being held on that day it was decided to change the night of performance at Orchard Street to Wednesday. This was taken as being a desire to prejudice the concerts, a charge which Palmer indignantly denied, pointing out that so far from that being the case, four or five of the principal per- formers were allowed to leave the Theatre "to the lessening of the entertainment there, and the improvement of the Concert, which is against it." This statement in vindication of the motive of the pro- prietor of the Theatre thus concluded—"The Theatre is as indepen- dent and well protected a property as any in this country, has never looked to or regarded any other patronage than that of the Public, and the performances will be exhibited there just as often, and on what nights may be thought most for its interest, without its being

thought necessary to consult any person or persons whatever."
Before Palmer relinquished his management of the Theatre a much
needed improvement was effected by the making of a good coachway
leading to it, together with a stand capable of accommodating from fifty
to sixty carriages.   This was in 1781, and in the following year, in consequence of the increasing expenses in connection with the Theatre, the
price of the boxes was increased to five shillings, among the reasons
given for this advance in price being "the enlargement of the
company, the band and servants, which have made weekly payments
nearly double to what they were only 10 years ago ; the extravagant
price of oil and candles * and almost every other of the numerous
articles used in a Theatre."
   Although neither played in Bath the deaths occurred of two very
noted actors during this period and deserve to be noticed.   Quin died
in Bath in 1766, and there is a monument to him in the Abbey with an
inscription written by Garrick, which is too well known to be quoted.
Garrick, who had on several occasions visited the city, died in 1779.

   *   The lack of comfort afforded by the Theatre to its patrons may be judged
from a complaint made in the newspapers by " a female correspondent " of the
way in which the clothes of persons in the pit were spoiled by the "spermaceti
candles " dropping on them.   That, however, should be said, was before the
younger Palmer assumed active management, and at a time when the curtain
had to be drawn up between the play and the farce on account of the intolerable heat if it were allowed to remain down.

E

CHAPTER IX.

SHERIDAN AND MISS LINLEY.

BATH IN 1772-74—DR. LINLEY AND HIS FAMILY—ELIZABETH
LINLEY—A STRANGE FATHER—ROMANTIC GIRLHOOD—"THE
MAID OF BATH"—SHERIDAN—AN ELOPEMENT—DUELLING—
A DISCREDITABLE AFFAIR—PRODUCTION OF "THE RIVALS"
IN BATH—"THE SCHOOL FOR SCANDAL"—MARIA LINLEY.

LTHOUGH Richard Brinsley Sheridan never had
any close connection with the Bath Theatre, yet his
name and that of his accomplished and beautiful
wife are both so closely associated with the drama
and with Bath that no excuse is necessary for introducing them here. Speaking of Bath in the years
1772-74, Mr. Percy Fitzgerald in his " Lives of the
Sheridans," says, " There were then a few centres which obtained a
sort of reputation for social attractions, of which the most leading
were Bath, York, and Lichfield. The diversions of Bath were akin to
those of some great foreign watering place. That handsome city,
with its fine situation, keen recovering air, salutary waters, its truly
architectural and imposing streets, to say nothing of its dramatic
nursery for the London stage, was at the height of its prosperity during
the last thirty years of last century."

At this time their lived in Bath a very talented family of the name
of Linley, the father, Dr. Linley, being a gifted musician, a native of
Wells, who had when a boy attracted the attention of Chilcot, organist
at the Bath Abbey, by his extraordinary talents. By Chilcot he was
adopted as a pupil, afterwards being placed under the tuition of a
well-known London master of that time. Eventually he returned to
Bath, where he established himself as a teacher of music, speedily
becoming the leading musician of the city, and the promoter of a series
of concerts at the Assembly Rooms which obtained great popularity
and were supported by the most fashionable among the visitors who
regularly resorted thither. Dr. Linley had a large family, all of whom
showed great talent, while his two daughters were remarkable for
their extreme beauty, especially Elizabeth, the eldest, who had a voice
as lovely as her face, and who was the prima donna of her father's
concerts, not only in Bath, but also in other cities, and especially
Oxford, where she is said to have fairly turned the heads of dons,

tutors, and undergraduates. Elizabeth, or Eliza Linley, as she was called, was born at No. 5, Pierrepont street, Bath, in the year 1754, and was about 16 years of age, the admired of all admirers, when Thomas Sheridan and his family came to live in Bath. The young gallants quarrelled over her, and vied with each other in the attempt to win her affections, while elder beaux were just as eager to obtain her favour. John Wilkes, who was visiting Bath about this time, wrote of the sisters, "The eldest I think still superior to all the handsome things I have heard of her. She does not seem in the least

spoiled by the idle talk of our sex, and is the most modest, pleasingly delicate flower I have seen for a great while." Garrick, too, was equally impressed when he stayed in Bath in 1770, so much so, in fact, that he made overtures to her father, with the object of securing her as an additional and valuable attraction for his theatre. Dr. Linley, however, declined his offers, and in doing so displayed a mercenary spirit which went near to ruining his daughter's young life, through his desire that she should marry an old but wealthy admirer who sought her hand. The ground upon which he refused Garrick's proposals was that, being her father, he was entitled to the full benefit of her

RICHARD BRINSLEY SHERIDAN.

talents. Colman made similar offers to take her to the Haymarket, but these were also declined upon like grounds, and it seems that Dr. Linley had some thought of bringing her out in London himself, though as a singer at concerts and oratorios only, for, wrote this strange man, "In regard to her engaging as an actress, I shall never do that, unless it were to ensure to myself and family a solid settlement, by being admitted to purchase a share in the patent on reasonable terms," or something adequate to this.

The whole of the letter to Colman from which this passage is extracted, tends to place Dr. Linley in a very unfavourable light, and makes it a matter of no surprise that he should favour the proposal of marriage of Mr. Walter Long, of Wiltshire, a man of considerable fortune, but with the weight of many years upon his shoulders. The story is, that Miss Linley, to whom such a match was repugnant, confessed her disinclination to her elderly admirer, who, generously responding to her request that he should continue his attentions no further, broke off the engagement, and satisfied the enraged father, who brought an action for breach of promise, by settling the sum of £3,000 upon the young lady. There is another side to the story, however, which puts a very different complexion upon it. According to Fitzgerald, Mr. Long was a notorious miser, who treated Miss Linley infamously, and his conduct having become a scandal in the city, Foote, during one of his visits to Bath, worked up the incidents into a highly personal play, entitled, " The Maid of Bath." So gross were the personalities in which he indulged that it was impossible to mistake the author's intentions (Foote himself played the part of the miser), and under this scathing attack Long was glad to retire and allow himself to be mulcted in the damages we have mentioned.

What is far more interesting, however, is Miss Linley's attachment to, and subsequent marriage with, Richard Brinsley Sheridan—a long and romantic story, which must necessarily be related here only in brief, though it is of unusual interest, inasmuch as upon it was founded that picture of life in Bath, the admirable play of " The Rivals," the attractions of which never tire upon genuine enthusiasts of the drama. A friendship was soon struck up between the Linley and Sheridan families. Miss Linley and Miss Sheridan became inseparable companions, and the latter's two brothers, Charles and Richard, both fell in love with the " Maid of Bath," but while the former failed to win her affections, the latter prosecuted his suit with far greater success. He seems to have constituted himself a sort of guardian over his enamorata, presuming to advise and direct her in various matters in which she was nearly concerned. They used to meet in what are now the Institution Gardens, where young Sheridan appears to have warmly protested against any encouragement being given to a Captain Mathews, who persecuted her with his attentions, and worked upon her feelings by threatening to destroy himself unless she listened to his suit. As a matter of fact, this Mathews was a married man, and a thorough scamp, who resorted at last to shameful threats which raised a scandal in the city. It was Sheridan who proved to Miss Linley the true character of her persecutor, and it was he who proposed that she should fly to France and take refuge in a convent for a while, until the danger should be overpast. The story of this strange elopement is well-known. It was conceived and carried out in quite a platonic spirit, although a ceremony of marriage was gone through at Calais. Miss Linley remained at the convent until she was taken from there by an English doctor in Lisle, who placed her under his wife's

care, where she was found by her father, who set out in pursuit as soon
as a clue was found to the fugitives. Dr. Linley appears to have
accepted the situation much more coolly than might have been
expected. He was not told of the Calais marriage but took the
explanations given him in good part, and even in Bath the runaways'
story was fully believed, which speaks well for a city where scandal is
supposed to have been so very rife. Mrs. Oliphant pertinently
remarks, " We doubt whether such faith would be shown in the hero
and heroine of a similar freak in our own day."

Sheridan, however, had to face an irate parent and a brother whose
rage knew no bounds. High words passed between the two brothers,
and their sisters feared that a duel would ensue, but instead they both
set out for London to seek out and fight Captain Mathews, who had
inserted an advertisement in a Bath paper, posting Sheridan as a liar
and a scoundrel for having, "in a letter left behind him for that
purpose," attempted " to account for his scandalous method of running
away from this place by insinuations derogatory to my character
and that of a young lady, innocent, so far as relates to me or my
knowledge." A challenge was sent to Mathews by Richard Sheridan,
which was accepted, and the parties met at Hyde Park, but being
there interrupted they adjourned to a tavern, where, in a private room,
so extraordinary a scene took place that Sheridan's account of it is
worth reproducing :—

Mr. Ewart took·lights up in his hand, and almost immediately on our entering the room we engaged. I struck Mr. Mathew's point so much out of the
line, that I stepped up and caught hold of his wrist, or the hilt of his sword,
while the point of mine was at his breast. You (the letter was addressed to
the second on the other side) ran in and caught hold of my arm exclaiming,
" Don't kill him " I struggled to disengage my arm, and said his sword
was in my power. Mr. Mathews called out twice or thrice, " I beg my
life." We were parted. You immediately said, " There, he has begged
his life and now there is an end of it." Mathews then hinted that I was
rather obliged to your interposition for the advantage ; you declared that
" before you did so, both the swords were in Mr. Sheridan's power." Mr.
Mathews still seemed resolved to give it another turn, and observed that he had
never quitted his sword. Provoked at this, I then swore (with too much heat,
perhaps) that he should either give up his sword and I would break it, or go
to his guard again. He refused—but, on my persisting, either gave it into my
hand, or flung it on the table or ground (which, I will not absolutely affirm).
I broke it and flung the hilt to the other end of the room. He exclaimed at
this. I took a mourning sword from Mr. Ewart, and presenting him with
mine, gave my honour that what had passed should never be mentioned by me,
and he might now right himself again. He replied that he " would never
draw a sword against the man who had given him his life ; " but on his still
exclaiming against the indignity of breaking his sword (which he had brought
upon himself), Mr. Ewart offered him the pistols, and some altercation passed
between them. Mr. Mathews said that he could never show his face if it were

known how his sword was broke—that such a thing had never been done—that it cancelled all obligations, &c. You seemed to think it was wrong, and we both proposed that if he never misrepresented the affair, it should not be mentioned by us. This was settled. After much altercation, and with much ill-grace, he gave the apology.

Notwithstanding that this apology was duly published in the Bath papers, the matter did not rest here, though the reasons for the quarrel being pursued further are by no means clear. One account says that the circumstances connected with the first encounter oozed out, and Mathews was obliged to again challenge his opponent to save his reputation, and another suggests that Sheridan continued to attack Mathews, and so brought about the second duel, while the *Bath Journal* of July 6th, 1772 (two days after the encounter), had the following :—

We are informed that the last affair between Mr. Mathews and Mr. Sheridan was not in consequence of any dispute concerning a certain young lady, but was occasioned by Mr. S. refusing to sign a paper testifying the *spirit* and *propriety* of Mr. M.'s behaviour in their former encounter. The latter gentleman then sent a challenge, which was accepted, and they went by agreement to Kings-down, in order to decide their quarrel. After a few passes they fell, by which means both their swords were broken, Mr. S.'s almost to the hilt ; Mr. M. having in that situation considerably the advantage, call'd to Mr. S. to beg his life, and upon his refusal, picked up a broken piece of sword, gave him the wounds of which he now lies ill, and leaving him (as he supposed) dead, set off immediately for London.

This account of the duel does not exactly tally with that given by Mathews's second, but there is no doubt that it was a most disgraceful affair, highly discreditable to both parties. Sheridan was seriously wounded, and it was some time before he recovered. In the convalescent stage he was sent by his father into Essex, with the hope, no doubt, that he would forget the cause of these quarrels, and, indeed, he promised his father that he would think no more of Miss Linley—a piece of deceit which it is to be feared he was only too ready to any time to practice. As a matter of fact, the romance was continued, and concluded on April 13th, 1773, when they were married with the consent of Dr. Linley, though Mr. Sheridan refused his consent, and maintained a stubborn spirit of unforgiveness.

Thus ends the story upon which "The Rivals" was founded. It was Miss Linley who supplied the idea of the romantic Lydia ; Captain Paumier, his second in the duel on Kingsdown, was Sir Lucius O'Trigger ; Mathews was the orginal Bob Acres ; Mrs. Malaprop was probably suggested by some pretentious vulgarian frequenting the Pump Room ; Sir Anthony Absolute, the elder Sheridan, and, for the rest, Fitzgerald says :—" The jealous and desponding Faulkland is founded upon himself, and long afterwards he used to tease his wife with the same morbid suspicions and imaginings. These, however, only supplied outlines and hints to be treated *secundum artem.* For while he drew hints from his own temper for Faulkland, he also presented himself to the Bath public as the gay and gallant Absolute, though it was scarcely loyal to represent the character he intended for Mathews, as a coward." " The Rivals " was first produced at Covent Garden on the 17th January, 1775. It was not at first a success, but after sundry alterations and a change in the cast for the part of Sir Lucius O'Trigger, it met with unqualified approval. A month or so later it was brought to Bath, where it was produced on March 8th, 1775, and the *Bath Chronicle* of the following day contains this note of the performance :—

Mr. Sheridan's Comedy of the Rivals was performed for the first time at our theatre last night ; and we have the pleasure to say, that it was received with every mark of approbation and applause from a numerous and polite audience.

In the same year Sheridan also wrote the farce entitled, " S. Patrick's Day," and this, too, was placed upon the stage in Bath very shortly after its first production in London. Portions of " The School for Scandal " undoubtedly had their origin in the gossip in which the scandal-mongers that frequented the Pump Room freely indulged, and this comedy also met with marked approbation upon its production in that city, when, says Fitzgerald, it was put on " with an excellent cast, while the author himself superintended the rehearsals, and took immense pains with the production. Principal actors were Bernard, Edwin, Dimond, Didier, Blisset and Rowbotham, men of ability and worth." Mrs. Candour was one of the first characters Mrs. Siddons appeared in at Bath (27th Oct., 1778), and she played the part eleven times during the season.

Of the after life of Mr. and Mrs. Sheridan we have little to do. Sheridan's career as a statesman and an orator is well known. Mrs. Sheridan died in 1792. Brief reference must, however, be made to Mrs. Sheridan's sister, Maria Linley, who married a friend of Sheridan's, Richard Tickell, then living at Beaulieu House, Newbridge Hill. She was also possessed of an exquisite voice, and the story ran that she died at her harpischord. This was incorrect, for Mrs. Tickell died from fever, but it is said that shortly before her death she raised herself in bed and sang a portion of the anthem, " I know that my Redeemer liveth," with a touching sweetness that went to the hearts of all who heard it, the physician who was attending her being so overcome that he was obliged to leave the room, exclaiming as he did so, " She is an angel." Her husband was the grandson of Addison's friend Thomas Tickell, and one of his daughters became the mother of John Arthur Roebuck.

CHAPTER X.

MRS. SIDDONS.

A Child of Bath — Early Life — Appears in London —
Dispiriting Blow — Engaged for Bath — A Discerning
Prompter — Growing into Favour — A Season's Work —
Salary—A Hard School.—Miss Kemble—Invitation to
Revisit London—A Triumphant Moment—A Memorable
Benefit—The Three Reasons.

OREMOST among the many notable names connected
with the Bath Stage, stands that of Mrs. Sarah
Siddons, the most celebrated of English tragic
actresses, whom Bath claims for a child of its own,
since it was in this city that she won the reputation
which gained for her the opening to the London
Stage through which she attained rank and fame.
Like many others of her profession, she failed at first to attract that
attention and favour which was subsequently so lavishly bestowed
upon her, and the lofty position which she held in the meridian of her
glory was largely due to the patient study and practice for which her
connection with the Bath Theatre supplied opportunities, and which
nurtured and directed her great natural talents.

Mrs. Siddons was a daughter of Roger Kemble, an actor, and
manager of an itinerant company, and she was born at Brecknock in
1755. She first entered upon her theatrical career as a vocalist, but
was soon induced to adopt a more serious line, and very early
attempted tragedy. At the early age of 18 she married Mr. Siddons,
and appeared with her husband at various places in the North of
England, where they obtained a good reputation, so that in 1775
Mrs. Siddons was invited to try her powers on the London stage, and
played Portia to Garrick's Shylock ; but the attempt was unsuccessful,
and her reception very unflattering. " She is certainly very pretty,"
said one who saw her, " but then, how awkward, and what a shocking
dresser ! " This would have been a depressing and dispiriting blow
to most beginners, but not so to Mrs. Siddons, who was only stirred
to greater and more persistent efforts. In 1778, she and her husband
were engaged to appear at the Bath Theatre, an engagement which
was due to the good judgment of Mr. Floor, the prompter, who had

seen her act at Liverpool, and formed an opinion of her abilities which was justified by time and events.* Her first appearance was on the 24th October, in the character of Lady Townly in " The Provoked Husband," other parts being taken by Dimond (Lord Townly), Blisset (Sir Francis) and Edwin (Squire Richard), and on the 27th she made her second appearance as Mrs. Candour in " The School for Scandal." Her friend, Mrs. Piozzi admitted that she did not shine in comedy, though she played Mrs. Candour very well, her facial expression being so significant. Mrs. Siddons complained that she was not allowed sufficient scope, but, of course, the principal comedy parts were by right allotted to the leading lady, besides which, Fitzgerald remarks, " Even here the disabilities attendant on failure pursued her for a while, for the manager was at first not very eager in her favour." But her abilities soon came into

MRS. SIDDONS
(After a Medallion.)

notice, and if slowly, at any rate surely, she worked herself into favour, and the management discovered what a treasure it had

* In the life of Mrs. Siddons, by Thomas Campbell, it is said that after her dismissal from Drury Lane she acted at Birmingham for the summer season of 1776, and it was there she played with Henderson, who was so struck by her merits that he recommended her to Palmer. The fact that her engagement was due to Floor is, however, gleaned from a contemporary newspaper.

alighted on. During her first season, which ended on the 1st June,
1779, she acted Lady Townly twice and Mrs. Candour eleven times ;
she played twice each the characters of Mrs. Lovemore, Belvidera,
Lady Brumpton, the Queen in " Hamlet " (Henderson playing
Hamlet), Portia (Shylock, Henderson), Countess of Salisbury,
Euphrasia, Juliet and Emmeline ; appeared once each in Elvira,
Lady Jane, Milwood, Rosamond, Queen in "The Spanish Friar,"
Imoinda, Bellario, Imogen, Miss Aubrey, Queen in "Richard III.,"
Indiana, Sigismunda, Lady Randolph, Jane Shore, Emmelina, and
six times as the Princess in "Law of Lombardy." She also twice
repeated Sheridan's Monody on Garrick.

Her salary at the Bath Theatre was £3 a week, "not a very liberal
amount," remarks Fitzgerald, " but respectable, considering her
modest claims, and the amount allowed at other Theatres." But it
was money well earned ; the number of different characters in which
she had to appear during a single season is alone sufficient to show
how arduous and exhausting was an actor's, or actress's, life in those
days, and in this instance it was not even as if the company appeared
at one theatre only, and had, therefore, a fair amount of time in
which to prepare their parts, but, as we have already seen, Palmer
was also proprietor of the Bristol Theatre, which was included in the
Bath " circuit," and it thus happened, that after a tedious rehearsal at
the Bath Theatre, lasting the whole morning, the members of the
company had to set out for Bristol, where they appeared the same
n ght, returning the next day probably to play some trying piece at
the Bath house. It was a hard, though good, school, but Mrs.
Siddons's heart was in her work, and she heroically laboured to gain
popularity, striving by hard study, not only to please the public, but
also to attain eminence in her profession. Mrs. Siddons has thus
described her life in Bath :—

"I now made an engagement at Bath. There my talents and industry were
encouraged by the greatest indulgence, and, I may say, with some admiration.
Tragedies, which had been almost banished, again resumed their proper
interest ; but still I had the mortification of being obliged to personate many
subordinate characters in comedy, the first being, by contract, in the
possession of another lady. To this I was obliged to submit, or to forfeit a
part of my salary, which was only three pounds a week. Tragedies were now
becoming more and more fashionable. This was favourable to my cast of
powers ; and whilst I laboured hard, I began to earn a distinct and flattering
reputation. Hard labour indeed it was ; for, after the rehearsal at Bath, and
on a Monday morning, I had to go and act at Bristol on the evening of the
same day ; and reaching Bath again, after a drive of twelve miles, I was
obliged to represent some fatiguing part there on the Tuesday evening.
Meantime, I was gaining private friends, as well as public favour ; and my
industry and perseverance were indefatigable. When I recollect all this labour
of mind and body, I wonder that I had strength and courage to support it,

interrupted as I was by the cares of a mother, and by the childish sports of my little ones, who were often most unwillingly hushed to silence, from interrupting their mother's studies."

Mrs. Siddons's second season in Bath opened on the 27th September, 1779, and closed on the 12th July, 1780, during which time she appeared in a number of characters, of which it will be sufficient to indicate a few. The Theatre opened with a performance of " Law of Lombardy," in which Mrs. Siddons played the Princess, and subsequently she sustained the parts of Jane Shore, Mrs. Candour, Isabella (" Measure for Measure "), Leonora (" Double Falsehood," acted for the first time), Mrs. Belville (" School for Wives "), Millwood (" London Merchant "), and Miranda (" Busy Body "). For her benefit, on the 12th February, 1780, Mrs. Siddons played Eleanora, in " Edward and Eleanora," Dimond playing Edward, and Master and Miss Siddons appearing as the children. Mrs. Siddons also recited the Monody on Garrick, the performance concluding with " Lethe "— Lord Chalkstone, Bonnor ; Old Man, Jackson (engaged from the Haymarket to supply the loss of Edwin) ; Frenchman and Fire Gentleman, Didier ; Mercury, Du Bellamy ; Fire Lady (with a song in character), Mrs. Siddons. For her second benefit, at Bristol, on the 26th June, the programme was " Isabella," with " Britons Strike Home,' and " Edgar and Emmeline "—Emmeline, Mrs. Siddons.

In the season of 1780-81, Mrs. Siddons brought out her sister, Miss Kemble, whom she have already noticed. She made her first appearance in " Jane Shore" on the 19th September, Mr. Brunton, from Norwich, also appearing for the first time before a Bath audience. By her benefit on the 17th January, 1781, Mr. Siddons realised £124, a very handsome sum. " Jane Shore" was the play presented, with "All the World's a Stage," the " entertainment to conclude with an address to the audience." On account of the expected crush, Mrs. Siddons announced that she was induced to " lay the pit and boxes together," reserving the front rows of the gallery " for the gentlemen of the pit," entreating " their indulgence for this liberty," and making most humble apologies for the innovation. The cast on this occasion was as follows :—Lord Hastings, Mr. Dimond ; Gloster, Mr. Blisset ; Belmour, Mr. Keasberry ; Ratcliffe, Mr. Rowbotham ; Catesby, Mr. Haughton ; Derby, Mr. Siddons ; Porter, Mr. Payne, and Dumont, Mr. Brunton : Alicia, Miss Kemble, and Jane Shore, Mrs. Siddons. Of Mr. Siddons's acting, Mrs. Summers, a member of the company, who was confidante to Mrs. Siddons in tragedies, and was very intimate with her off the stage, said that he was a very indifferent player, but a very good judge of acting. He took great pains in coaching his wife in her parts, " and was sometimes very cross with her when she did not act to please him." After the 11th June, 1781, the company removed to Bristol, and played there three times a week, and on 9th July Mrs. Siddons had a benefit which realised £100. During this season she again played in a variety of pieces, and her acting is said to have vastly improved by the experience which she gained at Bath. At any rate she had now become a fast favourite, and made so many friends that the parting which was very near at hand, was made all the more severe. In the course of the next season (1781-82) she received an invitation to re-visit Drury Lane, and "after my former dismissal from thence," she wrote, "it may be imagined that this was to me a triumphant moment." She attributed this honour in a great measure to the friendliness of the Duchess of Devonshire, whose acquaintance she had made during a visit to Bath, and who always spoke of her performances with unqualified approbation.   According to other accounts, however, her fame reached London through various sources, and her engagement was largely due to the influence and exertions on her behalf of the elder Sheridan, whose son was then proprietor of Drury Lane. How this occurred is thus told by his granddaughter, Mrs. Le Fanu :—

While at Bath for his health ; Mr. Sheridan, sen., was strongly solicited to go to the play, to witness the performance of a young actress, who was said to distance all competition in tragedy. He found, to his astonishment, that it was the lady who had made so little impression on him some years before in the "Runaway;" but who, as Garrick had declared, was possessed of tragic powers sufficient to delight and electrify an audience. After the play was over he went behind the scenes, to get introduced to her, in order to compliment her. He said: "I am surprised, madame, that with such talents you should confine yourself to the country ; talents that would be sure of commanding, in London, fame and success." The actress modestly replied that she had already tried London, but without the success which had been anticipated ; and that she was advised by her friends to be content with the fame and profit she obtained at Bath, particularly as her *voice* was deemed unequal to the extent of a London theatre. Immediately on his return to London, he spoke to the acting manager of Drury Lane, strenuously recommending her to him. Upon her being engaged, he directed her, with a truly kind solicitude, in the choice of a part for her first appearance. With the usual preference of a young and handsome actress for a character of pomp and show, she inclined to that of Euphrasia, in "The Grecian Daughter;" but the juster taste of Mr. Sheridan determined her in favour of the far more natural and affecting character of "Isabella;" and the judgment with which the selection was made was amply confirmed by the bursts of rapturous applause."

The accounts of her last season in Bath show how great a favourite she was, and with what reluctance the frequenters of the Theatre parted with her. Shortly after her engagement for Drury Lane, efforts were made to retain her services for the Bath stage, and a paragraph even appeared in the papers stating that Mr. Palmer was "in expectation of prevailing upon Mr. Sheridan to forego his engagement with Mrs. Siddons, at least to spare her a year or more to us."

Whatever was the nature of the negotiations they were not successful, and in the early summer she took a final farewell of the audience from which she had received so much encouragement, and such flattering testimonies of respect and regard. At her first benefit this season, on the 9th February, 1782, when she appeared as Zara in " The Mourning Bride," and, by particular desire, Nell in the farce "The Devil to Pay," the demand for places was so great that she was obliged to repeat the arrangement of the previous year, to turn the pit into stalls and partition off a portion of the gallery for the accommodation of the pittites. This benefit realised £146, and in a book which had been placed in the box office at the suggestion of friends, subscriptions were entered to the sum of twenty guineas. The practice of keeping a book in the box office "for those ladies and gentlemen who should wish to subscribe, who should wish to pay a compliment to the merits of any of the performers, and might be absent from Bath at the time of their benefits," was continued for some time after this. On May 21st Mrs. Siddons took another, and her last benefit, and the occasion was made a memorable one by her recital of an address, written by herself, introducing " Three Reasons " for quitting the Bath Theatre. The following is a copy of the advertisement of this performance :—

For the Benefit of Mrs. SIDDONS.

On Tuesday next being the 21st May 1782

Will be perform'd a tragedy (not acted this season) call'd

THE DISTRESS'D MOTHER.

At the end of the Play Mrs. SIDDONS will deliver a Poetical Address (written by herself) in the course of which she will produce to the Audience THREE REASONS for her quitting this Theatre.

After which will be perform'd a HOLIDAY FETE, or THEATRICAL MEDLEY: With a Farce called

THE DEVIL TO PAY.

Nell (by particular desire) Mrs. Siddons.

Tickets to be had of Mr. Siddons, at Mr. Telling's, on Horse Street Parade, and of Mr. Fisher, at the Box-Lobby of the Theatre, where places for the boxes may be taken.

☞ As the above bill of fare may to some appear tedious, Mr. Siddons begs leave to say that every possible despatch shall be made, and that the Entertainments between the Address and Farce are not only calculated to please, but to fill up the time, while Mrs. Siddons dresses, which otherwise would hang very heavy on the audience.

The "three reasons" were, as will be seen from the address, her three children, but what she intended to do was kept a profound secret ; not even the performers were taken into confidence, and the children were kept in her dressing room until they were required upon the stage :

MRS. SIDDONS'S THREE REASONS.

Have I not raised some expectation here ?—
Wrote by herself?—What ! authoress and player ?—
True, we have heard her,—thus I guess'd you'd say,
With decency recite another's lay ;
But never heard, nor ever could we dream
Herself had sipp'd the Heliconian stream.
Perhaps you farther said—Excuse me pray,
For thus supposing all that you might say—
What will she treat of in this same address,
Is it to shew her learning ? – Can you guess ?
Here let me answer—No : far different views
Possess'd my soul, and fir'd my virgin Muse ;
'Twas honest gratitude, at whose request
Shamed be the heart that will not do its best.
The time draws nigh when I must bid adieu
To this delightful spot—nay ev'n to you—
To you, whose fost'ring kindness rear'd my name,
O'erlooked my faults, but magnified my fame.
How shall I bear the parting ? Well I know
Anticipation here is daily woe.
Oh ! could kind Fortune, where I next am thrown,
Bestow but half the candour you have shewn.
Envy o'ercome, will hurl her pointless dart,
And critic gall be shed without its smart,
The numerous doubts and fears I entertain,
Be idle all—as all possess'd in vain.—
But to my promise. If I thus am blessed,
In friendship link'd, beyond my worth caress'd,—
Why don't I here, you'll say, content remain,
Nor seek uncertainties for certain gain ?
What can compensate for the risks you run ;
And what your reasons ?—Surely you have none.
To argue here would but your time abuse :
I keep my word—my reason I produce—
    [*Here three children were discovered : they were*
        HENRY, SALLY *and* MARIA SIDDONS.]
These are the moles that bear me from your side ;
Where I was rooted – where I could have died.
Stand forth, ye elves, and plead your mother's cause ;
Ye little magnets, whose soft influence draws
Me from a point where every gentle breeze
Wafted my bark to happiness and ease—
Sends me adventurous on a larger main,
In hopes that you may profit by my gain.

Have I been hasty?—am I then to blame ;
Answer, all ye who own a parent's name ?
Thus have I tried you with an untaught Muse,
Who for your favour still most humbly sues,
That you, for classic learning, will receive
My soul's best wishes, which I freely give—
For polished periods round, and touched with art,—
The fervent offering of my grateful heart.

The benefit yielded £145 18s., and a benefit at Bristol, on the 17th June, when Mrs. Siddons again produced her "three reasons," brought her £106 13s. Her last performance appears to have been as Mrs. Beville in the " School for Wives," on the 19th of June, for Mrs. Brett's benefit ; she was announced to appear in Bath as Zara, on the 22nd June, but she was taken ill and the play was changed. It was on the 10th of October she reappeared at Drury Lane, and from that day her great and exceptional abilities remained unchallenged. " I was truly grieved,"* she wrote, "to leave my kind friends at Bath, and was also fearful that the power of my voice was not equal to filling a London Theatre. My friends, too, were also doubtful ; but I soon had reason to think that the bad construction of the Bath Theatre, and not the weakness of my voice, was the cause of our mutual fears." Her salary at Drury Lane was ten guineas per week, and was raised in 1784 to be twenty-three guineas and seven shillings per week. Henderson said of her, " She was an actress who never had had an equal, nor would ever have a superior."

* "All through her Bath career," says Fitzgerald, "she seems to have been cherished with singular affection, and her letters to her friends give a very engaging portrait of a young and pretty woman, full of spirit and ingenuousness, and a gentle confidence, which is always sure to attract."

CHAPTER XI.

KEASBERRY AND DIMOND.

PALMER'S SUCCESSORS—WILLIAM WYATT DIMOND—KEASBERRY
—LOWERING THE PRICES—INTRODUCTORY ADDRESS—SUCCESS-
FUL SEASON.

ALMER'S labours in connection with the Post Office obliged him, in 1785, to decide upon relinquishing his proprietorship of the Bath Theatre, and the patent passed into the hands of Messrs. Keasberry and Dimond, with whose names we are already familiar, both having been members of the company for some years. Their reign was destined to be as brilliant and successful as their predecessor's ; the Theatre's star was still in the ascendant, it retained its position as a stepping stone to the London stage, and, indeed, it obtained greater popularity during the remaining years of the century than it had done previously. It was gradually getting into closer touch with the London Theatres, so that after a time we shall find, not only that members of the Bath Company were invited to appear upon the London boards, but that Metropolitan stars considered it by no means beneath their dignity to appear in Bath, where the audiences were noted for the justness and accuracy of their criticism. This, it must be acknowledged, was in great measure due to the excellent management of the new proprietors, who were both men of experience and ability.

William Wyatt Dimond continued to appear regularly as a performer until the end of the season 1800-1, when he took his farewell of the stage as an actor and devoted his attention entirely to the work of management. As an actor he is spoken very highly of, and Sheridan paid him the compliment of saying that his conception of the character of Joseph Surface was more consonant with his own ideas when writing the part than any other actor's he had seen. Joseph Surface and Lord Townly were his best and favourite characters, and he also appeared to great advantage as Don Felix, Posthumus, and Edgar ; he was also very great as Charles Oakly, for, though a particularly abstemious man, he was almost at his best when acting in a drunken scene. He is described as having been a very handsome man, of medium height, and in manners a perfect gentleman. In a notice of him which appeared in the *Bath Herald* after his death, in 1812, it was said :—

In every part he played, he always appeared in earnest and was always perfect. His action was elegantly spirited and appropriate. His voice was harmonious and finely modulated. With all these qualifications in their very zenith, he retired from the stage and devoted his mind to the duties of a manager. Perhaps no situation in life is more difficult than that of the director of a theatre. He has a variety of persons to contend with and control, and few of them but have a higher opinion of their own abilities than the public awards them, yet Mr. Dimond, by the gentleness of his manners and unassuming demeanour, had the power of reconciling their minds and making the business of the Theatre go smoothly on—they obeyed him more through the regard they had for him as a friend, than the awe he might have created as a manager.

Dimond lived at No. 1, Devonshire Buildings, where he had a room fitted up for dramatic performances,* a fact that proves what an enthusiast he was in his profession. He had a son, William, who was educated at the Bath Grammar School, and was brought up to the law. He was the author of several successful plays, and upon the death of his father succeeded him in the management, so that we shall have occasion to refer to him again.

Keasberry had occupied the position of manager under Palmer for several years before he joined Dimond in the proprietorship, filling the position with ability and good judgment, and being held in much respect not only by those belonging to the Theatre, but also by the public. He does not appear to have acted much after 1786, and as he continued to fill the duties of management he, no doubt, found them sufficient to wholly occupy his attention, but he is spoken of as being a good all round actor, excelling in some few parts which were more particularly suited to his style. About ten years after entering into partnership with Dimond he retired, that course being forced upon him by frequent indisposition. His son adopted the stage as a profession, and made his *début* under his father's management on the 4th November, 1789, playing in " Earl Goodwin." A sister of his married a gentleman of fortune named Peach, and was left a widow with three children, one of whom was Captain Peach, afterwards the city treasurer of Bath, and for some time stage manager of the Theatre. He married Miss Carr, a favourite Bath actress, of whom we shall have occasion to speak later on. Keasberry, we believe, lived in the large house which stands at the end of Philip Street.

The new proprietors made a preliminary bid for popularity by lowering the price of admission to the boxes, which had been a somewhat sore point for some time, as it was greater than was charged at

* " Historic Houses in Bath," by R. E. Peach.

F

the Bristol Theatre, and Bath playgoers naturally objected to pay for
the same entertainment a shilling more than their "wealthy neigh-
bours." Consequently, when the Theatre opened under the new
proprietors, on the 7th October, 1786, the prices charged for admission
were—boxes, four shillings ; pit, half-a-crown ; gallery, one shilling
and sixpence, and upper gallery one shilling. There was a crowded
house on the opening night, and when Mr. Dimond appeared to
deliver an introductory address, which had been written for the
occasion by Meyler, the applause was so great that it was some
minutes before he was enabled to proceed. The address, which was
as follows, was also very well received, particularly that portion
referring to the late proprietor, and the great work in which he was
engaged :—

"You, who th' historian's page have oft survey'd,
Behold this certain principle display'd—
'In every monarchy, through length of years,
A change of governors and laws appears ;'
Fate shall some empires to oblivion sink ;
To fame raise others from oblivion's brink ;
There prosp'rous Treason mounts the sceptred throne,
And Revolution calls the seat her own.
　　To bring the object nearer to our view
Than thrones and empires, or rebellion's crew,
Suppose this house of merchandizing fame,
Long carried on in but one trader's name,
Who grows or rich, or proud, or old, or great—
Or gets perhaps an office in the State ;
Retires—and leaves the labours and its fruits
To his long-tried and trusty substitutes ;
Who, to obtain continuance of favours,
Vow constant, grateful and increased endeavours.
　　He who of late reign'd o'er this dome supreme,
Retires, to perfect an applauded scheme—
To guard your persons—o'er your wealth to watch
Add wings to commerce, and to law dispatch ;
Old custom's stubborn maxims to control,
'And waft your fame from Indus to the Pole.'
His late possessions—patents, wardrobes, scenes,
His mimic thunder, lightning, kings and queens ;
The hero's truncheon, pantomime battoons,
Thalia's vizor, tempests, suns and moons—
Devolve on us—long agents in th' employ—
Me your obedient, and our late viceroy,
　　Be ours the task by every art to raise
The drama's splendour and the public praise.
T'enlarge the soul, Melpomene shall pour
Her copious streams in Grief's instructive lore ;
Shall teach mankind to prize a low estate,

By viewing woes attendant on the great.
Thalia here her magic wiles shall play,
To laugh your foibles and your cares away ;
And all confess that medicine's nicer art,
Which, while it cures the pain, delights the heart.
Here Music, too, shall greet the tuneful ear,
And with sweet sounds allay our grief and fear ;
Broad Farce and Pantomime shall oft peep in
To set our old acquaintance on the grin.
In short, our study, our delight, shall be
To blend true taste with sprightly novelty ;
Encourage merit—jealous envy shun,
Genius prefer—confess ourselves out-done.
Grant us fair trial—your protection guard us,
As we deserve—so censure or reward us."

The pieces produced on this auspicious occasion were "The Heiress" and "The Son-in-law." Mr. Keasberry played in the latter, and, like his partner, was accorded a most gratifying reception, being "welcomed," as a writer in a local paper put it, "with the affectionate congratulations that his most excellent character in public and private life has ever merited." The success of this first night was continued throughout the whole season, the various benefits were liberally supported, and when the theatre was closed on Midsummer Eve in the following year, it was recorded as an unusual fact that there was an overflow in every part of the house, and the audience, which included, among other titled personages, the Duke and Duchess of Devonshire and Lady Duncannon, was described as being "as large and as elegant " as was ever drawn together in the city. The energy which the new managers displayed was illustrated by the production during the season of a new play by Mrs. Inchbald, entitled " Such Things Are," a comedy that was attended with great success. The copyright of this piece was sold to a London bookseller, who paid a substantial sum for it, but it was deemed a play of such importance that it was re-purchased and became the exclusive right of Covent Garden Theatre. " Upon what terms then," remarks the *Bath Chronicle* (21st March, 1787), "did Messrs. Keasberry and Dimond obtain the privilege of presenting it at Bath is a question that suggests itself. Their interest must have been powerful to procure this early manuscript of so popular, so excellent a comedy."

CHAPTER XII.

INCLEDON AND MISS WALLIS.

FIVE YEARS OF SUCCESS—PROMOTION TO LONDON—BENJAMIN CHARLES INCLEDON—SKETCH OF HIS EARLY LIFE—A NATIONAL SINGER—WARD AND MIDDLETON—MOSES KEAN—MISS WALLIS.

HE first five years under the management of the new proprietors, although not remarkable for any very conspicuous incidents, are not without interest. They covered a period of unbroken success and popularity, during which many new names were introduced into the play bills, including one which was destined to become a star of the London stage. It was rarely that the company played in Bath to a thin or indifferent house, indeed, the Theatre was sometimes unable to accommodate all who wished to obtain admittance, and the receipts upon benefit nights show the desire of the playgoing public to encourage and stimulate the various performers.

A few words as to some of those who belonged to the company during this period will not be out of place. Of Dimond we have already spoken, both of his merits as an actor and a manager (though the actual work of management was at this time undertaken by Keasberry), but there were several members of the company in 1786 who were soon to be removed to the London stage. Among these were Mr. Blanchard and Mr. Murray. Blanchard appeared at Covent Garden in October, 1787, as a regular member of the company, and was looked upon as an acquisition in the line of comedy. He, however, ruined himself with drink, and was not engaged at Covent Garden after the season 1793-4. Murray, who came from Norwich, and made his first appearance in Bath in October, 1785, as Sir Giles Overreach, in "A New Way to Pay Old Debts," did not leave Bath until a later date than we are now dealing with, and at this time he was an established favourite at the Orchard Street Theatre. "We shall lose in him," said a local critic at the time of his departure for London, "a great actor—void of conceit or ostentation." He played Shakespearian parts with great ability, and his impersonations of such characters as Shylock and Iago were studied with much care ; the latter was said to approach as nearly as possible to Henderson's

SIMS REEVES.

representation of the character, and has been described as "detestibly
excellent." Two other members of the company, Mr. and Mrs.
Bernard, were also engaged at Covent Garden about the same time
as Blanchard, but they were apparently not thought much of, for
they were spoken of as "not bad performers," but "better suited for
Bath than London." Mr. Bernard was the author of a musical sketch,
entitled "British Sailors, or Whimsical Ladies," which was produced
in Bath with Mr and Mrs. Bernard and Blanchard in the caste, and
it was afterwards played at Covent Garden (May, 1789) for Bernard's
benefit, but it was never printed.

The name of Incledon figures conspicuously in the history of the
Bath stage during a number of years, reaching into the present
century. He was a vocalist of undoubted merit, but an exceedingly
vain and egotistical man, who, says Mrs. C. Mathews, "in pronounc-
ing his name, believed he described all that was admirable in human
nature." He was coarse, too, both on the stage and in private life,
but allowances must be made in view of the fact that some years of
his early life were passed on board ship. He was born at S. Keveran,
in Cornwall, in 1764, where his father practised as a surgeon. He
gave evidence of possessing an unusually melodious voice at a very
early age, and when only eight years old he was placed under the
tuition of the celebrated Jackson, of Exeter, in which city he became
the object of much admiration, and was accustomed to sing at public
concerts and private musical entertainments. He was articled to
Jackson, and was a chorister in Exeter Cathedral, but a roving
disposition induced him, at the age of 15, to leave his situation and
join the navy, and he became a midshipman on board the Formidable.
His naval career was not a long one, but he was in several engagements in the West Indies. His vocal abilities attracted the attention
of some of the officers, and, acting under their advice, he determined
to try his fortune on the stage. From Lord Mulgrave, Admiral
Pigot, and other naval officers, he received letters of introduction to
Coleman at the Haymarket, but, failing to obtain an engagement in
London, he joined a company at Southampton, and subsequently was
engaged for the Bath Theatre. There, however, he held only a
subordinate position in the company, until the musicians of the city,
discovering in him a vocalist of no ordinary merit, brought him
forward, and Rauzzini, at that time the conductor of the concerts,
gave him his patronage, as well as valuable instruction and training.
He appeared both at the Rooms and the Theatre, and was received
with rapturous applause, while his reception when he appeared in
Bristol was not less flattering. The news of his fame spread, and he
received, and accepted, an engagement at Vauxhall, which ultimately
led to his appearance at Covent Garden. where he made his *début* in
October, 1790, as Dermot, in "The Poor Soldier." His histrionic
abilities were not great, and this at first militated against his

advancement, but his power as a vocalist overcame this, and he is found taking the lead in operas, besides singing at the Lent oratorios, and in the provinces. Although a London favourite, he never forgot that it was to Bath he owed his introduction to the Metropolitan stage, and his appearances in the city were frequent, and his reception enthusiastic. The good people of Bath, apparently, always went into raptures over him whenever he came among them, and idolised and caressed him. Thus, we find him spoken of as "that British Orpheus, the incomparable Incledon," and in other equally flattering terms. One of his greatest friends in Bath was Dr Harington, the eminent physician,* and he was a great favourite with the members of the Catch Club, which he assisted in establishing.

Of the sweetness and charm of his voice there appears to have been no two opinions, though some writers are otherwise very uncomplimentary to him. "It is a pity," wrote Leigh Hunt, "I cannot put upon paper the singular gabblings of that actor ; the lax and sailor-like twist of mind with which everything hung upon him, and his profane pieties in quoting the Bible, for which and swearing he seemed to have an equal reverence." One of his peculiarities as a singer was the employment of a remarkable falsetto, said to have resembled the tones of a rich flute, and to have been particularly charming. His singing was described by one who often heard him as natural and national. "The hunting song, the sea song, and the ballad, given with English force and English feeling, may be said to have expired with Incledon."†

* Henry Harington, M.D., like his most famous ancestor, Sir John Harington, of Kelston, was endowed with versatile gifts of mind and great intellectual powers. He was physician to the Bath Hospital, for the benefit of which he not only exerted his professional skill, but made his literary powers and labours subservient to its pecuniary interests. Eminent as he was in his profession, Dr. Harington especially excelled in the walks of literature and music. He was a man of gracious, winning manners, easy in carriage and address, and free from the smallest vanity. He wrote with ease and accuracy, and his poetry is not without merit. Perhaps, however, it was in music and musical compositions that he displayed his highest power. In this he was *facile princeps*.—" Rambles about Bath."

† His vocal endowments were certainly considerable ; he had a voice of uncommon power, both in the natural and falsetto. The former was from A to G—a compass of about fourteen notes ; the latter he could use from D to E or F, or about ten notes. His natural voice was full and open, neither partaking of the reed or the string, and sent forth without the smallest artifice ; and such was its ductility, that when he sang *pianissimo*, it retained its original quality. His falsetto was rich, sweet, and brilliant, but totally unlike the other. He took it without preparation, according to circumstances, either about D, E, or F, or ascending an octave, which was his most frequent custom, he could use it with facility, and execute in it ornaments of a certain class, with volubility and sweetness.—" Dictionary of Musicians."

In their second season Messrs. Keasberry and Dimond introduced to their patrons, as a member of the theatre company, an actor who had already trodden the boards in London. This was Mr. Ward, who had played at Drury Lane some two or three years previously, and in the meantime had been the favourite comedian of the Edinburgh Theatre. He was engaged "for the first comic line," and his first appearance as Marplot, in "The Busybody," was a great success. Other new comers in this season were Mrs. Warrell, who possessed considerable musical powers ; Miss Harley, a young actress of much promise ; Mrs. Baines, Mrs. Prideaux, Mr. Fox, Mr. Bloomfield, Mr. and Mrs. Knight, and Mr. Middleton. The latter made his first appearance on any stage in "Othello" on 31st January, 1788, and in September, in the same year, played "Romeo" at Covent Garden. The following notice of his first performance, taken from a Bath paper, is not without interest :—

Of all the characters drawn by the great Master of Nature, to the Moor of Venice he has given the largest scope of varied and conflicting passions. Love, heroism, despair, doubt, rage, tenderness and jealousy hold everlasting war in his breast, and the actor who can portray the character with tolerable justice deserves to be held high in his profession. Veterans of eminence have beheld Othello with awe, and some even, after a trial or two, have relinquished him for the remainder of their lives. What then shall we say of a novitiate, whose first appearance in the theatric world, could give to so arduous a part its due force, and render it throughout tender, impressive and dignified. With peculiar pleasure we report that Mr. Middleton's performance of Othello on Thursday night last at our Theatre, every way merited the loud and lavish applause he received. His voice, though musically soft, and pleasing (conveying to those who had seen Barry, a perfect remembrance of his silver tones) is capable of the greatest exertions. To his judgment not the slightest objection can be made, he delivered every passage with sensibility, and to many gave a new, though far from pedantic illustration. The admirable tale before the Senate was well and pathetically spoken, no under evident marks of fear, but as his fears subsided he gradually rose to a climax of excellence ! We know not on what scenes to bestow our greatest admiration— those of a tender cast charmed, whilst the more compassioned ones roused and agonised us.

Mr. Middleton is said to be scarce 20 years of age—his person is tall, and appears well formed—his action was in general easy, and unembarassed—of his countenance we were not capable of judging ; the sooty visage preventing us from tracing those nice lines which indicate the feelings—but, whatever his face may be, we pronounce that his soul has received from the hand of Nature, a touch of her divinest inspiration.

In the following season new arrivals were Mr. Eastmure, from Norwich, Mr. Bates, "an excellent low comedian and principal harlequin and mechanist from the Theatre Royal, Drury Lane, also composer of the new pantomime at the Royalty Theatre," and Mr. Durravan. Durravan was spoken of as a young man of great

histrionic abilities, who gave promise of being a conspicuous figure
on the London boards, had not his career been cut short by death.
During this season we find the announcement that " Kean gave his
imitations of several of the London performers." This was probably
Moses Kean, uncle of Edmund Kean, who gained some notoriety as
a mimic and ventriloquist.

During the season 1789-90 Miss Wallis made her first appearance
in Bath, and became a regular member of the company, and a great
favourite, as may be judged from the fact that her benefit, in March,
1791, realised £126, while Dimond, a few weeks earlier, had only
£120 in the house. A year later her benefit brought in £136, and on
this occasion a very unpleasant accident happened. " Romeo and
Juliet" was the piece presented, but Dimond, who was cast for Romeo,
was so hoarse that he could not play, while Knight, who sustained the
character of Mercutio, in fencing with Tybalt (West) received a
severe wound in the thigh, which prevented him from appearing in
" The Romp," with which the performance concluded. The accident,
which was fortunately not attended with serious consequences, was
attributed to the stiffness and sharpness of the foil used by West.
At the end of the season 1793-4 Miss Wallis left the company,
having accepted a good engagement at Covent Garden, but the Bath
playgoing public reluctantly parted with her, and in an address which
she delivered on the occasion of her last benefit, she freely acknowledged the kindness which she had received in the city, and said,
" Nor can I think it just, at the moment when your fostering care has
given me strength to fly, that the first effort of my yet feeble wings
should be to fly from you. My only apology is—the duty I owe my
family compels me to depart." Then alluding to Mrs. Siddons's
" three reasons " she stated that she had seven brothers and sisters,
whose prospects in life were dependent upon her's. One of the
managers of the theatre she referred to as her "second father," and
the other as her "true friend," and there seems no doubt that the
parting was mutually regretted. Her subsequent return, a season or so
later, to play for a few nights was hailed with great delight, and the
Bath Herald thus spoke of her re-appearance :—" Her reception on
Tuesday night was a happy return, after a long absence, of a darling
child to its enraptured parents ; for loved, fostered and educated
under the eye of a Bath audience, we may exultingly call her the
child of our partial adoption." Contemporary local critics were lavish
in praise of Miss Wallis's tragic powers, some even going to the
length of declaring her equal, and in some respects superior, to Mrs.
Siddons.

CHAPTER XIII.

ROBERT WILLIAM ELLISTON.

First Appearance on any Stage — Engaged for York —
Again Appears in Bath — Popularity — Royal Favour —
"The Wandering Jew"—Marriage—In London.

OBERT William Elliston was another of those noted actors whom Bath has presented to the English stage. It was in the Orchard Street Theatre that he made his first bow to the public ; it was here that, during a number of years, he received that training and experience which enabled him to rank among English representative actors, and it was as a member of the Bath company that he first appeared in London. During the closing years of the last century, and the commencement of the present, he was the favourite of Bath audiences, and he only left the sunshine of their favours to become a conspicuous figure on the London stage.

Elliston was born in London in 1774. His father was a watchmaker, but Elliston, in whom Dr. Elliston and the Rev. Thomas Martyn, professors at Cambridge, took a great interest, was intended for the Church. He was educated at S. Paul's School, but when about sixteen years of age he left his school without the knowledge of his friends, and ran away to Bath, where he was able to gratify his ambition to tread the stage. On the 24th April " Richard III " was played at Orchard Street, and the part of Tressel was taken by " a young gentleman, his first appearance on any stage." The young gentleman was Elliston. On the following day he went with the company to Bristol and acted the same part there in the evening, and three days later he made his second appearance at Bath as Arviragus in " Cymbeline." " Elliston's reception," said Tate Wilkinson, manager of the York Theatre, " was wonderful, but as there was not a conveniency of engaging him at that late period of the season, Miss Wallis's father strongly recommended him to me. As soon as I heard him rehearse Tressel, I instantly engaged him."

His first appearance under Wilkinson was at Leeds, as Dorilas in " Merope," and he continued to appear in the York circuit for some months, meeting with much approbation. He then appears to have returned to London—dissatisfied, it is said, with the parts assigned to him—and made peace with his friends. He was introduced to John Kemble with the idea of getting an engagement at Drury Lane, but his ambition to appear at a London theatre was not yet to be gratified. Kemble advised him to study Romeo, and in that character he appeared at the Bath Theatre on the 26th September, 1793, having been engaged by Dimond. Wilkinson spoke of him as a young actor of "rising merit," with pleasing features and voice, and good address. He added, however, that his powers were not extensive, but here Wilkinson's judgment was certainly at fault, for it was his great versatility and tact that won for Elliston his after fame. The *Bath Herald* of 28th September, 1793, thus alluded to his engagement :—

The Theatre during the race week has been crowded, and all our old and respected performers have been received with hearty welcomes. The only novelty as yet produced is Mr Elliston, who performed the character of Romeo on Thursday night, with a degree of propriety and passion highly creditable to his abilities. His voice has force and melody, regulated by a sound and well-cultivated understanding. In such characters as Mr. Dimond may think proper to relinquish, he has found in Mr. Elliston a respectable successor.

During his first season he played a great variety of characters, and quickly sprang into favour, as may be judged from the fact that whereas his first benefit on 6th March, 1794, brought him £102, Dimond's was worth only £77, Mrs. Keasberry's £81 and Blisset's £92, and he was under the disadvantage of taking his benefit only two days after Miss Wallis's farewell, when there were £145 in the house. As a result of this popularity he gradually had all the leading business assigned to him, and in the following seasons we find him playing, among other parts, Macbeth for his benefit in 1796, Macheath in the " Beggar's Opera," Othello, Richard III, Dr. Pangloss, Henry V, Douglas, Hamlet, Lord Ogleby ("Clandestine Marriage"), Captain Absolute, King Lear, Benedick, Lord Townly, Marlow ("She Stoops to Conquer"), Wolseley ("Henry the Eighth"), and Harry Dornton ("Road to Ruin"). These, of course, are only a few selected characters out of a great number in which he appeared during his connection with the Bath Theatre, and we have mentioned them chiefly for the purpose of showing how versatile were the talents of this actor, for in all of them he gained applause, and evidently merited it. On the occasion of one of his benefits (9th March, 1802), he appeared in the same evening in " Oroonoko," " The Son-in-Law," " The Jew," and " The Doctor." Genest says, " He displayed a versatility of talent on this evening to which it would not be easy to find a parallel ; he acted all the parts well." Some of the characters we have mentioned he played with such stars of the first magnitude as Mrs. Siddons and Cooke.

By a curious arrangement, although Elliston remained a member of the Bath company until 1804, he was at the same time playing constantly in London, appearing there, either at the Haymarket or Covent Garden, about once a fortnight, by Dimond's permission. His first appearance in London was probably at the Haymarket in June, 1796, when he played Octavian in the "Mountaineers" on two occasions to overflowing houses with great success, and was rewarded with loud and general applause. It was a risky part to play, for the character was originally written for Kemble, and in it that noted actor had made a great impression ; Elliston's success in it was, therefore, deemed something extraordinary, especially by those who were previously unacquainted with his merits. Returning to his Bath and Bristol engagements, his popularity was further demonstrated by the fact that his benefit in the latter city secured for him the largest sum that had ever been taken in the theatre, namely, £146. A day or so after he received the following flattering letter from Mr. Colman of the Haymarket :—

London, July 14, 1796.

My Dear Sir,—I shall be very happy to see you again, the moment your affairs will permit you to return. I will either defer settling terms till we meet, or fix them with you by letter. If you prefer the latter, pray propose, and nothing that I am able to effect shall be left undone to meet your wishes.

Octavia and Sheva, you might, I am confident, repeat with increase of reputation to yourself, and advantage to the Theatre. Hamlet, too (of whom you seem a little afraid), has nothing in the character which is not within your scope. If you fancy my hints can be of service to you in any part, I think they may be so in this, for I have been reading "Hamlet" with no small attention, on your account, since your departure.

I am, my dear sir, sincerely yours,

G. COLMAN.

To show Elliston's independence, he neither accepted the offer or replied to the letter for some time. On the 21st September, he appeared for the first time at Covent Garden Theatre, playing Sheva in "The Jew," and on the 26th October he played with Murray, formerly of the Bath Theatre, in "Douglas," the bills expressly stating that his appearance was "by permission of the Bath manager." It was in consequence of his success at these performances that the London managers held out inducements to him to leave Bath and appear wholly on the London stage, but having signed articles with Dimond he was unable to accept the, no doubt, tempting offers, though, through the kindness of the Bath manager, he was able to undertake to appear in London, as we have stated, once a fortnight.

" An arduous task," wrote a local critic at the time, " but the professional zeal of this young man never tires."*

His exertions, however, were not limited to this arrangement, for
during one period of his connection with the Bath and Bristol
Theatres he was playing frequently at Windsor, being a great
favourite with their Majesties George III and Queen Charlotte.
On the 25th July, 1799, he played in " Don Felix" before the Royal
party at Windsor Theatre, and for a whole fortnight after that he
was playing alternately in Bristol and Windsor, the Bath Company,
as was usual at that season of the year, being located in the former
city. The immense strain which this must have been upon him, it
is not easy for us, in these days of express locomotion, to realise.
In the *Bath Herald* of 27th July, 1799, the following paragraph
appeared :—

> When Elliston played one night in London and the following day in this
> city, it was aptly observed that he was truly the " Wandering Jew." What
> will be said when we assert that he was obliged to set off after the entertain-
> ments of Wednesday evening at Bristol, to perform before their Majesties (in
> the characters of Dr. Pangloss and Young Wilding), return to the tragedy of
> Macbeth, this evening, for Mr. Paul's benefit, and must positively attend a
> second command at Windsor to-morrow night.

Five out of the six performances at Windsor were by command of
the King, who also directed that 25 guineas should be transmitted to
him for his benefit, and by the whole engagement Elliston is said to
have cleared over 100 guineas. "These daily transits between
Bristol and Windsor," says Raymond in his life of Elliston, "being
undertaken after each performance by night (for our hero slept like a
top within a coach, as sound and as vertical), were styled by his
companions " Night errantry." In 1802 he took the Weymouth
Theatre during the King's stay at his favourite watering place,
having his Majesty's express command to play there for a few nights,
and during the time, both he and his family were paid every attention
by their Majesties and the Princesses. Elliston married a Miss
Rundell, who was a dancing mistress in Bath, and it is said, eloped

---

* Elliston's popularity in London may be judged from the fact that on the
occasion of a benefit in 1804, while he was at the Haymarket, he took the
Opera House, and when the doors were opened the crush was so great that it
was impossible to take the money, the crowd rushing past the check-takers,
and filling the house. Elliston, therefore, came before the curtain, and pointing
out the loss this would mean to him, sent men round the house with pewter
plates to collect the entrance fees. When the curtain drew up, the stage was
discovered almost filled with people, which led to some uproar, but Elliston
appealed to the audience that as Madame Bouti, a foreigner, had been allowed
to place her friends on the stage, surely he, as an Englishman, might be
allowed to do so. The audience were satisfied, and Elliston cleared £600.

with her. - Such an assertion, however, is scarcely borne out by the following extract from a Bath paper of the 3rd June, 1796 :—

The following circumstance took place on the evening of Mr. Elliston's marriage, at our Theatre, and had so great an effect upon the audience, that the applause it occasioned retarded the performance of the Wheel of Fortune some minutes. Mr. Elliston played Harry Woodville, and Mr. Murray Governor Tempest, in which character the author observes " Here, Henry, take all I am worth in the world, a virtuous daughter, the joy and blessing of my heart," and as he was in the act of joining their hands, he stopped them, saying " Though I don't think I am acting the prudent part of a Parent either—for I am credibly informed you have this very morning married one wife already." It being the suggestion of the moment by Murray, and quite unexpected by Elliston, his confusion was great. After the tumult had somewhat subsided Murray proceeded, " But since, my dear boy, you have chosen this morning to realise the fiction of this evening, may I be permitted (who seldom take the liberty of digressing from my author) heartily to wish— may you both be as sincerely happy, as you are universally allowed to be deserving." This apostrophe was sensibly felt by the whole house, who appeared heartily to unite in the fervent ejaculation.

Elliston continued a member of the Bath company until 1804, in the early part of which year he bade farewell to his old friends and patrons, who parted with him with great reluctance, and took up his quarters entirely in London. His last benefit at the Bath Theatre was on the 28th February, 1804, when he acted Belcour in " The West Indian," Sylvester Daggerwood and Capt. Bebdare in a musical entertainment called " Love Laughs at Locksmiths," and his final appearance was on the 8th May, when he acted Rollo in " Pizarro," and Young Wilding in " The Liar."

On Kemble's retirement from Drury Lane Elliston became one of its most active and efficient supporters until it was burnt down in 1809, when he was nearly ruined. He then took the Royal Circus, which he gave the name of the Surrey Theatre, playing Shakespeare's plays under new titles, and with such alterations as would bring them within the license granted to a minor theatre. The venture was, however, by no means successful, and Elliston did himself no good by appearing in these pirated plays, though, on returning to Drury Lane, which he did in 1812, he continued to be the favourite comedian of the London playgoing public. In 1815 he again left Drury Lane and opened the Olympic Theatre under the title of the Little Drury Lane. In 1819 he became lessee and manager of Drury Lane, taking the theatre at an annual rent of £10,200, but the venture ended in his bankruptcy, though Genest asserts that it was "by his own fault, for with common prudence he might have been a rich man." Unfortunately he had become addicted to two of the great evils of his time, drink and gambling, and, indeed, it is said that it was probably only the earnings of his wife, who kept a dancing academy, first in Bath and afterwards in London, and had a large aristocratic connection, that saved him from ruin long before it came. " Broken, shattered in health, ejected from his great theatre," says Fitzgerald, " this wonderful elastic being removed to the Surrey Theatre, and with the well known " Black-eyed Susan " replenished his coffers again. He lived for several years, exhibiting his jaunty oddities to the end, and at last, worn out, died in July, 1831, at the age of 56."

As an actor there can be no doubt that his talents were very great. He was essentially a comedian, though some characters in tragedy were well suited to him, but his natural disposition was to be bright and gay, and he was nothing if not original. His Falstaff was a wonderful performance, so unlike the character as it was usually presented, yet convincing the spectator that he had caught the true meaning of Shakespeare.

CHAPTER XIV.

THE CLOSE OF THE CENTURY.

PROSPERITY AND PROGRESS — THE "PATRONESS OF BATH" —
PRE-EMINENCE OF THE BATH THEATRE — REASONS FOR ITS
POSITION—THE MANAGEMENT—MISS WALLIS—A FAREWELL—
TRANSFERENCES TO LONDON—MRS. SIDDONS—NEW ARTISTES.

CARCELY any period in the history of the Bath
stage is more interesting than that from about
1790 to the opening of the new theatre in Beaufort
Square in 1805. It was a time of prosperity, of
brilliancy and of progress. The theatre flourished
during these years in a greater degree than it ever
had previously, and it compares favourably with
any subsequent period ; indeed, it may be said that the Bath Theatre
was in the zenith of its glory during the closing years of the last
century and the early part of the present. The population of the
city was increasing, the city itself was gradually covering a greater
area, its visitors were numerous in the extreme, and consequently its
amusements were well patronised and prosperous. Rauzzini, with
his corps of vocal and instrumental performers, wielded his bâton
before large audiences, who crowded the Assembly Rooms to listen to
such singers as Braham, Storace and Mrs. Billington, and instru-
mentalists like Weichsell, Lindley, Schmidt and Herschell. Eminent
performers were always engaged for the twelve subscription concerts
which were generally given each season, and, like the balls and
dances, were never at a loss for support. H. R H. the Duchess of
York, styled by the inhabitants the "distinguished patroness of
Bath," was an annual visitor, and was intimately connected with the
city ; the theatre came in for a large share of her patronage, and
louder and louder became the cry that the house ought to be
superseded by a larger and more commodious building. Whereas,
not so very many years before fifty and sixty pounds were considered
a satisfactory receipt, and even a good house, the receipts for the
benefits of favourite performers now averaged nearly £150 a night.*
For instance, in 1799 Dimond realised £161 (Mrs. Siddons was
playing), and Elliston £146, while in 1800, in one month, Dimond's
benefit brought him £137, Elliston's £150, and Mrs. Edwin's £150,
and had the house only been capable of holding it, the sums would
undoubtedly have been larger.

* Mainwaring's "Annals of Bath."

G

It may safely be said that no other theatre out of London was
enjoying such prosperity as this ; Fitzgerald speaks of the York
Theatre (which attained distinction under Tate Wilkinson), as the
best specimen of the country theatre in the last century, for, he says,
the Bath Theatre held an exceptional position. This pre-eminence,
of course, was due, in a great degree, to its close connection with the
London theatres, so many of the first actors there having gained their
experience at Bath, and been transferred straight from that "pro-
bationary school of the drama" to the London stage. We must
remember, also, that Elliston was appearing during this period in
London, and making himself a favourite there, while he was still a
member of the Bath company, and no doubt this, coupled with the
fact that such stars as Mrs. Siddons (who never allowed her early
connection with the Bath stage to be forgotten), Kemble, Stephen
Kemble, and Cooke occasionally appeared at Bath, had the effect of
giving prominence to the theatre, while, most important of all, Bath
held an unrivalled position as the resort of what in these days we
term Society, and, therefore, was better able to support a theatre than
other places. One other reason must also be assigned for the proud
position which the Bath Theatre occupied, and that is the excellence
and thoroughness of its management ; other theatres in the country
were fortunate in having for their managers men of whose abilities
in this respect, and of whose enthusiasm in the drama, there can be
no doubt, but Bath was peculiarly fortunate in having a succession of
such men, and the share they contributed towards the brilliancy
which the drama attained in the city must not be overlooked.

During the period with which we are now dealing Keasberry, as
we have already stated, retired into private life, and left Dimond the
sole manager of the theatre. It is worthy of note that in the journals
of the time, in which the theatre was freely noticed, we find no
complaint of any moment raised against the conduct of the management. Praise there is in abundance ; complimentary references to
the liberal and generous manner in which new productions were
staged, and the care displayed in the engagement of new members
of the company, follow each other with marked frequency and are
couched in terms which show they were not mere flattery or empty
praise. At the commencement of almost every season we read of
improvements effected either in the house, or in connection with the
stage and its scenery, pointing to the fact that the management was
conducted in no niggardly spirit, but with every desire to make the
theatre worthy of its position as the first and highest place of
amusement in a city of pleasure. The only note of complaint we
find struck with any persistency, was that the size of the theatre was
not equal to its importance. Upon the retirement of Keasberry, Dimond
appointed Mr. Charlton as his assistant stage manager. This
gentleman had so happy a way of apologising to the audience when

From a Photo by]   [Elliott & Fry
                BARRY SULLIVAN.

through any unforeseen circumstance some alteration had to be made
in the programme at the last moment, that it was jokingly remarked
the audiences thought he sometimes prevailed upon members of
the company to be ill, in order that he might display his apologetic
skill.

Space will not permit of our dealing in detail with all the events,
interesting though they are, which marked the closing years of the
eighteenth century, and we must necessarily confine ourselves to
noting principal features only. Of course, the name of Elliston stands
in the front rank during these years of prosperity, but we have
already dealt fully with his connection with the city, and likewise
with that of Miss Wallis. An interesting incident, however, which
testifies to the regard in which the latter was held in the city, deserves
notice. Shortly before her departure she was presented, "in a large
and polite circle," to which she was invited for the purpose, with a
costly medallion, "representing Shakespeare inviting timid genius
from the shade, and holding to her view a sprig of laurel." On the
reverse was the inscription, " Presented to Miss Wallis, by the ladies
and gentlemen of Bath, as a small tribute to private virtue and public
merit." The medallion, which was enriched with clusters of
brilliants, was presented to this favoured actress by Lady Elizabeth
Noel. Several old favourites disappeared from the company before
the close of the century, and notably Mr. Blissett, whose name
had appeared in the bills for many years. In several parts he
attained distinction as a comedian, and his Hardcastle was
described as one of the best pieces of acting that the English stage
at that time could boast of ; he declined repeated offers of lucrative
engagements in London, and took his farewell of the stage at the
close of the season 1797-98, though he sometimes returned to it to act
for a few nights, or for a benefit. In 1795 Mr. and Mrs. Knight, who
had also been members of the company for some time, left for
Covent Garden, where they had received engagements. Mrs. Knight
does not seem to have acted in London after the season 1797-98, and is
said to have returned to Bath and rejoined the company there, but this
is a mistake. According to Genest she did return to Bath, and died in
the city, but her name never appeared in the Bath bills after she left
for Covent Garden. Miss Hopkins, another member of the Bath
company, obtained an engagement at Covent Garden in the autumn
of 1793, and to Mr. Murray's transfer to the same theatre we have
already made reference. In 1799 Mrs. Siddons returned for a few
nights to the scene of her early triumphs, and met with a most
flattering reception. Although "it was not till Saturday night," says
the *Bath Herald* of February 2nd, "that Mrs. Siddons was
announced to appear a few nights at our theatre, at an early hour on
Monday there was not a seat unlet in the boxes for any of her performances." The character in which she made her reappearance was

Euphrasia, in "The Grecian Daughter," (other principal characters being taken by Dimond, Elliston and Harley), and while her performance was watched with rapt attention, every time she left the stage rounds of applause followed her. The approaches to the theatre on this occasion were crowded by people anxious to get a glimpse of the unrivalled actress, and a like enthusiasm was manifested throughout the whole of her stay in the city. She appeared in "The Fair Penitent," "Jane Shore," "Isabella," "The Gamester," "Macbeth," "The Merchant of Venice," "The Distressed Mother," and "The Provoked Husband," playing Lady Townly in the latter, a part she had not ventured to attempt in London. For her benefit she played Zara, in "The Mourning Bride," and her last appearance on this occasion was as Millwood, in "George Barnwell," for Dimond's benefit, when Dimond played the title part for the last time. The scene at the theatre on this occasion was an unprecedented one ; people fought for places, and more money was crammed into the house than had ever been before. Many of those who had tickets could not get in, and the result was a tumult and uproar so great that the first scenes of the play could not be heard, and peace officers were obliged to interfere to prevent mischief. It was expected that when Mrs. Siddons appeared the uproar would cease, but, on the contrary, it was so great that it was impossible for the actors to play in anything but dumb show, and eventually Mrs. Siddons was obliged to retire. After a time the tumult subsided, and quiet and order having been obtained, the performance was commenced again from the very beginning.

A very large number of artistes new to the Bath stage were introduced during this period, and also an unusual number of novitiates. The latter, whose names were generally withheld, as they do not appear to have made any subsequent mark in the histrionic world do not call for mention here, but it will be interesting to briefly glance at some of the former. At the commencement of the season 1793-94 there were added to the company Mr. Sandford from York, Mr. Ainswick from York (a Bath man), Mrs. Coates from Dublin, and Mr. Taylor, who made his "first appearance on any stage" as Capt. Wilson in the "Flitch of Bacon," and remained a member of the company for several years, as also did Miss Biggs, who joined in October, 1794. Early in the following year Mr. and Miss Betterton were engaged ; the former had fulfilled engagements at several provincial theatres, and his daughter, who at that time was only 15 years of age, had made so successful a *début* in the north of England, that the managers of the Bath Theatre were strongly recommended to engage her. They did so, and her first appearance as Elwina in the tragedy of "Percy" justified their decision, for the youthful actress was received with applause as vociferous as that which greeted Mrs. Siddons's greatest efforts. She remained a member of the company until 1797, when she quitted the Bath stage for that of Covent Garden, and, on taking her farewell of the Bath audience, recited an address which had been written for her by Mr. Meyler. In February, 1796, Mr. H. Siddons, the son of Mrs. Siddons, played Othello, and was well spoken of by the local press, and in the same year Mr. Cooper and Mr. Harley, both from Covent Garden, were induced to join the Bath company ; the latter, who had left the London company through some disagreement as to salary, and was engaged in place of Murray, is said to have borne a great resemblance to a popular clergyman in the city at that time. Mr. Cunningham, from Dublin, and Mr. Hill, the possessor of "one of the finest voices on the stage," also joined the company during that season, and in the following year, 1797, Mr. and Mrs. Edwin were engaged. Mr. Edwin was the son of the celebrated John Edwin, who went from Bath to London, and is said to have greatly resembled his father, though he never made a similar name for himself. He remained in Bath till 1804, when he left for Dublin, where he died. His wife, then Miss Richards, appeared at Covent Garden in 1789, and subsequently played under Tate Wilkinson. She was received with great favour in Bath, and her impersonations of popular characters were much admired and applauded. In 1797 Miss Allingham, who had appeared at Covent Garden during the previous season, was introduced as an addition to the Bath company, but, although promising to become a conspicuous ornament to the stage, she quitted it in the earlier part of 1799, on the occasion of her marriage with a Bristol citizen. At the opening of the Theatre for the season in September, 1797, Mr. John Quick, from Covent Garden, played for two nights, appearing as Tony Lumpkin and Lovegold ("The Miser") and on the second occasion as Spado in "The Castle of Andalusia," and Barnaby Brittle in a piece of that name. He again visited Bath and played at the Theatre in the following year, during which Mr. Cherry, Mr. Richards and Miss Gough (from Dublin), became members of the company. Respecting the latter lady quite a romantic story is told. She was heiress to a very old family in Dublin, and had received a liberal education calculated to qualify her for the social position which she would have to take. But the imprudence of her father dissipated her property and she adopted the stage, not only with the purpose of gaining her own livelihood, but also to support the man who had squandered his own and his daughter's fortune. She remained at the Bath Theatre for about a twelvemonth only. The only addition to the company in 1799 which created any interest was that of Mrs. Johnstone, whose acting was described as "Siddonian." Mrs. Mountain, a well-known songstress, appeared for a few nights at the commencement of 1799, a year which saw the retirement of Floor, the prompter, who, after an honourable connection with the Theatre extending over 32 years, was obliged to relinquish his post owing to ill health.

CHAPTER XV.

LAST DAYS AT ORCHARD STREET.

FALSTAFF WITHOUT STUFFING — JOHN PHILIP KEMBLE — THE
WITCHES' DANCE— STOCK COMPANIES — THE BEGINNING OF
THE END — ANDREW CHERRY — NECESSITY FOR A LARGER
THEATRE—THE LAST PERFORMANCES AT ORCHARD STREET.

HE last five seasons at the Orchard Street Theatre
witnessed the introduction of several London stars
to Bath audiences. Mrs. Siddons twice paid the
city a visit during this period, the first occasion
being in April, 1801, when she played for seven
nights, and the second in September of the same
year, when she only appeared in three characters.
On each occasion she played to crowded houses, and the enthusiasm
exhibited was very great. In December, 1801, came G. F. Cooke,
who made his first bow to a Bath audience in " Richard III," playing
subsequently Othello to Elliston's Iago, Iago to Elliston's Othello, and
Shylock. He was very well received, and appears to have been
pleased with his brief engagement, for he wrote in his journal, " I
received the greatest sympathy and approbation from the audiences,
and every mark of politeness and attention from Messrs. Palmer and
Dimond, the proprietors of the Theatre." He appeared on three
separate occasions in the following year, and in June very generously
played " Richard III," gratis, for the benefit of the Bath Theatrical
Fund, to which reference will be made in a subsequent chapter.
Then, in November, 1802, came Stephen Kemble, whose reputation
as a man who played Falstaff without stuffing ensured him a good
reception. Every one was anxious to see him, and so many were
unable to, owing to the limited accommodation at so small a theatre,
that he was prevailed upon to appear three nights instead of one,
as announced, on two of which he played Falstaff in the first part
of " Henry IV," and on the third Falstaff in the " Merry Wives of
Windsor." The fact that he was the only man who had ever played
the part without the usual padding appears to have been his chief,
if not only attraction. He appeared again for one night at the
commencement of the last season at Orchard Street.

Then, early in 1802, came John Philip Kemble.* whose close relationship to Mrs. Siddons would alone have sufficed to fill the theatre, and when there was added to this his own reputation, and the fact that he was honouring Bath by making his first appearance there after a somewhat prolonged sojourn on the Continent, it may easily be imagined how great was the interest and excitement aroused by the announcement of his appearance. Within a few hours almost every place in the boxes was booked, and the scene presented upon the night of his first performance was only equalled by that on the occasion of Mrs. Siddons's return to her Bath friends, described in the preceding chapter. Mr. Kemble had visited the Continent for the purpose of studying the dramatic art as represented in the principal cities, and it was certainly a feather in the cap of the Bath managers to secure his reappearance on the English stage for the Bath Theatre. The character in which he was introduced was Macbeth, Lady Macbeth being played by Mrs. Johnstone. Genest mentions an incident in connection with this performance which is worth repeating. A dance by the Witches with their brooms had always been introduced in the play of " Macbeth," but Kemble objecting to it, Dimond very readily consented to with-draw it. However, no sooner did the audience discover this than they demanded the dance so vociferously (or at least the gallery did) that they rendered it impossible to proceed with the performance until their wishes had been complied with, and from that time to 1828 " Macbeth " was never played in Bath, or at Bristol, where the same thing occurred, without this most incongruous interpolation—" an exhibition," wrote Genest, " which would disgrace the lowest strollers in a barn." It usually drew more applause than the best scenes in the play, not from the gallery only, but also from those parts of the house where it might have been expected to find little favour. On an occasion in 1828 when " Macbeth " was produced, Bellamy, who was at that time the manager, decided to cut out the dance, though it was rehearsed in case of a repetition of the above incident, which happily did not occur. Kemble played also in " Hamlet," " The Stranger," " Merchant of Venice," " Wheel of Fortune," " Pizarro," " The Mountaineers " and " Richard III." He was induced to appear longer than was originally announced, and finally took his leave on the 10th of May in " Hamlet," the date of his first performance having been the 12th April, and on each occasion on which he played money was turned away from the doors, inducing a local paper to remark, " The sums returned to persons who could not accommodate themselves with even a sight of the stage, must again have convinced the managers of the necessity of an enlarged theatre."

* For portrait see page 41.

Kemble's visit had a bad effect upon the benefits which followed close upon his departure, and the regular members of the company received very indifferent support. That, however, was only the immediate result of one visit from a London star, whereas there was another and more important one, for the brief engagements of these renowned members of the dramatic profession wrought a great change in the history of the theatre. Hitherto, with very few exceptions, the audiences had been content to witness, season after season, performances given entirely by members of the stock company. The exceptions were generally in the case of the return of former members of the company who, having gained their laurels on the metropolitan stage, returned for a few nights to the scene of their probation, and were invariably met with encouraging receptions. Such instances as these were only natural, but, apart from them, Bath had hitherto made little acquaintance with the prominent members of London companies. The last years of the Orchard Street Theatre, however, wrought a great change ; with Elliston starring in London while still a member of the Bath company, and Siddons, Kemble, Cooke, Incledon, and other members of London companies making frequent appearances at the Bath Theatre, the taste of playgoers underwent a revolution, and instead of being content with ordinary fare they looked for stimulants in the shape of actors and actresses of great repute. As the *Bath Herald* remarked shortly after Kemble's departure, " Since Mr. Kemble has played here nothing will go down with a Bath audience but London actors." This has been the case in an increasing degree throughout the whole of the nineteenth century, until, in combination with other causes, it struck a death blow at stock companies, and made London more than ever the centre of the profession.

During the years with which we are now dealing Bath surrendered several members of its company to London. Among them must be mentioned Andrew Cherry, who accepted an engagement at Drury lane early in 1802. " Merry Andrew," as he was called, was the author of several dramatic pieces, including " Two Strings to Your Bow," and " The Soldier's Daughter." The latter piece was played at Bath shortly after its production at Drury Lane, and in a critique of the performance it was said, the author's " satisfaction would have been greatly heightened could he have witnessed its representation and reception. He would have seen those performers among whom he so recently held a place, animated with a generous emulation in the cause of a brother performer, and exerting themselves with uncommon zeal in their respective characters ; and he would have seen that audience, which he has so often contributed to entertain, rewarding their efforts by the most cheering and reiterated plaudits."* Every season brought about its changes in the company,

* Some time before Cherry went to London and, we believe, while he was

and among new members who joined it may be mentioned Miss
Grimani, who subsequently made herself a great favourite, notwithstanding that she was a foreigner, and never wholly succeeded in
speaking her lines without betraying the fact by her accent. She
played for the first time on any stage, on the 16th April, in " The
Grecian Daughter." She was the daughter of "a very ingenious
foreigner " in the city, who apparently combined the occupation of an
artizan with that of a teacher of languages. Miss Grimani's connection
with the Theatre was, however, comparatively short. In 1801 came
Mr. Talbot from Dublin and Edinburgh, Mr. Chalmers from York
and Edinburgh, Mr. Macartney and Miss B. Biggs, and in the
following year Mr. Lovegrove from Dublin, who is described by
Charles Lamb as the comedian " who came nearest the old actors."
He had the distinction of playing on his first appearance before
H.R.H. the Duchess of York, by whom he was complimented upon
his impersonation of Lazarillo in Cherry's farce, "Two Strings to Your
Bow." He subsequently was removed to Drury Lane, where in
November, 1814, he broke a blood vessel while on the stage. He
died at Weston, near Bath, on the 20th June, 1816. In 1803 the
company was strengthened by Mr. Bew from Margate, Mr. Egerton
from Edinburgh and Newcastle, and Miss Fisher, who made her first
appearance on any stage as Emma, in " Marriage Promise," 3rd Dec.
The opening of the last season at the old house saw an unusual
number of changes in the company, owing to the loss of Mr. Elliston,
Mrs. Johnstone, Mr. Eyre, Mr. and Mrs. Edwin, Mr. and Mrs. Taylor,
Miss Smith and Miss Daniells. In their places were engaged
Captain Caulfield, Mr. and Mrs. Phillips, Miss Smith from Edinburgh
and York, Mrs. Worthington* and Mr. Maddinson, two great
favourites from Norwich, Mr. Gatty (or Gattie) from York, and Miss
Jameson, locally connected, who made a first appearance. Miss
Smith was said to be "almost born to the stage, and educated from

in Bath, he received the offer of a very good engagement from a manager who,
on a previous occasion had not acted altogether fairly by him. Cherry replied
to the offer as follows :—" Sir,—though a little *black mazzard* like mine has
been exhibited upon your boards to the satisfaction of the public, yet as I was
cursedly bit by you, when you cobbled the fruits of your performers' labours,
I have made up my mind, that you never shall make ' Two bites of—A
CHERRY.' "

* The manner in which a new actress was sometimes introduced in the
press in the olden days would scarcely suit present day tastes. For instance, this
actress was announced in a local paper in the following terms :—" Mrs.
Worthington, who appears at our theatre next week, is particularly celebrated
for the beautiful symmetry of her person in the male attire. Indeed her
breeches figure is allowed to be the most perfect and admirably proportioned of
any upon the English stage."

early life with the sole design of becoming an ornament to the Bath
Theatre." That, it is acknowledged, she did become, but not for
long, for at the close of the season she received a liberal offer of an
engagement at Covent Garden, which through the kindness of the
Bath manager, who cancelled her agreement, she was able to accept.
  We have already alluded to the inadequacy of the Orchard Street
Theatre to meet the requirements of the city in the matter of accommodation. This had been felt for many years, and had convinced
the proprietors of the importance of providing a new home for the
drama, larger and more commodious than that in which it was then
located. Even as far back as 1796, on the occasion of a benefit to
Dimond, we read that could the house have contained the number, the
receipts would have been doubled—"a strong hint to that gentleman
and his colleague how necessary is the enlargement of the theatre,
and perhaps its removal to a more eligible situation, considering the
present state of the city." At that time, however, the managers by
no means saw their way clear to such enterprise, and some years
elapsed before the project assumed definite shape. Apparently, the
crush upon the occasion of Mrs. Siddons's visit in 1799, and the
increasing average in the attendance during that and subsequent
seasons, induced those interested in the conduct of the theatre to
take the matter into serious consideration, with the result that it was
eventually determined that a new house, in a more accessible
position, should be built, and that without delay. The building of the
New Theatre is a subject with which we shall deal in the following
chapter ; suffice it to say here that the matter was so heartily supported, that the Orchard Street Theatre was soon doomed, and
the year 1805 saw its close. The 29th June, when "The Honey-
moon" and "Three Weeks After Marriage" were produced, was
announced as the "last night of performing for some time," and, as a
matter of fact, the theatre was only once opened after that date. On
that occasion Mr. Harris, then the proprietor of the Theatre Royal,
Covent Garden, was present, and offered Miss Smith the engagement
which brought about her withdrawal from the Bath stage. Actually
the last performance at Orchard Street was on the 13th July, 1805,
when, after the programme arranged for that occasion had been
concluded, the curtain fell for the last time in a theatre which had
seen many vicissitudes, and the beginning of many a brilliant career.
The advertisement of the last performance was as follows :—

Last night of ever performing in the Old Theatre.
On Saturday July 13 1805, will be presented (by particular desire) the Tragedy
of
VENICE PRESERVED

| Jassier | - | - | - | MR. WRENCH | Priuli | - | - | - | MR. CHARLTON |
| Pierre | - | - | MR. EGERTON | Renault | - | - | - | MR. GATTIE |

Belvidera   -   - MISS SMITH
(The last night of her appearance in Bath)
End of the play (by particular desire)
COLLINS's ODE ON THE PASSIONS
BY MISS SMITH
With the new Musical Entertainment, called
MATRIMONY

The building is still in existence, and is now in the hands of the Free-
masons, who use it as a Masonic hall, while for many years it was a
Roman Catholic chapel.

CHAPTER XVI.

BEAUFORT SQUARE THEATRE.

SUGGESTED SITES FOR NEW THEATRE — BEAUFORT SQUARE
DECIDED UPON—PUBLIC SUPPORT—THE TONTINE PRINCIPLE—
A RAPID ERECTION—THE FIRST PLAY-BILL—DESCRIPTION OF
THE THEATRE— MEMBERS OF THE COMPANY—MASTER BETTY
—ITALIAN OPERA—A DISCREDITABLE INCIDENT—MRS. JORDAN.

AVING traced the history of the little Theatre in
Orchard Street, we must now turn our attention to
the building of the new theatre in Beaufort Square,*
on the site of that which now exists. We have
seen how insufficient was the accommodation of
the old theatre, and though that was the principal
reason why a new building was required, there were
also other reasons, of equal urgency. It was the threatened erection
of a competing theatre in the upper part of the city that induced
Palmer to obtain protection for his property, and it was the bad
approach and position of the theatre in Orchard Street that gave rise
to that project. The approach to Orchard Street was greatly improved during the years the theatre was open, but the unsuitability
of the position was an objection which could not be overcome, and
one that was increased by the continued growth of the northern
side of the city. A more central and more accessible situation was
urgently demanded. The proposal to build a new theatre was first
seriously entertained in the early part of 1802, but the negotiations
were carried on very quietly and undemonstratively, and when, in the
autumn, the Beaufort Square site was mentioned, it was subsequently
stated that the announcement was premature. Several objections to
the suggested site were urged, it being stated that the approaches were
not good, and that the nearness to the weighing engine would prove
a great inconvenience. Other possible sites were proposed, among
them the Bear yard, immediately below the General Hospital,† where,
it was urged, "a large theatre and a beautiful hotel could be erected
every way desirable, central and commodious," while others advised
the proprietors to pause before launching out into any extensive and
costly scheme, and to rather bear those ills they had, than to fly to

---

* Now called Beauford Square.   † Royal Mineral Water Hospital.

others they knew not of. It was also pointed out that it might be possible to improve the approaches to Orchard Street, enlarge the theatre, and better the neighbourhood. The objection of situation, however, still remained, and the proprietors did not abandon their intention of building another theatre. We say " proprietors," because although Palmer's name disappeared in connection with the theatre when it came into the hands of Keasberry and Dimond, there is no doubt he did not altogether lose his interest in the concern, and his name reappears with the scheme for a new theatre.

In 1804, the fate of the Orchard Street house was settled, and it was doomed to abandonment. After much deliberation, the Beaufort Square site was ultimately decided upon, plans were drawn out, and the matter so heartily taken up that, before the scheme was made generally known to the public, over £5,000 were subscribed. Rarely, if at all, has an important public building in the city been erected with such rapidity and completeness. In August, 1804, the proposal was informally announced in the papers, and in the following month work-men were on the site, pulling down the old premises, and digging the foundations. In December the foundation stone was laid, and ten months later the theatre was complete. It was built by subscription upon the tontine principle, the terms of which were to the following effect * :—One hundred shares to be created at £200 per share, the share to terminate with a life named and registered at the time of subscribing. Each shareholder to receive three per cent. per annum, and a right of admission to all performances, transferable once a year. The whole rent-charge of £600 per annum (that is, the three per cent. per share), to be paid so long as any one life remained, and to be equally divided among the survivors ; but the admission to cease with the life. There was also another class of subscriptions, not carrying free admission, which were £150 per share. The theatre and the whole property connected with it—the patent, wardrobes, scenery and furniture, together with its income—were vested in trustees for the security and interest of the subscribers. It was urged that the tontine was a most advantageous one in which to place the lives of young children, " as in the event of survivorship the income must gradually increase from the payment of a principal of £150 only to an annuity of £600." The subscriptions were rapidly taken up, and heading the list of subscribers were H.R.H. the Prince of Wales, H.R.H. Princess Charlotte of Wales, and H.R.H. the Duke of York, both the Prince and the Duke of York having manifested considerable interest in the undertaking, which was generally and rightly considered to be of great importance to the city.

On Saturday, the 12th of October, 1805, the theatre was opened, having been completed within the time proposed, and in a manner

* Mainwaring's " Annals of Bath."

superior to what was promised, so that the large audience which
assembled was more than gratified. The play which was performed
on the opening night was " Richard III " and the following is a copy
of the play-bill, which, it will be admitted, considering the importance
of the occasion, is a very modest production, since the fact that it was
the opening night of what was at the time described as " this elegant
and immense edifice," is but briefly recorded :—

New Theatre Royal, Beaufort Square, Bath.

WILL OPEN this present SATURDAY, OCTOBER 12, 1805;

KING RICHARD III,

With entire new Scenery, Dresses, Machinery and other Decorations.

RICHARD, DUKE OF GLOSTER - - -	BY A GENTLEMAN
(His First Appearance on the Stage)	
KING HENRY THE SIXTH - - -	MR. CHARLTON
PRINCE OF WALES - - - -	MISS MARTIN
DUKE OF YORK - - - -	MISS L. QUICK
DUKE OF BUCKINGHAM - - -	MR. CAULFIELD
(From the Theatre Royal, Drury Lane, His First Appearance on the Bath Stage)	
DUKE OF NORFOLK - - - - -	MR. EGAN
EARL OF OXFORD - - - -	- MR. ABBOTT
HENRY EARL OF RICHMOND - - -	MR. EGERTON
LORD STANLEY - - - -	MR. RICHARDSON
(His First appearance here these three years)	
LORD MAYOR OF LONDON - - -	MR. EVANS
SIR W. BRANDON - - -	MR. CUNNINGHAM
SIR RICHARD RATCLIFFE - - -	MR. CUSHING
(His first appearance here)	

SIR WILLIAM CATESBY	SIR JAMES BLUNT
MR. GOMERY	MR. EDWARD
SIR R. BRACKENBURY	DIGHTON MR. LODGE
MR. GATTIE	FOREST MR. SIMS
SIR JAMES TYRELL MR. KELLY	

QUEEN ELIZABETH - - - -	MISS FISHER
DUCHESS OF YORK - - -	MRS. CHARLTON
LADY ANNE - - - -	MISS JAMESON

The Scenes by Messrs. Greaves, Marchbank, French and Capon.
The Dresses by Mr. Quick and assistants—The female Dresses by Mrs. Jefferies.

To which will be added the MUSICAL ENTERTAINMENT of the

POOR SOLDIER

PATRICK - - - -	MISS WHEATLEY
(From the Theatre Royal, Covent Garden, her first appearance on this Stage)	
FATHER LUKE	CAPTAIN FITZROY
MR. RICHARDSON	MR. CASHING
DERMOT MR. WEBBER	BAGATELLE MR. GATTIE

DARBY   •   •   •   •   MR. MALLINSON
KATHLEEN   •   •   •   •   - MRS. SIMS
NORAH   -   •   •   •   - MRS. WINDSOR
Boxes 5s., Pit 3s., Gallery 1s. 6d.
Latter Account, Boxes 3s., Pit 2s., Gallery 1s.
Tickets and Places for the Boxes to be taken of Mr. BARTLEY, at his house in Orange-court Grove.
N.B. The Carriage Entrance to the Boxes is in the Sawclose, and Ladies and Gentlemen are particularly requested to order their servants to set down with their horses' heads towards Westgate-Street and to take up with their heads towards Queen Square, to prevent confusion. The Entrance for chairs is in Beaufort-Square, and the entrance to the Pit and Gallery is in St. John's-Court.*

The building was erected under the direction of Mr. Palmer, the city architect, Mr. George Dance being responsible for the ornamental parts of the building, and especially the "grand front" in Beaufort Square; the masonry work was carried out by Mr. Parfitt, the carpentering by Mr. Thomas Lewis. All concerned in the building laboured prodigiously to secure its completion within the brief allotted time, but though the work was hurried, it was not scamped, as the fact that portions of the old building, although they have passed through a fiery ordeal, are incorporated in the building which exists to-day testifies. Unlimited praise was bestowed on the arrangement of the building, which was at once spacious, elegant and convenient. The interior was planned from models of the first theatres in Europe. There were three lofty tiers supported by bronzed cast iron pillars, placed at distances of two feet from the front of each circle, so as to give the first row the appearance of a balcony. There were as many as 26 private boxes, four of which were taken from the first tier on each side next the stage, and were handsomely fitted with curtains, gilt rails, and chairs. The walls were covered with a dado of stamped paper, stuffed, of a rich crimson colour, surmounted by paper of the same colour, and of an Egyptian pattern, fringed with a gold stripe. The seats and ledges of the circles were covered with cloth, and the front of each was painted crimson with four broad stripes of gold, while the ceiling was divided into four compartments, in which were set the famous pictures by Cassali which had formerly adorned the picture gallery at Fonthill, and were purchased by Dimond at the celebrated sale at Mr. Beckford's mansion in 1801. †

* A copy of this play-bill, and many other interesting bills, both of Orchard Street and the new Theatre, are exhibited in the saloon of the present theatre.

† At the same time Dimond bought Mr. Beckford's State Bed, of crimson velvet, together with the accompanying chairs, sofas and curtains, adorned with burnished gold. This bed was originally made for Lord Melcombe, and is said to have cost £1,500, and when King George III reviewed the camp near Salisbury, during the American war, and visited Lord Pembroke at Wilton, it was borrowed for the king to sleep in. The upholsterer who took it to pieces on that occasion found a written paper in a drawer curiously

H

The arrangement of these pictures, and the artistic work introduced to connect them and finish the ceiling, was designed by Mr. Dance, and executed by Mr. Hayes. There was no lack of accommodation in the way of saloons and retiring rooms, and, to pass from the front of the house to the stage, the performers had not been neglected in the matter of dressing rooms, while other apartments such as the ward-robe and scene room were adequately provided. The stage itself—of which an uninterrupted view could be obtained from every part of the house—was as large as that of old Covent Garden Theatre, and the stage apparatus was said to be equal to that of a London theatre, while the scenery was thus spoken of :—" The new scenery cannot be sufficiently admired ; it astonished by its fine effect, and deluded for the moment the imagination, making that appear real which was only colours and canvas. The four painters employed in executing these happy specimens of the art were, Mr. Greaves, Mr. Marchbank, Mr. French, and Mr. Capon, who will be severally honoured by the plaudits of a Bath audience, whenever one scene is shifted for another, and while one atom of taste remains in the city."

There were three entrances, occupying exactly the same position as in the present theatre, namely, that for chairs in Beaufort Square, that for carriages in the Sawclose, and the pit, gallery, and stage entrances being on the south side. The extreme length of the building within the main walls was 125 feet, its width 60 feet, and its height 70 feet. According to Genest, the new house held between £250 and £300, but £200 was considered a very good house. " Such," says an old guide book, " is the new theatre at Bath, which has more the appearance of being the work of some luxurious favourite of fortune, for his own private gratification, than a place intended for the indiscriminate admission of the public. There is an air of warmth, comfort, and ease, about the house, not to be found in any other theatre in England."

Whoever the young gentleman was who figured in the playbill repro-duced in this chapter, and was entrusted with the arduous character of Richard III at the opening of the theatre, his appearance was not a success. As an amateur he had gained some reputation, and in the rehearsals for this important event he did very well, and promised to fulfil the anticipations of his friends ; but, alas ! when he found himself face to face with a crowded audience he was so overcome by nervous-ness, or stage fright, that his performance was a perfect failure. It will be interesting to examine for a moment the other names which appear on this bill In the first place, there are Mr. Charlton, who still held the position of deputy manager to Mr. Dimond, and Mr. Egan, a name

concealed in the dome. He replaced it, but when the bed came into Dimond's possession a search was made for it, and it was found to be a brief and ill-spelt history of one Thomas Lightfoot, by whom the canopy had been designed and executed in the year 1768, in Long Acre, London.

well known in the dramatic profession. Mr. Abbott was a talented actor who subsequently became a London manager, and who, in 1810, eloped to Gretna Green with a Bath lady. He, with Mr. Mallinson, during the summer season of 1809, conducted a theatre at Tenby, and so far interested the inhabitants that it was proposed to build a theatre for them by subscription. Mr. Mallinson was a leading vocalist in the West of England for more than 30 years. Mr. Cunningham afterwards went to London, and Mr. Richardson, who was a gentleman by birth, and whose real name was Richards, afterwards became a paymaster in the army, and died in Spain during the Peninsular War. Mr. Caulfield, who made a first appearance, was, as the bill states, from Drury Lane, and he has been confused with a Captain Caulfield, who also appeared in Bath, an officer in the Guards, who, having obtained some celebrity as an amateur tragedian, exchanged "the sash and gorget" for the sock and buskin. He afterwards played at Covent Garden, but became involved in a notorious intrigue and died in prison. The Mr. Caulfield who played at the opening of the theatre, however, afterwards went to America and died suddenly on the Kentucky stage. Of the other names, Mrs. Charlton was the wife of the deputy-manager; Miss Jameson, we have already alluded to as a native of Bristol; Mrs. Windsor, who was only temporarily engaged, became a permanent member of the company some few years later, and Miss Weatley was an actress of considerable ability.

We propose in this chapter to carry the history of the theatre to the end of 1809, and during the years which intervened between the opening of the new theatre and that date, it will be seen that the management arranged a succession of London attractions. The first of these were two precocious children, one being Master Dawson, aged six, "the celebrated comic Roscius," and the second, Miss Fisher, "the celebrated Roscia from Drury Lane." This young lady, who was a sort of rival of the famous Master Betty, was acknowledged to be very clever, but she made nothing like the impression which Master Betty did, and cannot be said to have become a favourite with Bath playgoers. In December, 1805, Mr. J. Johnstone, familiarly known as Jack Johnstone, appeared for a few nights by permission of the managers of Drury Lane, and acted in some of those Irish characters in which he was said never to have been approached. Early in 1806 Incledon once more appeared, and gained the applause of his many admirers. In this month, also, a Mr. Rae made his first appearance on any stage, in the character of Hamlet, and, after a brief connection with the Bath Theatre, he removed to London, and was the principal attraction at the opening of the Haymarket for the season in June of the same year. He was of prepossessing appearance, though somewhat small, and his original readings of the important parts which he undertook were very well received. In March, Cooke paid the city a short visit, and played to crowded houses. Alluding to this engagement in his journal, he said : " I played 13 nights at Bath and Bristol, at £20 a night, which was the sum I always received there, but the managers were so satisfied on this occasion that they paid me £300."

In the following month Master Betty, who was destined to become a great favourite, was introduced to a Bath audience for the first time, appearing on the 29th April as Orestes in " The Distressed Mother," and playing also in several other characters, including Hamlet. What were the terms upon which this boy was engaged we do not know, but he had been receiving as much as £100 a night at Drury Lane, and the desire to see him was so great that people would assemble at the doors of the theatre soon after mid-day, and when they were opened the crush was tremendous. Of his first appearance at Covent Garden, in 1804, it is said that "thousands pressed forward when the doors opened, and the house being immediately filled the crowd made ineffectual efforts to press back. The shrieks and screams of the choking, trampled people were terrible. Fights for places grew ; the constables were beaten back ; the boxes were invaded ; the pitway being narrow, many went round to the box-office, paid box-prices, and passed from the boxes into the pit. The heat was so fearful that men, all but lifeless, were lifted up and dragged through the boxes into the lobbies which had windows." In Bath, too, the desire to see this " Young Roscius " was so great that it was stated the theatre, had it been double the size, would not have had a seat unoccupied, and nightly numbers were turned away from the doors. Of Master Betty's acting there were many different opinions ; while some considered that his popularity was "a disgrace to our theatrical history," others saw in him premature but intrinsic dramatic power. In Bath, at any rate, he was received with every favour, and was always popular so long as he remained on the stage. There were, however, some who were unable to appreciate his abilities, and a dispute upon the subject which occurred at the theatre between two young officers very nearly resulted in a duel. A challenge was given and accepted, and a meeting arranged to take place on Lansdown, but information having been conveyed to the clerk to the Justices, the principals and their seconds were arrested just as they were about to repair to the appointed spot. Master Betty again appeared in December for several nights prior to his departure to St. Petersburg, and again in April, 1808, shortly before he retired from the stage.

At the end of the season 1806-7 Mrs. Didier retired from the Bath stage, after an engagement extending over 40 years, during the whole of which she had been a favourite with the audience, and had gained the title of the " Mother of the Bath Stage." She died in 1829, at the advanced age of 88. In March Mrs. Siddons commenced an engagement extending over several weeks, and was followed at intervals during the year by Mrs. Harry Johnston, Cooke, Elliston, Bannister

MRS. JORDAN.

and Young. In January, 1808, Mrs. Siddons fulfilled another engagement, which was announced as her last professional visit, as indeed it
was, the last character in which she appeared being Mary Queen of
Scots. The announcement of her speedy withdrawal from the stage
naturally increased the anxiety to see her, with the result that she
played on each occasion to overflowing houses. An effort was made
to induce her to give a farewell performance in Bath after she had
taken leave of the London stage, but this she considered would be
inconsistent, and would not consent to. Cooke and Young again
appeared during this year, and in January, 1809, Mrs. Dickons, from
Drury Lane, played for a few nights. In February Italian opera was
produced for the first time in the Bath Theatre, Madame Catalani,
who had been singing at the concerts at the Rooms, obtaining the
assistance of several eminent performers for the introduction of this
new feature in dramatic art—so far as Bath was concerned. Only
scenes from different operas were presented, but the departure met
with great success and unbounded applause. Yet, notwithstanding
the favour which was extended to these performers, and to Madame
Catalani in particular, when that lady again appeared towards the end
of the year she met with a disgraceful and unaccountable reception.
On this occasion she was only announced to sing in addition to the
ordinary performance, and the prices were as usual, but still she met
with a determined opposition. Upon the very walls of the streets,
and on the pavements, were chalked such inscriptions as "No cat,"
"Native merit," &c., and when the songstress appeared on the stage
she was hissed, slightly at first, but afterwards sufficiently to entirely
disconcert her, and to occasion "sudden and severe indisposition."
And yet this lady had given her services for the benefit of local
charities, and did so even after this occurrence. It was an exhibition
little to the credit of the city.

In April, 1809, the celebrated Mrs. Jordan, the mistress of the Duke
of Clarence, appeared as Peggy in "The Country Girl," her great
part, and other characters, and in fashionable Bath she naturally
proved a great attraction. From the time of the announcement of her
engagement "the box office was continually crowded with fashionables
eager to obtain places, and on the nights of her performance the theatre
overflowed." The attraction was said to have proved unprecedented,
and Mrs. Jordan "closed her engagement to the most crowded and
brilliant audience that ever graced its benches." Brief engagements
were also fulfilled during 1809 by Mr. and Mrs. C. Kemble; Joseph
Munden, a famous comedian, then of Covent Garden ; Miss Smith,
who went from Bath to Covent Garden, and Bannister.

CHAPTER XVII.

BRAHAM, MACREADY AND KEAN.

A CELEBRATED TENOR — DEATH OF MR. DIMOND — CHARLES MATHEWS — MR. LODER — WILLIAM CHARLES MACREADY — PICTURE OF LIFE IN BATH —EDMUND KEAN.

URING the latter part of the season 1809-10, John Braham, the celebrated tenor, was first introduced to a Bath theatrical audience. He was no stranger to the city, for his visits to take part in the concerts at the Rooms had been pretty regular, but he had never before been induced to try his remarkable voice on the stage of the theatre, and his appearance in opera proved, therefore, a very great attraction. He first played in the character of the Seraskier, in the opera of "The Siege of Belgrade," and it was considered that he was heard to far greater advantage than had been the case at the Rooms. Bath can lay some claim to having fostered the talents of this eminent vocalist, for, when about 20 years of age he first appeared at Rauzzini's concerts, that distinguished musician was so struck by his evident talent that he gave him musical instruction for three years. Braham completed his musical education abroad, but there is no doubt he profited greatly by the grounding he received under Rauzzini's able tuition. About two month's after his pupil's *début* at the Bath Theatre Rauzzini died, and Braham was among the numerous and representative body of gentlemen who attended his funeral at the Abbey. Braham and Signora Storace (another of his pupils) subsequently erected a monument to his memory, which, bearing an appropriate inscription, is still to be seen by the south-western entrance of the Abbey. Braham's voice, enlarged in compass by a falsetto, ranged over a scale of 20 notes, and was of wonderful power and sweetness, besides being always completely under command. He was no actor, but as a singer he had no rival.

Elliston appeared on two occasions before the close of the season, and other attractions were Mrs. Dickons, Mrs. Lichfield (late of Covent Garden) and Incledon. It would seem that the frequent

introduction of these "auxiliaries," as they were termed, was very
distasteful to at least some of the members of the regular company.
This is not to be wondered at, for it greatly lessened their opportunities, and in several instances had a deteriorating effect upon their
benefits, and so we find Miss Marriott, who had been a member of the
company some little while, complaining on the occasion of her last
benefit of the few opportunities that had been given her, in consequence of the "constant succession of auxiliaries," and stating that it
was this, "so mortifying and injurious to those performers who are
stationary," that induced her to retire from the stage. What the
public demanded, however, the proprietors were, of course, bound to
provide ; it is not likely that they would have gone to the great
expense entailed by these engagements with the first actors of the
day, were they not thoroughly satisfied that it was necessary in order
to maintain the reputation and position of the theatre.

The following season, 1810-11, presents very few points of interest.
The place of Lovegrove, who left the company at the end of the
previous season, was taken by Mr. Chatterly, who, with his wife,
were engaged from the Cheltenham Theatre. Chatterly, Genest tells
us, was so good an actor that the Bath audience had no reason to
regret Lovegrove's loss. He had been brought up to the stage, and
in some characters was scarcely to be equalled, though he had an unfortunate habit of introducing speeches of his own when at a loss for
his lines, and to such an extent that Stanley, another member of the
company, used to say, half jokingly and half in earnest, that if Chatterly gave him the right cue he was all astonishment. Johnstone
appeared when the theatre was opened in October, for two nights,
Bannister fulfilled an engagement in November, and was followed
before the end of the year by Mrs. Johnson and Elliston. In January,
1811, Mrs. Jordan paid Bath what was termed a farewell visit prior to
her retirement from the stage ; but it was not her last appearance.
Following this engagement came Elliston again, and in April the ever
popular Bath favourite, Incledon, played for several nights On the
11th May, Mr. Woulds, who subsequently became manager of the
theatre, made his first appearance on joining the company.

In the course of the season 1811-12, the management of the theatre
changed hands owing to the death of Mr. Dimond, one of the
patentees, who was succeeded by his son, Mr. William Dimond Mr.
Dimond, who was 62 years of age, was a member of the Corporation,
and his funeral at the Abbey was attended by a large and representative crowd of mourners, so generally was he esteemed and respected.
His remains were interred in the south aisle, near the monument to
Quin ; that, however, has in recent years been removed to the north-
east portion of the church, but the slab bearing an inscription to the
memory of Dimond is still to be seen in its original position. It is
somewhat curious that in one copy of Genest's work in the British

Museum, at the page where Dimond's death is recorded, some one has written the following marginal note :—

"He cut his throat in a frenzy of grief and despair at his son William's infamous propensities. It is singular that Mr. Genest suppresses all allusions to this, but continually throughout this work mentions the . . . in terms of respect."

That Dimond met his death in such a sad manner as this is not borne out by contemporary evidence, for the cause of death is distinctly stated in the *Bath Herald* of the 11th January, 1812, in a long obituary notice, from which we quoted in a previous chapter, to have been the rupture of a blood vessel upon the brain.

When the season opened in October, 1811, Miss Feron, described as the "celebrated English Catalani," appeared for three nights. Her first engagement was with Elliston at the Surrey Theatre, where her success was so great that the managers of Covent Garden secured her services, and it was by their permission that she played in Bath. There were several alterations in the company this season, as indeed, was the case now at the commencement of almost every season, and as to notice all these alterations would occupy more space than is at our disposal, we propose only to allude to them when of special interest. In November Elliston was again engaged to act for five nights, but in consequence of a domestic bereavement he was compelled to break off in the middle of his engagement. It so happened that at the time Charles Mathews and Incledon were appearing at the Lower Rooms in an entertainment entitled "The Travellers," with Mathews's imitations of celebrated performers, in which that great mimic was making his first appearance in Bath, and the management of the theatre, taking advantage of this, engaged these two performers for two or three nights, Mathews making his first bow at the theatre as Lord Ogleby in "The Clandestine Marriage," and Buskin in "Killing no Murder." Braham played for nine nights in January, 1812, mostly in opera, and, in response to very earnest solicitations, Mr. Betty—"Master" Betty no longer—appeared and played in most of his principal characters. He had not been acting for some time, and came to Bath without any intention of playing, but terms were offered him "beyond precedent," and several ladies seconding the efforts of the management by their persuasive powers, Betty consented, and the engagement proved very successful, the hero of the hour being "much followed and caressed by the fashionables of the place." In April he again appeared, and in May Mr. Fawcett, from Covent Garden, a masterly comedian, played two nights, the second being for the benefit of Mr. Loder, the leader of the theatre band, a name well remembered in the city even to the present day. Loder married Miss Mills, the daughter of Fawcett's wife, which probably explains Fawcett's coming to Bath for his benefit. Incledon also appeared again in May, and in the

WILLIAM CHARLES MACREADY.

same month, on Miss Summer's benefit, a new drama, entitled " The Castle of Montral," which had been performed at Drury Lane over 30 nights, was produced. It was from the pen of the Rev. Dr. Whalley, of Bath. Miss Duncan, from the Lyceum, was engaged for a week in June, and on the last night of the season, the 25th July, Bannister acted Col. Feignwell,

At the commencement of the following season, 1812-13, two members of the Bath company, Miss Marriott and Mr. Abbott, appeared at Covent Garden, to which theatre Mr. Terry, of the Edinburgh Theatre, a native of Bath, who now joined the company in that city, proceeded at the end of the season. Mrs. Weston "principal tragic actress at Covent Garden," Miss Duncan (who played Lady Ann Lovell in "The Sons of Erin," a comedy by Sheridan's sister, Mrs. Le Fanu), Braham, and Mrs. Childe were among the early attractions offered, and in November Mr. Vestris and Madame Didelot, " universally allowed to be the first dancers in Europe," with several other performers of the Opera House, were engaged for a few nights "at very great expense " to perform in a series of the most celebrated ballets produced at the King's Theatre. On the 24th November Kemble commenced an engagement which lasted until the beginning of January, Mrs. Weston playing such parts as Lady Macbeth to his Macbeth. He was followed by Mrs. Jordan, who acted for some nights and appeared as Rosalind for her benefit. Then, in February, Betty was again the attraction, and Mr. Sinclair, of Covent Garden, sang at Mr. Loder's benefit, cn the 6th March. Miss Jameson, a favourite member of the company, took her farewell of the stage on the 6th April, the occasion being Stanley's benefit. One of the pieces produced was " Tailors," which was at first received with a good deal of hissing, the tailors of Bath having, presumably, heard of the riot at Dowton's benefit in London. Considerable interest was excited by the return to the Bath stage, on the 10th April, of Mrs. Campbell (née Miss Wallis) and she played to crowded houses for six nights, Blissett re-appearing with her. During May Incledon and Sinclair appeared together, and on the 29th of that month Blissett appeared for the last time on the stage as Falstaff in the Merry Wives of Windsor. Before the close of the season, which was as late as the 24th July, Mrs. C. Kemble played for two nights, her first appearance in Bath.

The season 1813-14, is a somewhat uninteresting one, presenting no features of importance. Mr. Young and Mrs. Campbell appeared at the opening of the theatre, and Mr. Phillips, a vocalist of Drury Lane, and formerly a member of the Bath company, played Captain Macheath in "The Beggars' Opera " on the 4th November, when Miss Nash, a pupil of Mr. Loder, who was engaged as principal vocalist at a large salary in 1815, made her first appearance on any stage. A company of equestrians, who had appeared at Covent

Garden, were engaged to perform in several grand spectacles, but the innovation did not prove profitable. Miss Stephens, who at that time was the recipient of great favours at Covent Garden, Mrs. Jordan, Kemble (who played 15 nights), Mathews, Elliston, and Mrs. Dickons were among the special attractions, and it is worthy of note that the popular play of "The Miller and his Men" was produced for the first time during the season, and Mr. Warde, who subsequently became a great favourite, made his first appearance on the 28th December as Achmet in "Barbarossa." During the recess considerable alterations and improvements were carried out in the house. The box office was enlarged, and the whole of the interior newly painted, the groundwork being of light green, enriched with gold mouldings and appropriate devices, while the Fonthill pictures in the ceiling were carefully restored, and their setting redecorated and painted a rich salmon colour. The private boxes were ornamented with green velvet drapery fringed with gold. These alterations, it was hoped, would "be the means of restoring the lower tier to their former appellation, 'the dress boxes.' Bonnets, shawls and fur tippets being dispensed with, will allow of the advantageous display of costly ornaments, which have of late years been almost exclusively reserved for the ball-room or card party."

The following season (1814-15) is memorable, inasmuch as it introduced two such representative actors as Macready and Kean to the Bath public. The former, William Charles Macready, first played in "Romeo," on the 29th December. He was the son of Macready, formerly of Covent Garden, and was educated at Eton, being intended for the Church, his appearance on the stage being due to the intervention of Mrs. Siddons. He had received the offer of an engagement at Bath in 1812, when Mr. W. Dimond saw him perform at Birmingham. At that time, however, Macready was playing with his father, and was unable to leave him then ; Dimond told him that the Bath management would be willing to treat with him whenever he thought of changing his position. After a serious difference with his father in 1814, he wrote to Dimond, and after some negotiations with regard to terms an engagement was effected. In his "Reminiscences" he describes, at length, his first appearance in Bath, and, as his story presents an interesting picture of life in the city at the time, we give the following extracts :—

By coach and mail, I made the best of my way to Bath, where, on my arrival, I got a flutter at the heart on seeing my name in large letters in the play bills to appear as Romeo on the 26th of December. (?) This sort of nervous emotion at the sight of my name posted upon the walls never left me to the latest moment of my professional career, and I have often crossed over to the other side of the street to avoid passing by a play bill in which it might be figuring.

Amid the revolutions of the times which my life has witnessed, few places

can have undergone more extreme changes than the city of Bath. At this
time its winter season was to the fashionable world the precursor of that of
the London spring. Houses, lodgings, boarding-houses were filled ; rooms
in the hotels must be engaged at an early date. The hotels, of which there
were several, were of the first order, but conspicuous among them were the
York House and the White Hart. The *table d'hôte* at these houses were
frequented by military and naval officers, men of fortune of the learned
professions, and graduates of the Universities. The company in general was
most agreeable. and the dinners excellent, usually, with wine and dessert,
standing at half a guinea per head. Each day, a little after noon, the Pump
Room, a sort of exchange for news and gossip, was literally crammed full
with its throng of idlers. Monday and Thursday evenings were given to balls
(usually crowded) at the great rooms ; Wednesday and Friday to those (not
so well attended) at the lower rooms ; Tuesday to Ashe's concert, at which the
leading vocalists were engaged ; and Saturday to the theatre, where again was
a *reunion* of the votaries of fashion. Now all has disappeared. At about
three o'clock the pavement of Milsom street would be so crowded with gaily
dressed people, and the drive so blocked with carriages, that it was difficult to
get along except with the stream. I have of late years looked down the same
street at the same hour and counted five persons ! The Lower Crescent was
a Sunday promenade between morning and afternoon service, presenting the
same conflux of visitors. The life of the London world of fashion was here
on a reduced scale, and the judgment of a Bath audience was regarded as a
pretty sure presage of the decision of the metropolis. It is not therefore to be
wondered at, if, distrustful as I seem constitutionally to have been I should
have approached this trial with something like trepidation.

A neat little drawing-room opening into the bedroom, No. 5, Chapel Row,
Queen Square, was my new home. I felt its loneliness, nor did my introduction to the performers at the rehearsal tend at all to inspirit me. Being
announced as "a star" without having the London stamp, I was looked
upon with supercilious coldness, as if challenging my right to take such
precedence before my fellow actors. The stage manager, Mr. Charlton, was
a very kind gentleman, and enforcing all my directions, enabled me to get
through my rehearsals very smoothly. The romance of "Aladdin," expensively
got up, was the afterpiece, which on a Christmas night would ensure a full
audience, and every part of the theatre was crowded to overflowing. My
reception, if I had wanted heart, was hearty enough to give it ; but though
dejected and misgiving in the contemplation of my task, I was on my entry
into the lists always strung up to the highest pitch, and like the gladiators in
the arena, resolute to do or die. The applause increased in each scene, until
in the encounter with Tybalt it swelled into prolonged cheering, and, to use
a homely phrase, I then found myself firm in the saddle. The end of the
tragedy was a triumph, and I returned to my homely lodging, to write off to
my family the news of my success. "Romeo and Juliet" was repeated, and
followed by "Hamlet," "The Earl of Essex," "Orestes," &c. The newspapers, with one exception, were lavish in their praise.

In fact, Macready met with such success that Mr. Harris, of Covent
Garden, sent Fawcett, his stage manager, down to Bath to report to
him upon the young actor's abilities, and, as a result, he received a

very liberal offer from Mr. Harris, which, however, was not accepted. Macready concluded his engagement with the Bath management on the 18th February, when the play of " Riches " was presented for his benefit to a crowded audience.

The prosperous issue of this engagement, he wrote, was acknowledged very

cordially by the managers, who fixed its payment on the terms I had asked, and entered into a contract with me for the next season for a longer period and an increased rate of payment. To me the result of this visit to Bath was remunerative beyond its local influence. An engagement of £50 per week for seven weeks was proposed to me by the Dublin management, and was of course accepted without any hesitation. This, as an indication of extended reputation, and consequently of ample income, made me more independent of London managers.

On the 8th July the eminent tragedian,

EDMUND KEAN.

Edmund Kean, made his first appearance on the Bath stage, playing as Shylock, and long before the commencement of the performance every seat in the house was occupied, so great was his fame, and during the few nights on which he appeared he was received with much enthusiasm. Besides " The Merchant of Venice," he acted Othello, Macbeth and Richard III. Genest says : " Richard was Kean's best part, but he overdid his death. He came close up to Richmond, after he had lost his sword, as if he would have attacked him with his fists. Richmond, to please Kean, was obliged to stand like a fool, with the drawn sword in his hand, and without daring to use it." Among other notable engagements during the season were those of Mr. T. Cooke, from the Lyceum ; Grimaldi, the famous clown ; Mathews ; Mrs. Mountain ; Mrs. Davison (*née* Miss Duncan) ; Miss Booth, from Covent Garden, and Betty, who attempted Othello for the first time.

CHAPTER XVIII.

CHANGES.

ACREADY made his second appearance in Bath in December, 1815, and fulfilled an engagement which lasted until the following February. He wrote that the season was a dull one, and that all places of amusement suffered in consequence, but this, he says, "did not prevent me from using, as a means of study for my improvement, the practice it afforded me." He appears, indeed, to have studied very hard during his stay in Bath, and he was an actor who was little affected by seeing bad houses before him, for he made it somewhat of a boast, at that time at any rate, that he could make profit even out of a poor house by not neglecting the opportunity of improving and perfecting his represen-tation of the character for which he was cast. During this stay in Bath Macready made many valuable friends, and in his Reminiscences he gives an interesting account of his first meeting with Mrs. Piozzi at the house of Dr. Gibbs, and tells the following amusing story at the expense of a well-known amateur :—

One of the very worst, if not the worst (amateur) who owed his notoriety to his frequent exposure of himself in the characters of Romeo, Lothario, Belcour, &c., was Coates, more generally known as "Romeo Coates." He drove a curricle with large gilt cocks emblazoning his harness, and on the stage wore diamond buttons on his coat and waistcoat. He displayed himself, diamonds and all, this winter at Bath in the part of the West Indian, and it was currently believed on this occasion he was liberally paid by the theatre, which profited largely by his preposterous caricature. I was at the theatre on the morning of his rehearsal, and introduced to him. At night the house was too crowded to afford me a place in front, and seeing me behind the scenes he asked me, knowing I acted Belcour, to prompt him, if he should be "out," which he very much feared. The audience were in convulsions at his absurdities, and in the scene with Miss Rusport, being really "out," I gave him a line which Belcour has to speak, "I never looked so like a fool in all my life;" which, as he delivered it, was greeted with a roar of laughter. He was "out" again, and I gave him again the same line, which again repeated was acquiesced in with a louder roar. Being "out" again, I administered him the third time the same truth for him to utter, but he seemed alive to its application, rejoining in some dudgeon, "I have said that twice already." His exhibition was a complete burlesque of the comedy, and a reflection on the character of a management that could profit by such discreditable expedients.

During this time Macready had under consideration offers both from Drury Lane and Covent Garden, but he did not go direct from Bath to the Metropolis. There were several important engagements during this season. Grimaldi appeared in November, when he took the clown in a pantomime of Mother Goose, played after a piece entitled "Love and Gout, or Arrivals from Bath," the original MS. of which was lent to the manager by the proprietors of the Haymarket Theatre; it proved a very popular play in the city, being repeated on several nights. Mr. J. Cooke was engaged in November to appear in comic opera, and towards the end of the year Mr. Sinclair appeared

JOSEPH GRIMALDI.

for a few nights. Then, in January, 1816, Mathews gave several performances, and in the same month Mrs. Alsop, a daughter of Mrs. Jordan, made her first appearance in Bath. Macready, wrote of her, "Some tones of her voice recalled for an instant her incomparable mother, but there all resemblance ended." In March Miss Hughes appeared, followed in April by Mr Young (Covent Garden), and Mrs. C. Kemble, who played for a fortnight early in May. On the 25th of that month William Dowton, the celebrated comedian from Drury Lane, played Sir Anthony Absolute in the "Rivals" for Mr. H. West's benefit, this being his first appearance in Bath, and on June 8th Mathews acted Dr. Ollapod in "The Poor Gentleman" on the occasion of Mr. and Mrs. Egan's benefit. It appears that when Mathews was in Bath earlier in the year he gave a supper to several members of the Bath company, and they kept it up till the early hours of the morning, when it was time for Mathews to go off in one of the coaches, but Egan had the misfortune to fall going home and break his leg. Mathews, therefore, offered to play for his benefit, and the result was a bumping house. The season ended with Kean's second appearance in Bath.

The following season (1816-17) opened on the 5th October with " The School for Scandal," in which Mr. Foote, from the Haymarket, who, with Mr. Green and Mrs. Heywood, now joined the company, played Sir Oliver Surface. Another member of the company during this season was Mr. Henry Kemble, a nephew of Mrs. Siddons. Incledon again appeared on the 19th October for a few nights, and gave his last performance in England before leaving for a tour in America. On the 29th November " Guy Mannering," a musical play by Mr. D. Terry, a native of Bath, was produced for the first time, and met with considerable success. Kean paid the city another visit in December, and on the 7th January, 1817, Kemble commenced his farewell visit previous to his final retirement from the stage. His last performance in the Bath Theatre was in the character of King John, and of a representation of " Coriolanus " on the 14th January, Genest wrote : " He was truly great on this·evening ; he said himself that he had never played the part so much to his satisfaction." In April, Mr. Howard Payne, " the American Roscius," drew good houses for a few nights, and he was followed by Booth, whom Genest described as " little more than Kean at second hand." The engagement was, however, only effected, if we may believe the playbills, at "extraordinary terms." Miss Somerville, at that time the first tragic actress at Drury Lane, gave one performance in " Isabella " in June ; Kean also appeared for one night as Selim in Barbarossa, and the theatre closed for the season with Booth as Richard III. At the end of this season the connection between the Bath and Bristol Theatres, which had existed for so many years, was severed, the lease of the Bristol Theatre having expired and the management declining to renew it, though upon what grounds we do not find stated. Stanley, who had been a member of the company for some years, now went to Drury Lane and subsequently left England for America.

The Theatre did not open for the ·season 1817-18 until the 1st of

November, a later date than had usually been the case, and the performance was now commenced at seven instead of half-past six,
the ordinary days of performance being Mondays, Wednesdays,
and Saturdays, though this arrangement was subject to frequent
alteration. The play with which the season opened was "Belle's
Stratagem," in which Mr. Warde played Dorincourt, and Mr.
Butler, from the Haymarket, and Mrs. Hill (late Miss Kelly, of
Bath), appeared. Among the new performers were Mr. Meadows,
from the Theatre Royal, Birmingham, and Mr. P. Farren, from
Dublin, a brother of W. Farren, the noted performer. On the 22nd
November Miss Somerville and Mr. Conway commenced an engagement, and in January a new tragedy by Mr. Hillman, entitled
"Fazio," was produced, and met with such success that it was
soon after acted at Covent Garden. The Bath management, however,
dropped in for a reprimand from the Lord Chamberlain for playing
the piece without a licence, but the offence was committed owing to
its having been previously acted at the Surrey Theatre, from which
it was supposed that it had been duly licensed.   "Cerberus,"
says Genest, "received his sop, and all was well," at any rate the
tragedy was repeated with equal success, and was very well received
both by the public and the press. Miss Bryne, a vocalist from Drury
Lane, and Young, from Covent Garden, fulfilled engagements during
March, and in Lent an entirely new departure was taken, several
oratorios being rendered, under the conductorship of Mr. Loder, the
principal vocalists being Miss Bryne, Mrs. Ashe, and Mr. Leoni Lee.
The child actress, Miss Clara Fisher, Betty Braham, and Miss O'Neill,
who had made a tremendous impression at Covent Garden, also performed during the season. In August, 1818, Palmer, who played so
great a part in the history of the Bath stage, died at Brighton, after a
long illness. He was, it will be remembered, the original patentee of
the Theatre, and to his taste, discrimination, and liberality must be
greatly attributed the high position which it occupied. He had been
twice Mayor, and was an alderman of the city, which he had also for
some years represented in Parliament. His remains were brought to
Bath and interred at the Abbey, his two sons, Col. Palmer, M.P., and
Capt. Edmund Palmer, R.N., C.B., being the chief mourners, and the
Mayor and other members of the Corporate body attending.
    The next season opened on the 31st October, when the comedy of
"Wonder" was produced. Among the performers engaged for the
season were Mr. Conway and Miss Penley, from the Windsor Theatre.
Conway, who was a remarkably handsome man, was a great favourite
among the ladies of Bath, but so also was Warde, who still remained
a member of the company, and they became therefore rival candidates
for the ladies' favours. The following amusing extract referring to
this is taken from ":The Life and Theatrical Times of Charles
Kean":—

Conway and Warde, when rival heroes in the Bath Theatre, had each a patronizing dowager, who sat in opposite stage boxes and led the applause for their respective protégés. The red and green factions of the circus at Constantinople, in the reign of Justinian, or the feuds of the Ursinis and Colonnas, during the middle ages, at Rome, never raged with greater intensity than the " Vereker " and " Piozzi " parties which divided " British Baiæ " in support of their respective favourites of the buskin. When Warde was locked up in " durance vile " under a merciless creditor he was fed daily with eleemosynary turkeys, fowls, and rounds of beef. When Conway fell sick from over-exertion, three physicians were despatched daily to his door ; and no sooner was he pronounced convalescent, than turtle, venison, and pineapples poured in to re-establish his physical man.

Miss Rosina Penley also divided the playgoing public into two factions, but in a different way. She was a very young actress, and her abilities became the subject of fierce discussion during the season. Numerous letters were written to the papers, and while some assailed her with adverse and even bitter criticism, others declared this to be unjust, and extolled her acting in many characters.* Mrs. Humby, from York, was another addition to the company. In consequence of the death of the Queen the theatre was closed during the greater part of November, and did not re-open until the 5th December. Shortly afterwards Mathews played for a few nights. Other attractions were Miss Kelly, Mr. Bologna and Mr. Kirby, from Drury Lane, W. Farren, Young, Mrs. Edwin, Mrs. Dickons, Miss O'Neill, and Booth. The patronage bestowed on the various performers at their benefits this season was very liberal, and the following were some of the receipts :—Conway, £160 ; Loder (leader of the band), £214 ; Miss Kelly, £160 ; Brownell, £266 ; Chatterly, £143 ; Leoni Lee, £110 ; Warde, £264 ; Mrs. Humby, £112 ; Cunningham, £164 ; Charlton, £216 ; Miss Tree, £98 ; Green, £166 ; and Farren, £150. Miss Maria Tree joined the Covent Garden Company before the following season.

During the recess the theatre was entirely re-decorated, the work being carried out with great taste and liberality. The prevailing colour was a delicate salmon relieved by cream coloured designs executed in bass relief :—

The former angles in the Proscenium are converted each into an elegant ellipsis by the introduction of rich and highly ornamented cornucopias, in the centre of which is an Apollo's head, in alto-relievo, finely executed in burnished gold ; and in the long panels immediately over the stage doors, the rose, thistle, and shamrock, are picturesquely entwined around a lyre, emblematic of the harmony of our National Union. The pilasters which support the cove are enriched by light ornaments, and the pedestals exhibit a classical caducous in

* Miss Penley, who was connected with the stage for many years, died at Budleigh Salterton, Devon, in 1879, in her 83rd year. She was a sister of Mr. Belville Penley, of Bath.

the centre of a panel.   In the centre of each stage door, which is richly
panelled, is a superb lyre, encircled with au oak wreath.   The two upper tiers
of Boxes are embellished with a strikingly chaste running design, formed by
lozenges, composed of oak husks, enclosing a superb red aud white Norman
rose.   The Dress Circle is divided into panels, with a chaplet in the centre
and leaves at the corner.   The private boxes present a most beautiful appearance, having handsome ruby-colour fluted silk curtains, with an antique
drapery, enriched with gold fringe, supported by Thyrces, with carved gilt
pines at each end.   The lining of the boxes is a rich crimson and ruby satin-
striped paper (purposely manufactured for the occasion), with burnished
mouldings and rosettes of gold in each corner.

During this season (1819-20) Kean played for several nights in
various of his best characters, and Yates and Young also acted for a
few nights. W. Farren appeared for his brother's benefit, and the
latter left at the close of the season to undertake the management of
the Dublin Theatre. Mr. Phillips, from Covent Garden, starred in
opera in the early part of the season, and Miss Greene, a pupil of
Bishop, the celebrated composer, made her first appearance on the
stage in "The Beggar's Opera." She possessed an excellent voice,
and sang with taste and artistic execution, her *début* occasioning no
little sensation. Miss Eliza Blanchard also made her first appearance
in Bath in November, and the attraction for her benefit in the following spring was the presence of her father from Covent Garden. In
consequence of the death of George III. the Theatre was closed for
some days in January and February. A very old member of the
company, one who had belonged to it for over half a century took a
farewell benefit in May, namely, Miss Summers, who, Mr. Dimond
said on the authority of the books of the theatre, had never been
absent for a single night. Although on the Theatrical Fund and
allowed a ticket night each season, she appears to have had a hard
struggle after severing her connection with the theatre until her death,
and Genest, who evidently interested himself in the case, gives a long
account of the efforts made on her behalf to induce the management
to deal more liberally with her. The season closed on the 5th May,
when Warde took his farewell of the Bath audience, appearing as
Rob Roy and John of Paris, and playing to a crowded house. He
had been seven years in the city, and now left to take a more lucrative
engagement at Dublin. Mr. Bedford, who joined in 1815, and Miss
Greene, left for London engagements.

Among the engagements for the following season were those of
Mrs. Weston, Mr. Mude, Miss Johnson (engaged to replace Miss
Greene), and Miss Carr. The inimitable Liston gave six performances
in April, and was said to have been more attractive in Bath than in
London. Miss Stephens, afterwards Countess of Essex, Young
and Broadhurst also appeared. At the end of the season Meadows
(who was engaged at Covent Garden), Mude, Pritchard, Younger,

Mrs. Weston, and six other performers of less note, left Bath.
Although the company lost so many of its members at the end of this
season it was strengthened in the next (1821-22) by the addition of
such performers as Hamblin, who married Miss Blanchard, F. Vining,
from Norwich, Mrs. Bunn, and Miss Lydia Kelly. Still such actors
as Meadows and Younger, could not but be missed. Miss Wilson, a
rival to Miss Stephens, was announced to appear at the commence-

ment of the season
for five nights, but
she was too ill to
fulfil the engage-
ment, and Mr. Loder
c o n s e q u e n t l y
entered into an
arrangement with
Madame Catalani
to give a grand
concert on the 27th
O c t o b e r , t h e
o p e n i n g n i g h t.
After the concert,
Madame Catalani
returned to Mr.
Loder every shilling
of her stipulated
engagement, declar-
ing it "a small
tribute of regard
for his private
worth, and high
professional skill."
   On the 15th
December, a new
p l a y , e n t i t l e d
"Kenilworth; or
England's Golden
Days," was pro-

JOHN LISTON.

duced very elaborately, and at great expense. Writing of the
production Genest says, "Kenilworth was very successful; it was
the grandest spectacle ever exhibited at a provincial theatre. Mrs.
Bunn was excellent as Queen Elizabeth, and the whole play was well
acted.   No expense had been spared : several new scenes were
painted by Grieve ; the canopy had been really used by George III.
This play and the ' Heart of Midlothian,' as acted at Bath,* are by

* Produced in 1819.

far the best pieces which have been compiled from the novels of
Sir W. Scott ; it is a pity that they are not printed." The play was
acted several times during the season, and probably would have
been produced once a week, but that Mrs. Bunn had to leave to fulfil
an engagement in Ireland. The principal engagements in 1822 to
the end of this season were those of Charles Kemble (who failed to
draw good houses), Liston, Miss Dance, from Covent Garden, Kean,
and Warde, who played during the race week. Miss Dance, who is
said to have borne some resemblance to Mrs. Siddons, was so well
received that she was offered by the management a liberal engagement for the next season. Miss Jarman, who was a great favourite
with Bath audiences, left to appear at Dublin, where she had
accepted a profitable engagement.

When the following season opened on the 2nd November Mr. Blood
made his first appearance on any atage in "The Duenna," by permission of the proprietors of Covent Garden, he being engaged to
appear at that Theatre at a later date. David Fisher, from Drury
Lane, was engaged as a member of the company but, although he is
said to have been a good sound actor, he did not give satisfaction, and
consequently did not remain throughout the season, Hamblin taking
his place in December. On the 20th November a play, entitled "Life
in London ; or the days and nights adventures of Tom and Jerry"
was produced, and proved such a success that it was frequently repeated. Then came engagements with Young, Madame Bellegrade,
prima donna of the Royal Opera, Naples, Miss Brunton, Macready,
Miss Clara Fisher, and Miss Paton (afterwards Mrs. Wood) a talented
voca'ist from Covent Garden, who was engaged at great expense in
the place of Liston, unable to fulfil an engagement in consequence of
a domestic bereavement. On the 4th June, Miss Lydia Kelly's benefit,
Mr. Henry Field, a prominent name in Bath musical circles for many
years, made his first appearance on the stage as the Seraskier in "The
Siege of Belgrade." His rendition of the part was very successful, and
subsequently he made frequent appearances on the Bath stage. At
the close of the season both Hamblin and Miss Dance were discharged, the former because he refused to play parts for which he was
cast, and the latter for neglecting to make herself perfect in her parts,
through her love for amusement. Vining also left the company,
having received a London engagement. The season was not altogether a success, there being but poor houses nearly every night, but
when the adventures of Tom and Jerry were put on, with the introduction of pugilists in one scene, the house was crowded, a fact which
indicated a great change in the tastes of the Bath playgoing public.
The following extract from the *Bath Herald*, of the 5th April, 1823,
deals with this fact :—

It is true, our managers have been most zealously employed through the
season, in their multiform endeavours to suit the taste of the public ; good

farces and good plays have in their turns been performed ; Shakespeare and
Sheridan have been produced—but often to barren benches ; other specimens
of the "legitimate drama " have been revived for a night or two, but have met
with sudden deaths through their chilling reception in the late cold winter ;
ventriloquism has been tried, but in vain—for the voice of the celebrated
artiste reverberated through every corner of the almost deserted house.
Thalia's smiles and Melpomene's tears have been disregarded, and even melo-
drama has lost much of its influence !   At last a lucky hit has been made—
the managers engaged the undoubted Champion of the Fistic Art, Mr. Neate,
with one of his compeers in that fashionable science ; and on Monday last they
displayed their sparring gymnastics at the Theatre Royal, Bath, before an
audience *crowded to an overflow* in Gallery, Pit—aye, and in Boxes ! ! !   Let
not the Managers be blamed—for, to resort to a rather hacknied couplet,

> "The Drama's laws the Drama's Patrons give,
> " Since they who live to please, must please to live."

When the season for 1823-24 opened on the 4th November it was
under different management and proprietary.   Mrs. Dimond died in
June, and her son then relinquished the management, in which he was
succeeded by Mr. Charlton, the stage manager.   After Keasberry's
death, Palmer and Dimond, senior, bought his share, and became
equal proprietors.   Dimond left his share to his wife, who in turn left
it to her four sons.   Mainwaring says that upon Mrs. Dimond's death
the theatre became vested in Palmer's two sons, but, according to
Genest, Palmer's share was left to his son, Col. Palmer, to whom
the Dimonds sold their shares, so that he became the sole proprietor.
" Never, perhaps," wrote Genest, " did a theatre belong to any
gentleman who was so little theatrical.   In a preceding season he had
asked a friend what sort of a play 'Hamlet' was."   The season
opened under favourable auspices, the company being strengthened
by several new members, including Mr. Bellamy, from Norwich,
Mr. Balls, from Birmingham, Mrs. Green, Mrs. Bailey, from York, and
Mr. Osbaldiston, from Norwich.   Early in the season there were
several performances of Italian opera, and in December Mr. and
Mrs. Yates fulfilled an engagement, and were followed by Sinclair,
Liston, and Young.   Miss M. Tree came from Covent Garden to
assist at her sister's benefit, W. Farren played for the benefit of a
member of the company named Sheppard, and for Mr. Loder's benefit,
the last night of the season, the *bénéficiarie* was fortunate enough to
secure the services of Fawcett, Sinclair and Miss M. Tree.

CHAPTER XIX.

DECADENCE.

THE DRAMA UNDER A CLOUD—MR. BELLAMY'S MANAGEMENT—
WANT OF PATRONAGE—REASONS FOR THE CHANGE—THE
THEATRE CLOSED—A PLAN OF SUBSCRIPTION—PRINCIPAL
PERFORMERS.

O far we have had to deal with a history that has
presented little but success, and has been a story of
continued prosperity and fame. It was only to be
expected, however, that there should come a break
in this brilliant career, for it was too brilliant to last,
and the changes to which all mundane institutions are
subject, especially those which are dependent upon
the vagaries of fashion and the fluctuations of the fancies of the public,
were bound at length to make themselves felt even upon the
prosperous history of the Bath Theatre.   It is somewhat strange that
this change should come at a time when the management of the
Theatre passed from the hands of those who had been responsible for
the welfare of the institution for so many years, but it is not to that
fact that any alterations in its fortunes are to be entirely attributed.
No doubt it had something to do with it.   Charlton, who, as we have
seen, succeeded Dimond in the management, although he had proved
a valuable assistant, and an excellent stage manager, did not possess
the qualifications necessary for a successful manager, and became so
careless, and so inactive in providing attractions for the public, that it
was found necessary at the close of the season 1826-27 to dispense
altogether with his services.   Genest even throws a doubt upon his
capabilities as an assistant manager, and says that Dimond did much
that it was really his business to do, and dared not trust him with the
direction of either scenery or dress in a new production, could never
depend upon him in difficulties, and that, in fact, " he was little more
than a prompter, on whose punctuality and regular attendance the
proprietor might always rely."   It is some contradiction to this,
however, that Charlton should have continued to hold such a responsible position at the Theatre for a period of over thirty years, but
there seems no reason to doubt that as a manager he was a failure,
and that he did not exert himself to secure the patronage of the public
as he might have done.   At any rate, on the 28th May, 1827, he made

his last graceful speech as manager, and was succeeded by
Mr. Bellamy, a member of the company, who possessed sufficient
energy to restore the theatre to its lost prestige had only the fates
been with him. His very first season was, however, from a variety of
causes, one of continued disaster, one of the first of these causes being,
as he stated in his speech on the last night, that from the commencement there had not been one hour in which some important department
of the drama had not been paralysed by the absence of some principal
performer through accident or illness. Notwithstanding these difficulties, however, the pecuniary results of the season were stated to
have been satisfactory, and Mr. Bellamy promised that his exertions
should not be relaxed, but that everything should be done to place
before the public a programme for the next season (1828-29) in every
way worthy of the city, and the traditions of the Bath stage. And he
appears to have kept his word ; the number of London stars was not
so great as usual, but a number of new pieces was produced, revivals
were very numerous, and the resources of the company must have
been severely taxed, especially as it was by no means a strong one,
and was wanting in actresses capable of taking the leading parts,
either in comedy or tragedy. Again Mr. Bellamy had to inform the
audience, after the last performance of the season, that it had been ,
one of disaster, inasmuch as it had "afforded but little cause for
exultation in a pecuniary view," but he continued to take a hopeful
view of things, trusting "that the cloud which now obscures the
drama will pass away, and show that its glory has not departed."
The cloud, however, was too thick and heavy to be dispelled by
Mr. Bellamy's exertions.

It will be interesting to examine the reasons for this change in the
fortunes of the Theatre, as far as may be possible. In the first place
the temper of the times had turned against the drama. It was no
longer the fashionable amusement that it had been for more than half
a century. Fashion is notoriously fickle and uncertain, therefore it is,
perhaps, strange that it should have remained faithful to the drama
for so long, but at last the change came, and the fact that it had become the fashion to adopt a later hour for dinner was one of the
principal causes that contributed to it. But while dramatic
amusements suffered from the neglect of fashion, they also suffered at
the hands of those who denounced fashion, and who made it their
business also to denounce the stage and assume an attitude of active
hostility towards it. That is a form of antagonism which the stage
has frequently had to combat, but it has always been a struggle from
which it has issued triumphant in the end. There was another cause
which contributed to the want of interest in the drama, and that was
the agitation caused throughout the country by the question of reform,
which, of course, during the period with which we are dealing, reached
a high pitch. With elections, and such events as the Bristol riots to

LIONEL BROUGH.

think about, it may easily be understood that the drama stood a poor chance of securing the attention of the public. In Bath, however, there were many who recognised that the want of adequate support for the chief amusement of the city was a serious matter, and they did their best to bring home to those who were interested in the city, that should it become necessary to close the theatre, the popularity of Bath as a resort for fashionable society would gradually dwindle away, that, in fact, the interests of the city materially depended upon the prosperity of its theatre. "Without the theatre," said one writer, "the splendour of the fullest season will be thrown into eclipse, that being the only establishment where the great bulk of the population have the opportunity of witnessing its gaieties," and in the *Bath Herald* we find the following remarks : "The stranger who visits Bath cannot instantaneously make arrangements for giving or partaking of those brilliant and expressive private parties which at present usurp the place of public amusements ; and if neither balls, concerts, theatres, nor any other public entertainments whatever, are to receive further patronage, Bath, from being the very throne of gaiety, elegance, fashion and good taste, will settle down into one of the dullest and most insipid places in these dominions." In 1830, it was suggested that an attempt should be made to revive the custom of having a recognised fashionable night in each week, and the management, falling in with this idea, decided to set apart Tuesday as such a night, and announced that on every Tuesday an operatic entertainment would be placed upon the bill (for the public taste, until lately favouring tragedy, had now decidedly changed in favour of opera), and the result was in some measure satisfactory, though the effort was not attended with the success that was hoped from it. Mr. Bellamy's speech on the last night of the season seemed to have despair for its key note. "No exertion," he said, "has been spared—every species of entertainment has been tried—Italian and English opera, tragedy, comedy, spectacle, pantomime—stars of various magnitudes have glittered in our dramatic hemisphere." "For the future," he added, "I will make no promises." The following season was somewhat brighter than its predecessors, but the season of 1831-32 was so bad that the spirit was taken out of all who had to do with the conduct of the Theatre. We take the following extract from the *Bath Herald* of 21st July, 1832 :—

Thus was terminated a season in which the exertions of our respected and zealous manager to procure attractive novelty have been incessant and successful ; while the labours of the whole company in the study of those numerous novelties must have been severe and trying in no common degree. From a variety of combining causes, of which public distress, public agitation and the fickleness of fashion, are a few, these exertions must have been but inadequately repaid. We hope, however, for better times, and a return of fashionable patronage to this elegant and rational recreation. As a proof that the worthy manager, Mr. Bellamy, has earned the esteem of his brother performers, as much as the respect of the public, we are informed that a letter of thanks has been transmitted to him signed by the whole company. A testimonial which will prove some little consolation to him, we trust, under many trying and vexatious disappointments.

The proprietor now determined to close the theatre, which, under the circumstances, was undoubtedly the only and best step that could be taken. It was, of course, not to be expected that the theatre could be kept open at a loss, and the fact of its being definitely closed roused those interested in the welfare of the city into action. Consequently, in December, 1832, a representative meeting of the professional and trading inhabitants of Bath was held in the saloon of the theatre, for the purpose of submitting to the public a plan by which it might be opened by subscription, it being understood that there would be no difficulty in securing the services of capable professionals if they were guaranteed against loss. A plan of subscription was, therefore, decided upon, the sum subscribed to be considered payment in advance for a certain number of tickets to any part of the theatre at the regular prices of admission. The money so subscribed was to be paid into Messrs. Tugwell and Co.'s Bank, in the names of Mr. Soden, Mr. R. Savage, and Mr. Davis, as trustees for the subscribers, and paid to the order of the lessee, or lessees, of the theatre, in ten weekly instalments of ten per cent. on the whole sum. In case, however, the theatre should have to be closed for want of patronage, it was provided that the trustees should audit the account and divide the unemployed balance in just proportions among the subscribers. It was also resolved "That this meeting, having used their utmost endeavour to organise a plan for renewing an important feature in the amusements of Bath, respectfully ask the co-operation of the nobility and gentry, inhabitants and visitors, on whose influence and patronage the success of every place of public entertainment must principally depend ; " and it was further urged that subscribers should, as far as possible, use their tickets on Saturdays, since by so doing they might "essentially and permanently serve the interests of the theatre, because a full attendance on that evening may gradually revive the ancient practice of Bath when fashion always devoted Saturday evenings to dramatic entertainment, and thus ensure the prosperity of the theatre." At a subsequent meeting it was decided that Mr. Brownell, the treasurer and box office keeper, should personally call upon the usual visitors to the boxes with the object of soliciting their support of the plan proposed. These efforts on the part of the citizens where so far successful—greatly it should be mentioned through the public spirit displayed by the tradesmen of the city—that on the 10th of January, Mr. Bellamy became the lessee for the season, and the theatre opened nine days later. Commencing so late, the season was naturally a brief one, but although there was a marked absence of "stars," when it closed on the 3rd of June, the lessee had the gratification of announcing that it had been "the most prosperous season known in Bath for many years," the result being a balance, though a small one, on the right side.   Mr. Bellamy took the opportunity of thanking the public for " their energy and zeal in resuscitating the almost sinking drama," and especially thanked the " ladies of fashion who by their example and influence have restored the almost forgotten custom of appropriating the Saturday evening to dramatic entertainment."

The following is a brief notice of the principal performers appearing at the theatre during the time with which we have been dealing in this chapter.

1824-25.—Warde was engaged for the season, and Mr. Montague, from Edinburgh, joined the company.   Very early in the season Madame Catalani was prevailed upon to appear for a few nights, and it is satisfactory to find that her reception was very different to what it was on a previous occasion.   In January, 1825, Braham was engaged for the purpose of producing the opera of "Der Freyschutz" in which he played four times, and then came an engagement with Liston. Braham also fulfilled a second engagement in the course of the season. For Miss E. Tree's benefit her sister, Miss M. Tree, appeared, and on the occasion of Mr. Loder's benefit there appeared Mr. Sapio, from Drury Lane, who, and also Mr. Henry Field, played in the opera, "Fall of Algiers," and Mr. John Reeve, of the Adelphi, a well known mimic, appeared in a new farce, in which he introduced imitations of various actors.

1825-26.—Before the Theatre really opened for the season Mathews gave his "At Home" entertainment.   New members of the company included Messrs. Cooke, from Cork, Kent, and Hamerton, from Dublin. Mr. Perkins, from the Opera House, London, appeared for a few nights, and was followed by Mr. Sapio and Master Burke, a child who displayed much precocity.   On the 14th December "Paul Pry" (by special permission of the proprietors of the Theatre Royal, Haymarket) was produced in Bath for the first time, the title rôle being taken by Woulds.   Mr. J. Vining, from the Haymarket, brother to a former member of the company of that name, joined for the season on Boxing Day.   During January, 1826, Miss Paton, Pearman, from Covent Garden, and Macready appeared, and on the 1st February, Liston, the original Paul Pry, appeared in that character, playing to a house thronged to the roof, while numbers were refused admission.   Miss Foote fulfilled an engagement towards the end of February, and Young and Macready also appeared during the season. Charles Kemble and Miss Tree appeared for the benefit of the Misses E. and A. Tree, and for Loder's benefit Miss Love, from Covent Garden, was introduced to the Bath audience.

1826-27.—The stars engaged during this season were Miss Kelly, Mr. Bartley (Covent Garden), Sinclair, Miss Foote, Madame Vestris,

K

who first appeared as Mrs. Ford in the " Merry Wives of Windsor,"
on the 18th April, and Yates. Liston played for Charlton's benefit,
and also for Mr. Loder's.

1827-28.—Extensive decorations were carried out before the Theatre
was opened for this season, such as to "leave no room for critical
comment, even to the most fastidious taste." But the most important
improvement was the substitution of gas lights for oil lamps as foot-
lights, a reform which was thus spoken of at the time :—

> The effect of the gas in the new footlights on the stage at our Theatre was
> tried last evening, and far exceeded any expectation, however sanguine, that
> we have formed of it. Not only the proscenium and scenery generally, are
> improved by it, but an air of splendour and animation is thrown over the
> whole house, no part of which is, however, more assisted by it than the ceiling.
> The new and exquisitely beautiful drop-scene would never, in our opinion,
> have been justly appreciated but for this judicious change.

Among the new members of the company were Miss Foote, of
Drury Lane, a vocalist who had been a great favourite at Dublin,
Mrs. Darley, from York, Miss Brooke, from Hastings, Miss Taylor,
from the Theatre Royal, Richmond, Messrs. Popham, from Chelten-
ham, Mason, from York and Birmingham, and Henry, from Bristol.
The company was said to have been better than for some seasons.
Among the "auxiliaries" engaged were Miss Paton, Miss Foote,
Madame Feron, Madame Vestris, Miss Hallande, Pemberton,
Macready, and Sinclair. Charlton was allowed a benefit in April, at
which Warde and Green appeared, and Mr. Loder secured Fawcett
and Madame Vestris for his benefit.

1828-29.—The addition to the company included Miss Bitts (English
Opera House), Mr. Stuart, from Birmingham, and Mr. Reynoldson,
from the Haymarket. Madame Catalani, Miss Fanny Ayton,
Miss Foote, Madame Vestris, Braham and Macready were engaged
during the season, and in February, 1829, a series of Italian operas
was rendered by Signor de Begnis and pupils of the Royal Academy
of Music. Mr. Loder never failed to present an attractive programme
on the night for his benefit, and for the 11th May he was able to
announce the appearance of Warde, Green, Meadows, Miss Forde
(Covent Garden) and J. R. Addison.

1829-30.—The theatre was opened on the 30th October with an
entertainment by Mr. J. Henry, of the Haymarket and Adelphi
Theatres, and before the season properly commenced Mr. Loder gave
a grand concert at the theatre, at which Madame Malibran Garsia
was the principal vocalist. One of the first pieces produced was the
popular " Black Eye'd Susan," which was played for a first time on
the 18th November, "the overture, entre-act, and melo-dramatic
music, selected from Dibdin's melodies, and arranged expressly for
this theatre by Mr. E. Loder," son of the leader of the band. On the

20th November a "musical prodigy" was introduced, in Miss Coveney, a child twelve years old, with a voice of exquisite sweetness, power and expression, who became a great favourite with Bath audiences. On the 13th January Mr. Bianchi Taylor made his first appearance as a member of the company, from which he withdrew at the end of the following season, and took up his residence in Bath as a teacher of music. Among those who played during the season were Miss Paton, Miss Foote, Macready, Young, Perkins, and for the last four nights Charles and Fanny Kemble, while for Loder's benefit two former members of the company, Miss Ellen Tree and Mrs. Humby (Haymarket) appeared. Though the benefits were neglected this season, some performances by an elephant drew crowded houses—an instance of the change which had come over the theatre.

1830-31.—Kean made his first appearance in Bath for nine years, previous to his departure for America, and Mrs. Humby, Miss Foote, Madame Vestris, Mr. and Mrs. Wood (late Miss Paton), Mathews, Braham (who appeared in "Masaniello"), Macready, J. P. Cooke (in "Black Eye'd Susan"), and Power from Covent Garden were among the "auxiliaries" engaged. Mr. Mason, a member of the company, went to Covent Garden at the close of the season.

1831-32.—A great number of operas were presented during this season. New performers were Messrs Bennett, M'Keon, Mellon, Howard, Broadfoote, Miss Turpin, from Edinburgh and the Haymarket, Miss Weston, from Edinburgh, and on the 5th November Mrs. Macready made her first appearance as Meg Merrilies in "Guy Mannering." Dowton and Kean appeared in November, and in January an actor of colour, named Keene, called "the African Roscius," played a number of characters, commencing with "Othello." He was followed by Miss Coveney and Macready, and on the 20th March Young commenced his final engagement before leaving the stage, his last performance being in "Man of the World." In April Mr. and Mrs. Yates played, and in July Warde, Meadows and Miss F. Jarman, from Covent Garden, appeared, when the "Hunchback" was performed for the first time.

1833.—The season did not commence, in consequence, as we have shown, of the proprietor determining not to carry it on on his own account, until the 19th January, and the company which Mr. Bellamy got together included, Messrs. Stuart, Howard, Clement White (from Edinburgh), Mulleney, Woulds, Bedford (from Edinburgh), Connor, Hooper (Drury Lane), Johnson, Miss Crisp (from Cheltenham), Mrs. Ashton, Mrs. Darby, and Miss Turpin (who went to the Haymarket at Easter) while in March, Miss George, who had been to America, returned to the Bath boards. Madame Vestris was the only star engaged, except for Loder's benefit, when Miss Shirreff, Bennett, and G. Stansbury, from Covent Garden, and Paul Bedford, from Drury Lane, appeared.

CHAPTER XX.

FTER his one short season as manager, Bellamy severed his connection with the Theatre entirely, subsequently (1835) becoming lessee of the Assembly Rooms, and there being nobody to carry on the management, both the Bath and Bristol Theatres were, in August, 1833, advertised to be let by tender. In November it was announced that Mr. Barnett, of the Reading and Newbury Theatres, had become lessee, the announcement being followed by an address to the public, in which the new lessee stated that though he was well aware of the cloud which for years had obscured the theatrical horizon, yet, "as a sincere lover, as well as professional follower of the drama," he was determined to do his utmost "to dispel the mist." Having no local connections to recommend him, he relied upon the kind feeling of the Bath public, and added that it was his desire to associate himself permanently with the Bath Theatre. Notwithstanding this flourish of trumpets and protested determination to persevere in the attempt to restore the Theatre to its former prestige, one season proved quite enough for Mr. Barnett, who showed himself by no means anxious to renew his management for the next season. He was succeeded in the lesseeship by Mr. Woulds, who, with his wife, had been playing in Bath for several seasons, but his reign, though plucky and stubborn, resulted at length in insolvency, by reason of the apathy of the public, who failed to support his enterprise in anything like the manner which was necessary in order to keep going so expensive an establishment. The fact that Woulds was not, at any rate for a part of the time, entirely dependent upon his own resources, only makes the ultimate result of his connection with the Theatre all the more deplorable. When he opened, on the 26th December, 1834, there is no doubt that it was with Macready at his back, for the fact is admitted in the latter's Reminiscences. Macready commenced

an "engagement" on the 5th January, 1835, playing constantly in
Bath and Bristol, and under date of the 6th January, the following
was written in his diary :—

Occupied at the Theatre from ten till quarter past three—saw old Mr.
Taylor, who seemed very sanguine, good old man, about the success of the
speculation.   I certainly am not.   On a rough calculation of my expectations
from the prospect afforded by the present receipts, I think the chances are
rather against a balance in favour than for it, and if in favour, I think it must
be very small, and not at all worth my time and trouble.

Then two days later he speaks of being told by Woulds that he
had heard from Mr. Field that there was much discontent at the
prices, and several references to the receipts subsequently occur and
appear to express satisfaction.   With the commencement of the
following season Woulds announced a reduction in the prices in
consequence of representations which had been made to him, but
remarked that it would only be an experiment, as he could not reduce
his expenditure, feeling assured that a company of inferior talent
would not satisfy the Bath public, so that it became a question of
whether, if he reduced the prices for admission, the difference would
be made up to him by increased attendances.*   At the close of this
season, in the customary farewell speech to the audience, the lessee
stated it had been unprofitable, though not to such an extent as to
deter him from continuing the management, but the same melancholy
announcement had to be made when he again addressed the audience
at the end of the 1836-37 season, though on that occasion he said he
could not attribute it to the lack of inclination on the part of the
public to support him, "but to various other causes, a protracted
winter of inclement weather, and a long-continued epidemic, which
confined nearly two-thirds of the population of Bath to their houses."
The epidemic, it may be interesting to state, was influenza.   The
next season the now usual tale of want of support is conspicuous by
its absence, but only to recur in June, 1839, when Woulds, addressing
the audience on the night of his benefit, said " From the present state
of theatres and theatricals in this country, believe me, a manager's
situation is no sinecure."   However, though the season had been
"attended with considerable loss," he said he did not despond, but
when the time came for the opening of the next season to be talked about,
no announcement on the subject appeared until early in December,
when it was learnt from an advertisement which appeared in the
papers that Woulds had relinquished his interest in the establishment
as lessee, and that the Theatre was again to let, the advertisement

* The prices thus altered were :—Private Boxes and Dress Circle, 4s. ;
second price, 2s. 6d.   Upper Boxes, 3s. ; 2s.   Pit, 2s. ; 1s.   Gallery, 1s. ;
no second price.

also stating that upwards of £600 had been expended during the
recess in placing the building in complete repair and re-embellishing
and decorating it under the superintendence of the Messrs. Grieve.
The unfortunate Woulds, who had also been running the Swansea
and Cardiff Theatres, became insolvent early in 1840, and subsequently
returned to his old position, as we shall presently see, as an ordinary
member of the company.

The theatre did not long remain in want of a lessee, notwithstanding
the unpromising record of nearly twenty years, the new comer being
Mr. Davidge, the manager of the Surrey Theatre, London, who,
besides being not altogether unacquainted with the Bath stage,
occupied a position of some influence and experience in his profession.
His advent was hailed with much satisfaction by those who were
really interested in the welfare of the theatre, because it was felt that
if the public were to be induced to restore it to its former eminence by
increasing their patronage it would be by one having such an
extensive theatrical connection as Davidge. Disappointment, however,
was again in store for those well-wishers of the drama, for, after a
season and a half, the lessee was compelled, in consequence of
" continued and increased indisposition," to determine the tenancy of
the theatre. Whether this sudden termination was wholly due to ill-
health seems a somewhat doubtful point. Undoubtedly Davidge
became greatly shattered in health during his tenancy of the theatre,
and when, on the last night, he appeared to make a speech he had to
be supported by Woulds, but at the same time his management had
been to a great extent carried on by deputy, and it is noticeable that
in his valedictory address he commented upon the causes of the
decline of the drama in London and the provinces, attributing it in a
great measure to the system of "starring" and the neglect of keeping
up an efficient company at each theatre. It was almost in the middle
of a season (March, 1841) that the theatre was thus closed, but it was
opened for the remainder of the season through the energy of two
citizens, Mr. J. R. Newcome* and Mr. J. Bedford, who became joint
lessees for the time being and brought the season to a fairly successful
conclusion. We will now proceed to note the principal points of
interest in the seasons included under these successive managements.

1833-34.—Among the company engaged by Barnett were Mr. and
Mrs. Woulds, Messrs. Aldridge, Montague (stage manager), Mulleney ;
Mrs. Ashton and Mrs. Darley, and the new comers included
Miss Gordon, Miss Weston, Miss Atkinson, from Covent Garden,
Miss Malcolm, from the Queen's Theatre, Mrs. Barnett ; Messrs.
Harrington, Lee, W. Keene, Wyatt, Edmunds, and Stuart. The
Theatre was opened on the 26th December with James Wallack, from

* The name of Mr. Newcome is well known in theatrical circles, for he
was lessee of the Plymouth Theatre for many years before his death, in 1888.

Drury Lane, an actor who had successfully taken Kemble for his model. There were but few " stars " introduced during this season, the most notable, perhaps, being Sheridan Knowles and Miss Jarman, who appeared together, while for Loder's benefit Mr. Perkins and Miss Coveney played in the opera of " Gustavus the Third." Lord Byron's tragedy of " Sardanapalus " was produced for the first time on the night of the benefit of Mr. Stuart and Mr Harrington, on the 19th May, the season closing with the lessee's benefit on the 23rd May.

1834-35.—When Woulds opened the season on Boxing Day the following new members of the company were notified :—Messrs J. Webster, from the Haymarket, Norwich, and Brighton Theatres; Hughes, from Exeter; Thompson, from Drury Lane and Covent Garden ; Saville, from Birmingham ; Grainger, from Bristol ; T. Green, from Drury Lane and Covent Garden; Strickland, from the Haymarket ; Mrs. F. Conner, from the Dublin and Belfast Theatres ; Mrs. Lovell, from Drury Lane and Covent Garden; Mrs. Belville Penley (née Miss

MRS. LISTON.

Field), also from Drury Lane and Covent Garden ; Miss Fanny Healy, from the English Opera House, London ; Mrs. Woulds and Miss Russell. Macready's appearances (we have already alluded to the fact that he was probably lessee in all but name at this time) were very frequent during this season; in January he appeared with Dowton, and on the 24th February, in the " Merry Wives of Windsor," he and Mrs. Wood played Mr. and Mrs. Ford, Mr. Wood

was Fenton, and Dowton assumed the character of Falstaff. The
same four also appeared in "Rob Roy" and "The Quaker," and in
March, W. Farren, Dowton, and Mrs. Lovell played together. During
an engagement of Sinclair and Miss E. Romer, for opera, in March,
the "Mountain Sylph" was produced very successfully. T. P. Cooke
fulfilled an engagement in April, and in the following month Miss
Turpin appeared on the occasion of Loder's benefit. With the benefit
of Mr. and Mrs. Woulds, on the 14th May, concluded a season, which,
according to a contemporary print, had been attended with a "ruinous
loss." The following extract from the *Bath Herald* (21st March) is
interesting, as showing what were an actor's labours in those days :—

The life of an actor is one of intense mental application and exertion, accom-
panied by bodily fatigue little inferior to that of the day labourer. We will
just recapitulate, as correctly as we can, the number of *new* pieces produced
by the manager since the period of opening, a little more than ten weeks :—
*Secret Service, Werner, Married Life, In the Wrong Box, Fra Diavolo, Beau
Nash, The King's Seal, Sardanapalus, the second part of Henry the Fourth,*
(never before done here) ; *Uncle Fooyle, Tam O'Shanter, the Minister and the
Mercer,* and *the Old Country Gentleman.* This rapid succession of novelties
could not fail to impose severe study upon all the members of the company—
but mere study was only part of the labour—rehearsals commencing at 10 in
the morning, and *never* terminating before 3 o'clock and often protracted till
half-past five in the evening—their arduous public duties commencing in little
more than an hour after that and prolonged till past midnight—four nights in
the week—all these things, being duly considered, would lead the harshest
censor of dramatic performances and performers to make some indulgence with
his reproofs, and to pass the mildest sentence that the fault will permit of.
For our part, after this view of the difficulties of the profession, and the
excessively brief period left for study, we are only astonished the company
acquit themselves half so well.

1835-36.—The new members of the company this season included
Messrs. Shaw, from Edinburgh ; Chippendale, from York ; Frazer,
from Liverpool ; Houghton, from Cheltenham ; King, English
Opera House, London ; Miss Somerville, English Opera House, and
Mrs. Hamerton, from Exeter. On the 1st February Charles Kean,
who became a great favourite in Bath, and frequently played at the
theatre, made his first appearance, and was well received in the character of Richard III. Macready followed in March, after which
the dramatic performances were diversified by a tight rope and acro-
batic entertainment by the Ravel family, who had played at the London
theatres with great success. On Easter Monday a grand operatic
spectacle, entitled the "Jewess," was produced, with entirely new
scenery by Mr. Thorn, and with Mrs. Yates as the heroine, and after
that Miss Betts appeared in opera. Owing to disagreements with the
lessee, Mr. J. D. Loder, who had occupied his seat in the orchestra for
37 years, separated himself from the theatre, and, after much corres-

pondence between them, each party published a letter in the newspapers regarding their differences. Mr. Loder in his said :—

I will not indulge Mr. Woulds by recording the various instances in which
I have submitted to mortification and professional insult during the period he
has been Manager of the Bath Theatre ; he knows that I renewed my engagement on his solicitation and promise that those evils of which I complained
should be amply redressed ; but—alas ! for "integrity and honour "—they
have been multiplied forty-fold, until, no longer able to bear the degradation
heaped upon me, I have been compelled to withdraw from a theatre, to which
I have been attached the greater part of my life ; and this sacrifice of my
feelings and interest may serve to show, how unbearable has been the conduct
of Mr. Woulds to a man who for upwards of twenty years was his active and
zealous friend.

In his reply Woulds characterised the contents of Loder's letter as
"groundless lamentations and vague generalities." He had called
upon him, he said, "to leave the mystery with which he shrouded his
pretended injuries, and come forward with clear and specific charges,"
which he had refused to do. In fact, wrote Woulds, "he has no real
grievances to record, his discontent being merely the result of an
unfortunate temper, which gives a jaundiced colour to every object he
looks upon, and which has generated that vindictiveness of disposition
his most intimate friends had such reason to deplore." Whatever
were the faults which led to this rupture, it seems certain they were
not all on one side.

1836-37.—The company was reinforced by Mr. Addison, from
Brighton ; Mr. Robson, from Worthing ; W. Dowton, jun. ; Mrs.
Martyn, from Covent Garden, and Miss Invevarity, from Edinburgh.
Mrs. Owen (née Miss Beaumont) a vocalist from Covent Garden,
played in the comic opera "John of Paris" early in January, after
which a company of French comedians were engaged for a few nights.
Charles Kean played from the 6th to the 25th February in various
characters, his last performance being as Macbeth. He was suffering
from indisposition, and after the fight with Macduff he sank upon the
stage with a groan, causing considerable alarm in the house. There
were loud calls for him to appear before the curtain, but it was some
time before he was able to do so. When he did he was hailed with
tremendous enthusiasm. He was to have left for London the same
night, but the journey was forbidden by medical advice, and he was
confined to a sick room for some time. Others who appeared this
season were Mr. Morris Barnett, from St. James's Theatre, London ;
Mrs. Waylett, from Drury Lane ; and Mr. Butler, from Covent
Garden.

1837-38.—The theatre, which had been re-decorated, and had a
new proscenium painted by Mr. Turner, the scenic artist, opened on
Boxing Day, when Mr. W. J. Hammond, from Covent Garden, and

proprietor of the Strand Theatre, London, appeared, the principal part which he played being Sam Weller in a piece founded on the "Pickwick Papers." Mr. R. Guy was now the leader of the orchestra, in place of Loder, and the following comprised the company for the season :—Messrs. Addison, H. Bedford, Bower, Bartlett, Cowle, Dowton, Edmonds, Fitzjames, Grainger, Gough, Hughes, Hoskins, King, Ludford, Land, M'Mahon, North, Shaw, Webster and Woulds; Mrs. Woulds, Mrs. Ashton, Mrs. Darley, Mrs. J. Faucit, Mrs. Bartlett, Miss Ellis, Miss M'Mahon, Miss Hibberd, Mlle. Eloise, Mlle. Juliette, Miss Webster and Miss Bartlett; prompter, Mr. Montague. With the exception of Mrs. Waylett, Mlle. Celeste, a French actress, and Sinclair, there were no engagements of any note this season, but there were several successful amateur performances.

1838-39. — Before Woulds opened the Theatre for his last season very extensive alterations were carried out.

A somewhat unsightly portico at the box entrance was superseded by one of much larger dimensions, enabling arrivals in carriages to alight under cover. The stage was reduced by seven feet, thus nearly doubling the extent of the separation between the pit and the stage, and the orchestra being confined to a square in the centre of the front of the stage, the space obtained at each side was made into stalls—sixteen on either side of the orchestra—accessible by private entrances from under the stage. It was intended that these "sittings," as they were termed, should be let for the whole season. A large gas chandelier suspended from the ceiling was another new feature. Mr. Edmund Glover, from the Haymarket ; Mr. Coleman Nantz, from Norwich ; and Miss Noel, from S. James's Theatre, London, were accessions to the regular company. Kean appeared during the season prior to his departure for the Continent, and other stars engaged were Braham, Henry Betty (son of W. H. W. Betty, formerly known as the Young Roscius), Mr. and Mrs. Wood, Mr. and Mrs. Yates, Walter Lacy, of the Haymarket, Benjamin Webster, lessee, manager and principal comedian of the Hay-market, and on the 27th May, four popular vocalists, Mr. Stratton, Mr. Franks, Miss Poole and Miss Middleton.

1840.—In consequence of Woulds having relinquished the lessee-ship it was not until the 18th January that the theatre opened under Davidge. His company was practically the same as that engaged under Woulds, additions being Messrs. Strickland, from the Hay-market ; Robson, formerly of the Bath company ; Rogers, from Dublin ; Boyce, from Edinburgh, and Mrs. East and Miss Adeline Cooper. Mr. Russell, from Drury Lane, was the acting manager, and Mr. Charles Perkins, of the English Opera House, stage manager, while the band was led by Mr. J. F. Loder, the musical arrangements being under Mr. Loder, who, on the opening night, received an enthusiastic reception, described as " one of the most vehement and long continued bursts of popular feeling " ever seen in the theatre. Davidge himself appeared on the 14th March as Justice Woodcock in the opera " Love in a Village," Mr. and Mrs. Wood also playing. During the season, which terminated on the 13th June, there appeared Miss Ellen Tree ; George Bennett, from Drury Lane ; Dowton, his last appearance ; Wallack, upon his return from America ; King, from Drury Lane, and Mrs. Keeley, Yates and Paul Bedford, members of the Adelphi Company, in " Jack Sheppard." Davidge gave Woulds a benefit on the 6th May, when Miss M. Woulds, second daughter of the *bénéficiaire*, appeared, and Mr. H. Bedford, Mr. and Miss Saunders, Mrs. B. Penley and Mr. Henry Field gave their services.

1840-41.—Davidge, who had been abroad for the sake of his health, opened the season on the 14th November (acting and stage manager, Mr. Stirling), and before he retired from the management, Mrs. Waylett, Kean and T. Green fulfilled engagements. The 20th March was the last night under Davidge, and on that occasion an amateur performance of "Money" was given, it being the first production of the piece in Bath. When the theatre re-opened for the remainder of the season, on the 12th April, under Newcombe and Bedford, by arrangement with Mr. Yates, who was now proprietor of the Adelphi, several of the popular Adelphi performances were produced, including

"Robespierre," "Agnes St. Aubyn," Buckstone's "Poor Jack," and "Old Curiosity Shop," the principal characters being sustained by Mr. and Mrs. Yates, and Messrs. Paul Bedford, Wright, Weilard and Lyon. The company which the managers got together was a strong one, and the acting and stage management was given to Mr. Woulds, so that, naturally, the name of Loder again disappeared from the orchestra, Mr. R. Guy being once more the leader of the band. The season closed on the 22nd May, but offers no incident of particular interest. On the 29th of May the proprietor permitted Woulds, who had a suit between himself and his wife pending in the Ecclesiastical Courts, and who had been arrested for contempt of court during the season, to take a benefit.

CHAPTER XXI.

MRS. MACREADY.

N the whole history of the Bath Stage, there has been no season so disastrous as that of 1841-42. Messrs. Newcombe and Bedford having only taken the theatre to fill the gap caused by the retirement of Davidge, the building was again to let, and was taken by Mr. Hay, the manager of the Exeter and Plymouth Theatres, who opened it early in December with the usual promises, few of which, however, he fulfilled. He announced it as his intention to avail himself of the facilities of the railway to procure the best metropolitan talent, whereas fewer London stars were engaged than had been the case for some seasons, while instead of restoring the theatre to " what it once was," he left it worse than he found it. Whatever were the difficulties against which his predecessors had to struggle, they, at least as far as we know, dealt honourably with those in their employ, and even if they suffered loss themselves we do not find that they permitted those whom they engaged to suffer also. Hay, however, when the season closed on the 23rd May, left his company entirely in the lurch, their salaries in arrear, and most of them absolutely without means. Some had no engagements, but even those who had could not raise sufficient to defray the expense of their journeys. Down to the 7th May the salaries had been paid in a very irregular fashion—a few shillings at a time being the most that any one of the company received—while from that date they were paid nothing, the total amount in arrear, to members of the company and servants in the theatre, being nothing less than £350. Under these distressing circumstances a committee was formed to see what could be done, and the trustees of the theatre offering the use of the building, it was decided to give two performances, the proceeds to be appro-

printed, as far as the amount would go, in making up to the actors
their arrears in salaries. Messrs. Newcombe, J. Bedford, C. Perkins,
Herring, Cooper (stage manager at Covent Garden) and Bianchi
Taylor, were among those who appeared for the benefit of the distressed comedians, and Charles Kean was also asked to do so, but his
engagements preventing him, he wrote a very kind letter to that effect,
enclosing £20. The public did not display an equal liberality, for the
receipts of the two performances only amounted to £97 15s. Among
those who had been engaged by Hay were Miss Vinning, Miss R.
Penley, Miss Woulds, Miss Carr and Messrs. Woulds, Wilsone and
Taylor.   Of these Miss Carr and Mr. Wilsone received engagements
for the Haymarket during the season.   Mr. and Mrs. Kean, it should
be noted, appeared together in Bath for the first time on the 23rd
April, 1842.*

After such a fiasco as this it would not be surprising to find the
theatre remaining tenantless, but it was again opened in the early part
of January, 1843, this time by Mr. Hooper, formerly of Drury Lane
and S. James's Theatres, London, who continued in the management
until 1845. During his first season a number of London artistes
appeared, including Mr. and Mrs. Kean, W. Farren, Wallack, Webster,
Strickland and Buckstone (who made his first appearance before a
Bath audience on the 20th March), and when the season was closed
Hooper stated that he was satisfied with it, remarking that though all
provincial theatres were more or less affected by the pressure of the
times, he believed the Bath Theatre had been as prosperous as any of
them.   He attributed the difficulties under which provincial managers
laboured in a large measure to the heavy expense entailed by the
engagement of metropolitan stars. "In times gone by," he said,
"when the provincial theatres were favoured with such stars as
Kemble, Siddons, Liston, Edmund Kean, Miss O'Neil, and a long list
of others, these distinguished actors were satisfied with dividing the
profits of the house with the manager ; but he was sorry to say that,
according to the system now pursued, this liberality was not evinced,
and little less than the whole receipts was considered sufficient as a
remuneration for stars of the present day."

In the following season (1843-44) he was benefited in an unexpected
quarter, not by the exertions of those who were interested in the
welfare of the drama, but by those who looked upon the theatre as an
evil to be denounced and discouraged.   The Bath stage has on two
notable occasions been the subject of pulpit attacks, one being of
recent years, when the late Rev. W. E. Littlewood preached a sermon
at S. James's, which drew forth a vigorous defence of the stage from
the Rev. James Wright, at Trim Street Chapel, and the other being a

---

* Charles Kean married Ellen Tree, for some time a member of the Bath
company, and a great favourite.

sermon delivered at S. Michael's on the evening of the 7th January, 1844, by the Rev. John East, then rector. The sermon, which was afterwards published in pamphlet form, was strongly condemned in many quarters, as well it might be, considering the extraordinary statements which it contained. The excuse for preaching on the subject was a letter which Mr. East stated he had received from " an

From a Photo by]   [*London Stereoscopic Co.*
JOHN BALDWIN BUCKSTONE.

old actor," in which the writer desired to hear him " speak conscientiously upon the errors of either following or supporting the theatre." " My opinion is," said the Rector of S. Michael's, " that the character of the theatre is strongly marked, and marked with almost every variety of evil ; and that, therefore, in proportion as it is adapted to the intellectual character of man, and as it is calculated to interest his passions, and to make a deep impression on his heart, it is a dangerous enemy to his virtue and happiness." The literature and performances of the stage he declared to be "hostile to the doctrines and morals of Christianity, degrading to the professors of the art, and destructive of the present and eternal happiness of man ; " and, in concluding, he expressed himself satisfied that if his hearers considered and thought out his statements in private, those who had never been inside the theatre would thank God and be fixed in their determination never to cross its doors, or if any had been "a frequenter, a supporter, or a professor of theatricals," they would "go to the fountain open for sin and for uncleanness, to wash away the stain of precious time so vainly and so guiltily spent." The result of this remarkable discourse was twofold ; in the first place it produced weighty and well-reasoned replies in the form of pamphlets, and exposed the preacher to no little personal abuse, and in the second, it proved the best advertisement the theatre could possibly have had. Instead of empty houses, we have it on the authority of one of the pamphleteers, that the house was crowded nightly after the attack—"all have gone, to prove they participated not in your most ungenerous aggression,"—the Mayor gave a special bespeak, on which occasion the house looked quite like old times, and performances were given under the patronage of the "Association for increasing the attractions and promoting the interests of Bath."

But though this season, thanks greatly to Mr. East, did not prove altogether unsatisfactory, the same cannot be said of that which followed. The theatre did not open until the 11th of January, when Mr. and Mrs. Kean played in "Money," and before Easter it had collapsed, according to some opinions owing to mismanagement, and a want of respect and confidence in the public, and, according to others, as the result of a decline of dramatic taste in Bath. Perhaps the true cause was to be found between these suggestions, for while there was an undoubted falling off in the support of the drama, we do not find that Hooper carried out his promises, made at the commencement of the season, when he stated that arrangements had been effected with popular artistes, whose names he gave, but who did not visit Bath during the period. Hooper took his benefit on the occasion of the last performance before Easter, the 8th March, and that was practically the last performance under his management. In the following month Mrs. Macready, who for some eleven years had been successfully managing the Bristol Theatre, brought the Bristol company over for one night, when the American tragedian, Mr. Edwin Forrest, appeared, and subsequently three benefits were held at which the Bristol company also appeared, namely, for Woulds, who had been stage manager for Hooper during the season, for Brownell, who still occupied the position of box office keeper, and for John and Miss Quick, the former of whom had been for sixty-four years tailor and wardrobe keeper to the theatre.

For the first and only time in the history of the Bath Theatre its fortunes were now to be directed by a woman, Mrs. Macready, who, as we have stated, had successfully managed the Bristol Theatre for some years, becoming lessee, with the intention of conducting the two establishments concurrently, as was done years before, though with great difference, for as before Bath had been the head of the circuit, now the headquarters of the management were at Bristol, and the Bath Theatre presented a lamentable falling away, both in respect to the character of the audience and the abilities of the company which appeared before it. No longer was the theatre the fashionable amusement of a fashionable city, no longer was it thronged with the very cream of society, assembled to applaud a Siddons, an Elliston or a Kemble, an

MISS HELEN FAUCIT.

audience whose approval meant success, and possibly fame to a young actor. Now crowded houses were the exception, not the rule, and it was only by affiliating the theatre with that in the neighbouring city that it was kept open at all.

In granting Mrs. Macready a lease of the theatre for five years, determinable on her part at three, the trustees inserted a provision that the performances during each season should not average less

L

than ninety nights, so that the holders and purchasers of tontine tickets might not be treated, as had been the case, with short and abruptly terminated seasons. Consequently Mrs. Macready opened her first season on the 2nd September, 1845, or three months earlier than had been the case for some years, the intention being to close for a period before Christmas, and then to re-open and remain open until the end of the season. The ordinary nights of performing were Tuesdays, Fridays and Saturdays. Charles Mathews and Madame Vestris performed in October, and made several subsequent appearances during Mrs. Macready's management, and in the following May "Field Marshall Tom Thumb" was introduced to a large audience. During the next season Buckstone and Mrs. Fitzwilliam fulfilled an engagement, and that gifted actress Miss Helen Faucit (Mrs. Theodore Martin), made her first appearance in Bath. Macready, also, in January, 1847, renewed his acquaintance with a Bath audience after an absence of eight years, and he appeared on four different occasions during Mrs. Macready's lesseeship, the last being in January, 1850, when he bade farewell to his Bath friends, previous to his final retirement from the stage. Alluding to one of these visits John Coleman tells the following amusing story :—

Being the leading man in the company, I had the honour of acting "Othello" to Macready's Iago. Talk about being nervous ! I was a bundle of nerves during every night of his engagement. The "Othello" night was a proud one for me—indeed, I had reason to be proud to be permitted to try my prentice hand besides such an Iago. What a masterpiece it was ! what a revelation of subtle, poetic, vigorous, manly, many-minded develry ! The audience were more than usually kind, and after I had got my first plunge over, I took heart of grace, and by the time I had reached the third act I forgot that he was anything more than "mine ancient." I remembered only that I was Othello. Neither then nor now could I act with gloves on my hands. I had removed, as I thought, all traces of the pigment with which I had "made up" from the palms of my hands, but as my excitement increased, the wretched stuff seemed to ooze out of my very pores. When I came to the famous speech, "Villain ! be sure you prove my love is false," I sprang upon Iago and seized him by the throat. I remembered nothing until I found that I had literally flung him bodily down upon the stage and stood above him erect and quivering with wrath. On his part he growled like an angry lion. The incident was as unprecedented as it was unpremeditated, and its effect upon the audience was electrical. They got up and cheered, and for some time the progress of the play was interrupted. This gave me time to collect myself, when, to my horror, I perceived that, in the tempest of my rage, I had torn open Iago's vest, and, worst still, left the marks of my ten fingers on his beautiful white cashmere dress. When we came off the stage together he glared at me, and growled : "Err—well sir, what have you to say ?" "I'm very sorry, Mr. Macready." "Err—sorry, sir. By ——, you sprang upon me more like a young tiger than a human being ?" "I was carried away by the passion of the scheme ; I must ask you to remember the novelty of the position in which I have been placed, being permitted to attempt so great a part besides so distinguished an actor as yourself." "'Don't humbug me, sir !'" "I scorn to attempt it, nevertheless, the honour you have done me to-night might well have turned an older head than mine. Pray, sir, make some allowance for my excitement." At this he relaxed into a grim smile, and growled : "Say no more—say no more—only remember the next time you play this part with me, confine your excitement to your mind, and not to your muscles."

Coleman speaks highly of the company at that time performing in Bath and Bristol, and says that had it not been both numerous and efficient, the pieces produced could never have been got through. During a single engagement Macready acted Macbeth twice, Hamlet twice, Iago twice, Werner once, Virginius once, Richlieu twice, Lear twice, and Lord Townly and Henry IV (the fourth act from part II) for his benefit, and as an example of what an actor's life in those days was, we will again take the liberty of quoting from Coleman :—

Macready kept us day after day from ten to four o'clock, following every situation, every scene, every line, every word of the text, with an interest as eager and unabated as if he had been acting each play for the first instead of the last time. It was true that he flurried, and worried, and bullied us, but his petulance was peppered with brains ; his irascibility arose more from dyspepsia than bad temper, and everything he touched was inadiated with the sacred fire of genius. "Hamlet," "Othello," "Macbeth" (the latter with music) were rehearsed letter perfect, words and music, with only one rehearsal, but for the other plays we had two. Only think of this, young ladies and gentle-men, who nowadays have a hundred rehearsals for one part ! I acted Othello, Macduff and the Ghost before ; but Ulric, Icilius, De Mauprat, Edgar and the Prince of Wales were all new parts, which involved sitting up half the night with wet towels on my head and strong coffee in my stomach. It was a matter of honour to be letter perfect in these great works, and, indeed, the imputation of being imperfect in the text was considered a grievous stigma upon an actor's professional reputation in those days. There was a strong feeling of *esprit de corps* amongst us too. We all assisted in the music of "Macbeth." As leading man, I set the example and rushed off from the murder scene, and the next minute was on the stage as a witch. We had four leading ladies : Mrs. Pauncefort, then a young and lovely girl, the beautiful Mrs. Maddocks, Mrs. Marcus Elmore, and Mrs. Faucit Saville. When the latter lady played Macbeth, the other three Lady Macbeths sat on in the banquet scene as speechless gentlewomen !

On the 28th September, 1847, the renowned Jenny Lind sang at the theatre, and the house on that occasion was crammed in every part, hundreds being unable to obtain admission. The cantatrice, who was received with rapturous applause, her every appearance creating a scene of enthusiasm almost unrivalled in the building, was accom-panied by Signor F. Lablache, Madame Lablache, Madame Solari and Mr. Balfe. In the following February, Mr. and Mrs. C. Kean made their first appearance after their return from America. Before the theatre was properly opened for the season in 1849 (and, by the bye, the management had returned to the old plan of commencing on Boxing Day), Hay, whose connection with the theatre was not, it will be remembered, a very creditable one, gave two or three performances of an entertainment *à la* Mathews, in which he was assisted by his daughters. Not only did this season (1849-50) witness the final performance of Macready, but it also witnessed the first appearance on the Bath stage of Sims Reeves.* Macready played for the last time on the 19th January, as King Lear, and on the Monday following Sims Reeves played with an opera party, with which he was touring, in "Lucia de Lammermoor." During the engagement he also appeared in "La Sonnambula," "Puritani," and "Ernani." It should be understood, however, that this was not his first visit to Bath, for he had previously appeared at the Assembly Rooms. One feature of the season, 1850-51, deserves to

JENNY LIND.

be specially recorded, and that is the production, on Boxing Day, of the first Christmas pantomime, that is to say, the first pantomime produced as the sole attraction. Pantomimes had often been performed, both at Christmas and at Easter, Grimaldi and other noted clowns appearing in them, but they were always played after some drama, while on this occasion it was the principal attraction,

* For portrait, see page 69.

Mr. T. Salmon, the leader of the band, composed and arranged the overture and music, and the harlequinade was supported by Metropolitan performers, Mr. Grammani being clown. Local allusions abounded in the piece, those in authority being pointedly referred to, and many of the leading tradesmen being mentioned by name. The production was well received, and was finally withdrawn on the 8th February, but after the first few nights it was played, as its predecessors had been, after some play. After the close of this season, Professor Anderson, the Wizard of the North, proved a great attraction for a week or more.

In the season 1851-52, under the patronage of the Mayor and a committee of gentlemen, performances were given entitled " The drama for the people," standard plays being presented at popular prices, namely, dress boxes, 2s. 6d. ; upper boxes, 1s. 6d. ; pit, 1s. ; gallery, 6d. ; it must be inferred that these prices were found by the management to be profitable, for they remained the prices of admission during the whole of the following season, the last under Mrs. Macready, who died on the 8th March, 1853. For some years her health had been very indifferent, but at the last death came somewhat suddenly and unexpectedly, and her loss was mourned by a very large circle of friends and acquaintances. Death took place in Bath, and on the 14th March the body was removed to Bristol, and there interred in the Cathedral by the side of the remains of her husband, which had been placed there some twenty-four years previously. The principal mourner was her son-in-law, Mr. J. H. Chute, who carried on the theatres until the close of the season, and subsequently became lessee. Mr. Chute was stage manager for Mrs. Macready in her earlier Bath seasons, but in 1848 he became lessee of the Assembly Rooms.

Among the metropolitan performers who appeared during Mrs. Macready's lesseeship, in addition to those names already mentioned, were Messrs. Benjamin Webster, the liberal lessee of the Haymarket Theatre, Arthur Webster, Hudson, Stretton, Warner, Ranger, Bunn and Wigan ; Madame Celeste, Mrs. Butler (Miss Fanny Kemble), Mrs. Nesbitt and her sister Miss Jane Mordaunt, Miss Cushman, Miss Rainforth, Miss Missent and Miss B. Fane. Amateur performances were frequently given during the latter part of the period dealt with in this chapter.

CHAPTER XXII.

UNDER MR. J. H. CHUTE.

AN ENERGETIC AND ENTERPRISING LESSEE—TOURING COM-
PANIES — WELL-KNOWN NAMES — LIBERAL PRODUCTIONS —
" MIDSUMMER NIGHT'S DREAM "—" THE DEAD HEART."

R. James Henry Chute, who succeeded Mrs. Macready
in the lesseeship of the theatre, was undoubtedly
the best manager the theatre had had since those
days in which it enjoyed its full measure of
popularity and success.   Not only was he enterprising and energetic, thoroughly and practically
acquainted with all theatrical matters, accustomed
for years to cater for the public amusement, but he was widely known
in dramatic circles, and possessed, therefore, great advantages for
obtaining the services of the first in the profession, an advantage
increased by working the Bath and Bristol Theatres together.   Had
it been possible to restore the Bath stage to its halcyon days, it would
undoubtedly have been accomplished under his management, but
circumstances had entirely altered, and the two essential features
which had contributed to its former glory were absent, that is to say,
the city was no longer the centre of fashion that it was in those days,
and the drama did not occupy the position that it did—that of being
the most fashionable amusement.   But, although Mr. Chute could not
succeed in restoring the fame of the Bath stage, he did what was the
next best thing, he kept the theatre open every year throughout a full
season, provided an excellent stock company, produced new and
attractive pieces and revived others of genuine merit, and frequently
introduced London stars and metropolitan attractions.   The visits of
prominent artistes were not so frequent as they had been under previous
managers it is true, but no doubt the support which the theatre received did not warrant their recurring oftener, besides which the
starring business was undergoing a change, for the period of the first
portion of Mr. Chute's management may be said to have witnessed
the birth of the touring company system.

Touring companies, as we know them to-day, completely supplant-
ing the old stock companies, were yet a long way off, but we find that
entire London companies were now visiting provincial theatres, after

a manner which had not obtained previously. Hitherto, except in the case of Italian, and in some instances English, Opera, London stars travelled by themselves, or in some cases in couples, while at times as many as half-a-dozen minor luminaries might be found travelling in company. Thus, we have already noted the visits of members of the Haymarket Company, but we believe, at all such performances, the assistance of members of the local company was necessary. Now, however, we have arrived at a different state of things. In August, 1854, we find Madame Vestris and Charles Mathews appearing with the principal members of the Royal Lyceum Company, and later in the same month twenty-seven members of Mr. Charles Kean's Royal Princess's Company paid the theatre a visit. Again in June of the following year there was an engagement of Madame Vestris, and the Lyceum Company, followed in September by an English Opera Company. Italian Opera companies

From a Photo by]   *[Barraud.*

MRS. KENDALL.

visited the city in 1856 and 1857 (on the latter occasion with the fascinating Mlle. Piccolmini), in August, 1857, we find Mr. and Mrs. Leigh Murray and a London dramatic company producing various pieces, and in 1861 Mr. G. Meville appeared with a London Company. To the facilities for travelling offered by the railway this new phase of theatrical business must be largely attributed, but it is not for a moment to be supposed that theatrical managers of that day foreshadowed the full growth of the touring system, and the revolution it was destined to produce. Now that we are able to realise the full effects of that revolution, and pronounce them good or bad according to our personal views, it is interesting to look back and observe its small beginnings.

We have already pointed out how the Bath Theatre has owed its good fortune in a very great degree to having for its managers men who exhibited great acuteness in the perception of the early signs of talent, and in this particular Mr. Chute was in no way behind his predecessors. There was not a Siddons or an Elliston for him to find out and culture, but among the names of those who composed his companies are to be found several who have since become well-known in the dramatic world. If there was not a Siddons to be discovered, we are able to point out that Mr. Chute secured for his company the early services of one who is generally acknowledged to be the leading actress of the present day—but we are proceeding

From a Photo by]   *[Vander Wede.*
MRS. BANCROFT.

too rapidly, and must confine our remarks in this chapter to the old theatre, and it was in the present structure that Miss Ellen Terry appeared. Among those who figured in the play bills of the old theatre under Mr. Chute's management we find such names as George Melville, a great favourite in Bath, Arthur Stirling, George and William

Rignold, Miss Marie Wilton (Mrs. Bancroft), Miss Henrietta Hodson
(Mrs. Labouchere), formerly of the Manchester and Edinburgh
Theatres, who joined the company at the commencement of the 1861-2
season, and Miss Madge Robertson (Mrs. Kendal) ; also John Rouse,
Fosbrooke, Arthur Wood, Wilton, F. J. Cathcart, Mrs. Robertson,
Mrs. Wilton, Miss E. Wilton, Miss E. Thorne, Miss Margaret
Eburne, Miss Adelaide Bowering, Miss Mandlebert, &c., all of whom
have made their mark in the profession.   In 1861 a London manager
said of the Bath company : " So good a company does not exist out
of London."
    Of those who appeared as stars during the last years of the old
theatre, under Mr. Chute, may be mentioned the Bath favourites, Mr.
and Mrs. C. Kean, Madame Vestris, Charles Mathews, B. Webster,
Madame Celeste, Wright, Miss Cushman, Samuel Phelps, Mr. and
Mrs. Sims Reeves (the former both in English and Italian opera),
Charles Pitt, Sir William Don, bart., and Lady Don, and Charles
Dillon (who made his first appearance in Bath on the 21st April,
1855, when he played Belphegor for the benefit of members of
an opera company which had been playing in Bath for some time), all
of whom appeared on more than one occasion, while the following
paid only one visit each, Paul Bedford, G. V. Brooke, T. C. King,
Swinburne, McKean Buchanan, John Coleman, Miss Vandenhoff,
Miss Marriott, Mrs. W. C. Forbes (American tragic actress), Miss
Amy Sedgwick, and Mr. and Mrs. F. B Coleman, of America, the
former being a son of the old Bath actor of that name.   Among those
who appeared in opera were Mlle. Titiens, Mme. Grisi, Mme. Gassier,
Mme. Borchardt and Signor Giuglini, besides a number of others.
    In the production of plays Mr. Chute always exercised great
liberality, and mounted the pieces with considerable attention to
detail.   The scenery possessed by the theatre was abundant and
excellent both in design and execution, while its wardrobe and library
ranked among the best in the kingdom.   Productions were so
numerous that it would be a matter of impossibility to mention
even of a part of them in the space at our disposal, but allusion may
be made to two, one as an example of the completeness with which
the lessee did his work, and the other because it is of some special
interest at the present time.   In the first place, we refer to the production, on the 27th November, 1858, of the " Midsummer Night's
Dream," which was said to surpass all his previous efforts.   It was
a close copy of Kean's revival at the Princess's, which had been
played for 150 nights, and was spoken of as an " unique and romantic
entertainment."   New scenery and appointments were provided, and
on a scale of magnificence that would probably have made Keasberry
and Dimond stand aghast.   The following description of the production, taken from the *Bath Express*, will serve to convey an idea
of the impression which it made on the playgoer of that day :—

When the curtain draws up a view of Athens presents itself in the period
of its highest splendour. To make the scene more striking, the actual
topography is departed from. The deeply and deliciously blue Ægean is not
seen in the distance with a long plain of some five miles intervening between
the harbour of the Peræus and the city, as there is in reality; but Athens is
here made to stand on the very edge of the waters, which flow in front of the
city and wash the very base of the Acropolis. This liberty taken with fact is,
of course, excusable, and makes a more effective picture. The marble palaces
and the purple ocean in immediate juxta-position produce a most entrancing
effect. This scene does great credit to Messrs. W. and George Gordon.
They did well to dispense with topographical accuracy in order to produce
effect. Scene 2 represents the workshop of Quince, the carpenter, the
furniture and workmen's tools being copies from discoveries at Herculaneum.
Such is the truthful and artistic spirit which Charles Kean has carried into all
his revivals. The past is no longer a cold ideal, but glows with life and
colour under his magic touch. Act 2 opens with a view of a wood near
Athens, the fairies' haunt by moonlight. Here Oberon and Titania appear
with their fairy trains, some score nymphs most gracefully attired. The effect
of moonlight here produced is a perfect marvel. It seems to be managed by
some side reflectors, and the illusion is complete. The shadow dance, where
the fairies chase their own shadows, is an enchanting scene. How completely
we are taken out of this weary work day world, and see realised before us the
brightest visions of our fancy! To the mystic radiance of moonlight succeeds
a thick fog, caused by Puck, which soon disperses, when we have another
dance of the fairies. The palm of poetical beauty certainly belongs to the
moonlight scenes, but for magnificence Titania's bower is unequalled. Its
appearance was greeted with a burst of applause. But every successive scene
was more or less thus received, and the whole drama was a march of triumph
from first to last. A moving diorama is a novelty in dramatic representation,
but here it was resorted to. The scenery of the fifth act is by Lennox, and
brings before us an apartment in the palace of Theseus and closes with a view
of the galleries and illuminated gardens. This is most gorgeous, and the
kindling of the fires enhances the effect to the utmost verge of scenic possibility.
The closing tableau was the climax of magnificence.

The music, chiefly Mendelssohn's, was arranged by Mr. J. L. Hatton
and Mr. T. H. Salmon, the conductor of the orchestra, and of the cast, it
may be mentioned that John Rouse was Bottom ; Fosbrooke, Flute,
the bellows-mender ; Mr. Vincent, Lysander ; Miss Cleveland,
Helen ; Master Robertson, Puck. The piece was played a number of
nights, but scarcely sufficient, we should think, to have rendered it a
pecuniary success. The other piece to which we alluded was " The
Dead Heart," which has lately been brought prominently under the
notice of the play going public, and which was first produced in Bath
on the 7th March, 1860, when Mr. B. Webster appeared as Robert
Landry, Miss Woolgar impersonated Catherine Duval, and the Abbé
Latour was played by Mr. Arthur Stirling.

HENRY IRVING AS HAMLET.

CHAPTER XXIII.

THE DESTRUCTION OF THE THEATRE.

A GOOD FRIDAY SCENE — DESCRIPTION OF THE FIRE — ITS ORIGIN A MYSTERY—COMPLETE DESTRUCTION.

N Good Friday, the 18th April, 1862, the Bath Theatre was destroyed by fire. The event was a memorable one, for it was one of the largest fires that Bath has ever seen, and one of the most destructive and unaccountable, involving lamentable loss, and depriving the city of a building which, had it not fallen a prey to the devouring element, would have become historical—indeed, was so at that time. All the circumstances surrounding the conflagration are somewhat remarkable—the mystery of its outbreak, the rapidity with which the building was consumed, and the escape of surrounding property from impending destruction. The scene upon that fatal morning was not one to be readily forgotten by those who witnessed it, but those to whom a description of the event is new should bear in mind that the position of the building and adjacent property was practically the same then as it is now.

It was just half-past ten in the morning when the fire was discovered, smoke being seen to issue from the back of the theatre by a resident in Monmouth Street, by whom an alarm was at once raised. One of the scene shifters happening to be near at hand, promptly obtained the keys from Miss Quicke, the wardrobe mistress, who lived in one of the adjacent houses, and on entering the building found that a large body of fire existed in the north-west corner, in close proximity to the dressing rooms and the carpenters' shops. In the meantime messengers had been despatched to the Police Station, where, fortunately, a number of men were parading, and on the point of starting for the various places of worship in the city, for the bells were already ringing for morning service. Small, however, were the congregations which assembled that day ; the news spread rapidly, and crowds flocked towards the Sawclose, where thousands of people were shortly assembled to witness the grand but awful sight which presented itself. There was abundance of aid, and within a quarter of an hour from the discovery of the fire every available hose in the city was employed in bringing water to bear upon the "beds of raging fire," for the flames spread with such rapidity that almost the whole building was by this time in the fire demon's grasp, and it was evident that there was no hope of saving the premises. Had the fire occurred at night, the scene would have been a terrible one ; even as it was, with the sun shining brightly, it was fearfully grand. By eleven o'clock, says one account, " the view over the stage entrance resembled the orifice of a vast furnace, so grandly solid was the

hurricane of flame." From the stage the flames spread wildly to the box fittings and the house generally, until the whole building became wrapped in "steep-down gulfs of liquid fire," and presently, with a dull alarming thud, the roof fell in, and huge sheets of flame and myriads of sparks rose high into the air. " Then," we are told, "the scene from the Sawclose was sublimely fearful, and we wondered not at the dead silence which fell on the panic-stricken crowd, by this time swelled to many thousands. Scarce had the impression thus produced died away, when a

From a Photo by]   *[London Stereoscopic Co.*
HERMANN VEZIN.

murmur of suspense ran through the multitude in S. John's place. The fire had penetrated to the front, where the scenery is deposited, the roof had given way, and the stone wall, at that part thinner than at any other, bulged ominously forward at the summit. The police, firemen, and crowd withdrew, and in another instant a gaping crack and totter was seen and the heavy wall, with its massive coping, plunged down on the spot where the people were standing just previously." It was a narrow escape, but fortunately no lives were lost, no injuries sustained.

The attention of those who were attempting to "qualify the fire's extreme rage" were now directed entirely to the property surrounding the theatre. The building itself was irrecoverably lost, and the adjacent premises at every quarter were in the utmost danger, for the flames were licking the walls and seizing upon the vulnerable parts ; in fact, the danger of the fire assumed gigantic proportions and causing a wholesale destruction of property was at one time so great that a message was telegraphed to Bristol for assistance, but it so happened that there was no one at the telegraph office in that city to receive it. Other than human agencies, however, were at work, and confined the conflagration to the theatre. When the fire broke out the wind fanned the flames and directed them right into the main block of the building, but no sooner was this thoroughly on fire than the wind completely changed, veered right round and blew the fire back again upon the part whence it had worked such havoc that there was nothing upon which it could spend its force. Mainly in consequence of this the fire was confined to the theatre and the buildings around were saved from sharing its fate. The house once occupied by Beau Nash, in the Sawclose, was in imminent jeopardy for some time, and but for the utmost exertions of firemen and police would probably have been included in the destruction. The last portion of the theatre to fall a prey to the fire was the extensive frontage of the building in Beauford square ; as this side of the theatre consisted of a number of rooms it had offered a greater resistance than other parts of the premises, but at length the fire gained the mastery, and the valuable wardrobe and other property belonging to the lessee perished. So wonderfully rapid was the course of the conflagration that in less than an hour from the first alarm being given the whole of the theatrical premises were either consumed or burning themselves out, and by one o'clock all fear of the fire extending was passed. The burning of the Covent Garden Theatre, some time previously, was, in the opinion of one who had witnessed both, "a dilatory affair in comparison." When the flames had died away, all that remained of the elegant Bath Theatre, upon the boards of which some of the greatest names in the history of the English stage had added to their laurels, and with all its old associations, was the gutted frontage in Beauford square, portions of the solidly built walls, the box entrance and staircases, and some rooms above ; all the rest and its contents were reduced to ashes. To make matters worse, the lessee was uninsured, and, therefore, sustained a heavy loss, and the building itself was only insured for a moiety of its value, the policies having been considerably reduced only about two years previously.

The origin of the fire was never satisfactorily accounted for.

Nothing certain was known, and although several theories were advanced there was not much dependence to be placed upon any of them. The last performance in the house was on the previous Wednesday, when the company appeared in a drama, entitled " Peep o' Day," which Mr. Chute had mounted with much care and expense, and had played for several nights. After the performance the theatre was closed and every-thing apparently safe, as it appeared also on the following day when a sweep and his assistant were engaged in sweep-ing all the chimnies in the house, and a charwoman was engaged in cleaning until the evening, all these people averring that they perceived no trace or smell of fire, nor did any of them employ any artificial light. So far as was known, no one entered the theatre after the charwoman left until after the alarm of fire had been given on the following morning. A portion of the fire when first discovered was burning in one of the gentlemen's dressing rooms, and it was surmised that possibly some burning wadding from pistols used during the performance on Wednesday night had lodged in one of the dresses, and so had

From a Photo by]   [C. Watkins.
CHARLES J. MATHEWS.

smouldered until it ultimately broke into flame, but this theory, like so many others, was exploded by a subsequent statement to the effect that all the dresses used in the piece had been removed to Bristol. The most probable theory propounded appears to be that a beam of the building was in some way connected with a flue of the brewery at the Theatre

Tavern,* and that the fire was communicated in this way. Even this, however, was a mere speculation, and considerable doubt was thrown upon it at the time, so that the origin of the fire remains wrapt in mystery.

There were two singular circumstances in connection with this fire. In the first place the fact did not escape the notice of those opposed to theatrical representations that, whereas the theatre was burned down on Good Friday, the performance on the prevoius Wednesday was the first occasion on which the theatre had ever been opened during Passion week. It is also a curious coincidence that one of the first to perceive the fire, and to telegraph to the lessee, was Charles Kean, who, with Mrs. Kean, was passing the premises when the alarm was given, and witnessed the destruction of the building in which they had so often appeared. Only about a year previously an alarm of fire was raised while Kean was playing Henry VIII, at the Bath Theatre—though, fortunately, the cause was not serious, it being only some paper which had become ignited and created a quantity of smoke—and exactly twelve months before the destruction of the Bath Theatre, a similar alarm, fortunately a false one, was raised at the Theatre Royal, Bristol. Mr. Chute did not arrive in Bath until the work of destruction was complete, and all that was to be seen of his handsome theatre was some blackened walls and glowing embers.

* The site of the Theatre Tavern is now occupied by a handsome building used as a Mission hall for St. Paul's parish.

M

CHAPTER XXIV.

THE PRESENT THEATRE.

SUGGESTED SCHEMES FOR A NEW THEATRE — A COMPANY
FORMED — PLANS THROWN OPEN TO COMPETITION — THE
PREMIATED DESIGNS—MR PHIPPS'S SELECTED—·OPENING THE
THEATRE—THE FIRST PLAY-BILL—MISS ELLEN TERRY.

EFORE a week had elapsed after the destruction of
the old theatre, two or three projects were on foot
for providing the city with a new home for the
drama. One scheme suggested was to abandon the
old ground and erect a theatre on the site of the
White Hart Inn, where the Grand Pump Room
Hotel now stands, and another was to construct a
theatre in conjunction with the Assembly Rooms, by some ingenious
plan of economising the space occupied by the entrances, cloakrooms
and vestibule, but it is not surprising that neither of these suggestions
met with approval, the first because it was felt no advantage would be
gained by the proposed change of site, and the second because it was
unworkable. A third scheme, proposed by Major Davis, the city
architect, was to secure the old site and the adjacent premises held
by the trustees of the theatre, to clear away the Garrick's Head, Beau
Nash's house, and the block of houses to the east of Beauford Square,
increase the width of the street, and build a large hall capable of
holding an audience of about two thousand, and suitable for concerts,
lectures, and similar purposes. The seats were to be planned fronting
towards the western side, giving the position for the orchestra as
nearly as possible on a line corresponding to that of the proscenium
of the old theatre. Then, in order that it should be also available for
dramatic performances, it was proposed that an arch should be constructed at the back of the orchestra to form the proscenium of a
theatre, the old stage being refitted, the floor of the concert room
being made moveable by means of hydraulic pressure and disclosing
a pit and sunk orchestra, with entrances from Beauford Square. The
estimated cost of this scheme was £10,000, but, though at first it met
with approbation, various objections were urged against it, and it was
ultimately abandoned altogether.

There was little delay in taking steps to definitely ascertain the state of public feeling on the question of restoring the theatre, and on the 7th May, 1862, a large and influential meeting was held in the Guildhall, under the presidency of the Mayor (Mr. T. Fuller), at which the proceedings were very unanimous and enthusiastic. Charles Kean, who it was hoped would be present, wrote expressing sympathy with the object in view, and the attendance was very representative. The first resolution, affirming the necessity and importance of a theatre to the best interests of the city, and proposing the erection of a new theatre on, if possible, the old site, was moved by Mr. George Monkland, seconded by Mr. H. J. Walker, and carried amid applause without a dissentient voice. It was next agreed, on the proposition of Mr. Thomas Jolly and Mr. Hooper, that for the purposes of carrying out this resolution a limited liability company should be formed with a capital of £12,000 in £5 shares, and this having been carried with similar unanimity, Captain Ford moved a third resolution, which is worth preserving on account of the names that it contains :—

From a Photo by]   [A. Bassano.
E. A. SOTHERN (Lord Dundreary).

"That the following gentlemen be requested to act on the Provisional Committee, with power to add to their number, and that Mr. Powell and Mr. G. J. Robertson act as their secretaries : The Mayor, Mr. W. Appleby,

T. Barrett, Esq., M.D., W. H. Breton, Esq., W. H. Brace, Esq., Mr. John Broadley, Mr. Bishop, C. Bradford, Esq., Mr. G. Butcher, Colonel Blathwayt, Colonel Cronin, N. Cumberledge, Esq., E. Coates, Esq., M.D., Mr. R. D. Commans, Mr. J. Chaffin, Mr. J. H. Chute, R. Cook, Esq., Captain Callaghan, C. F. D. Caillard, Esq., Captain Dumergue, Sir T. Dancer, Captain J. Dolphin, D. M. Dunlop, Esq., A. Durham, Esq., Sir A. H Elton, Bart., Mr. R. P. Edwards. Captain J. R. Ford, R. W. Falconer, Esq., M.D., Mr. George Field, W. F. Farrar, Esq., Mr. E. R. Fuller, W. S. M. Goodenough, Esq., R. T. Gore, Esq., Mr. W. Green, Mr. J. Green, W. Hunt, Esq., Mr. J. D. Harris, Mr. G. Hancock, Mr. Hayward, A. Hinnuber, Esq., C. Holworthy, Esq, — Hooper, Esq., G. A. Jones, Esq., General Jervois, T. Jolly, Esq., Mr. Jameson, — Janvrin, Esq., Jun., V. Jenkins, Esq., C. J. Jones, Esq., Mr. J. B Keene, W. C. Keating, Esq., Charles Kearn, Esq., A. Kinglake, Esq., J. A. Lloyd, Esq., M.D., Mr. Moger, Mr. Jacob Maggs, Captain K. R. Murchison, Captain R. M. Murchison, J. Murch, Esq., Mr. F. Morris, N. H. Nugent, Esq., Mr. C. W. Oliver, Bruce Pryce, Esq, Captain Peach, Mr. Peach, Captain Phayre, R.N., Colonel Pryor, Mr. Ellis Reynolds, Mr. J. Rainey, J. Ricketts, Esq., Mr. G. Sturmey, P. C. Sheppard, Esq., Sir C. Style. H. D. Skrine, Esq., J. Soden, Esq., Mr. H. Simms, Mr. T. Salmon, E. Salmon, Esq., J. Stone, Esq., R. N. Stone, Esq, Sir V. Stonehouse. W. Tite, Esq, M.P., J. Taylor, Esq., H. Tugwell, Esq, W. Thompson, Esq, Mr. J. S. Turner, B Taylor, Esq., Mr. Vezey, Mr. Whitfield, Mr. H. J. Walker, Mr. G. H. Wood, Captain Wemyss, A. E. Way, Esq, M.P., J. W. Yeeles, Esq."

This was seconded by Mr. George Butcher, and also carried, and it was left to the committee to take what steps they thought fit towards procuring plans for the new building. A meeting of the Provisional Committee was at once held, and an executive appointed, of which Mr. G. Monkland was chairman, and Mr. J. Murch and Mr. K. R. Murchison, vice-chairmen. Negotiations went forward with the trustees of the old theatre for the purchase of the site, and in June it was announced that the purchase had been provisionally effected, and included besides the site, the ruins of the old theatre and certain adjacent property belonging to the trustees. The price of the whole was £2,500, and the purchase was confirmed on the 3rd July, when it was decided to open the plans for the new theatre to competition, with the offer of a premium of twenty guineas for the best plan not accepted, and ten guineas for the one next in order of merit. The committee, it should be mentioned, after the first flush was over, did not meet with that support, which from the enthusiasm of the first public meeting, they had a right to expect, and it was announced at another public meeting, held at the Guildhall on the 10th July, Mr. Thomas Jolly presiding, that the sum subscribed in shares amounted to 1,126 shares, representing £5,630, the donations to £510, total £6,140, whereas the total estimated cost of building the theatre was £8,000. It was decided at that meeting that local committees should be formed for the purpose of promoting subscriptions, and the Provisional

Committee, nothing daunted, continued their exertions. The first meeting of the shareholders of the new company was held on the 9th August, when the chair was occupied by Mr. J. Murch, and the following directors were appointed :—Messrs. K. R. Murchison, H. Tugwell, G. Butcher, J. Murch, T. Jolly, J Taylor, E. Dowding, G. Hancock, R. P. Edwards, John Rainey, J. Soden, and T. W. Saunders. It was also decided that holders of twenty shares should be entitled to a free admission for life to self or nominee, and that holders of fifty shares should be entitled to the same privileges, or a yearly transferable free admission.

In August the plans sent in were examined for selection by a committee consisting of the directors, aided by seven gentlemen from the former Managing Committee, and Mr. Chute. There were five plans, or rather six, for one architect sent in two, and they were each distinguished by a motto. The final order in which they were placed was as follows : — Mr. C. J. Phipps, Bath and London (selected), motto, "Midsummer Night's Dream ;" Mr. W. J. Green, Bath and London (twenty guinea premium), "Invidiam virtute vincam ;" Mr.

WILSON BARRETT.

C. Hansom, Clifton (ten guinea premium), "Labor omnia vincit;" Major C. E. Davis, city architect, "Much Ado About Nothing ;" and Messrs Finch, Hill and Parailo, London, "Britannia." The method of procedure by which the committee arrived at this decision came in for some adverse criticism, but the selection met with general satisfaction, and the work was speedily in hand, tenders being accepted in September, which were to be completed in five months.

One of the principal features in Mr. Green's plan was an iron stage and the greater introduction of iron in the building generally. All the plans were very meritorious, especially that of Major Davis, who had been to immense trouble not only in working out his design, but also in promoting the formation of the company, and whose plan was in several respects preferred by some to that accepted. Of Mr. Phipps's plan there is no occasion to say many words, for the present theatre is a standing proof of the ability and skill which he exercised in its construction. Since the erection of the Bath Theatre the name of Mr. Phipps has become very familiar in connection with theatre building, and it was his first theatre that brought him fame. The old theatre was looked upon as a model building, but it was far surpassed, alike in beauty and convenience, by the new erection ; the model of the former house was taken as a basis, and the old walls were greatly taken advantage of, and in such a manner as to add considerably to the safety of the building, for the corridors and staircases are really built outside the former theatre, and, therefore, are doubly secure. The important matter of exits was carefully considered, and great improvements were made upon the former arrangements, while the additional precautions since adopted by the directors render the building one of the safest in the Kingdom. There has happily been no panic experienced in the history of the present building, but there would be little to fear in such case, for the exits from all parts of the house are amply sufficient. The acoustics of the building are admirable, and there is no part of the house that has not a full view of the stage. The building lends itself to decoration, and this department being placed in very capable hands, the theatre presented a striking appearance on its opening night. Behind the curtain, as well as before, the building is a model of convenience ; the stage, which was constructed by Mr. Sloman, of Her Majesty's Theatre, is one of the largest in the country for the size of the theatre, and there is excellent accommodation in the matter of dressing rooms, &c.

It was announced early in December that Mr. Chute would be the lessee, and in that month he was made a presentation of plate by Bath friends as a token of sympathy for his loss in the fire, and of their esteem for the manner in which he had for so many years conducted the affairs of the theatre. At a largely attended meeting of share-holders held during December, it was reported that there was still a deficiency of £1,878 to be made up by means of fresh exertions, but the directors were very sanguine that this would be done, and even at the meeting, headed by Mr. George Butcher, several agreed to take additional shares, amounting in all to £550.

On Wednesday, the 4th March, 1863, the theatre was opened with a grand production of "Midsummer Night's Dream," which, it will be remembered, was the architect's motto. This was the date originally fixed upon for the opening night, and it was greatly to the credit of the various contractors that the building was prepared for the reception of an audience in so short a time. As a matter of fact, it was a very near shave, and it was even said that as the audience was coming in by the front doors the workpeople were going out at the back. There was a brilliant attendance, including, among other influential visitors, the Mayor (Mr. T. Barter), the Recorder (Mr. T. W. Saunders), the Master of the Ceremonies (Mr. W. L. Emerson), Lord and Lady Powlett, Sir C. and Lady Style, Sir Thomas Dancer, Sir Henry and Lady Bayly, Sir Vansittart and Lady Stonhouse, &c. Mr. Salmon was the first to receive a hearty welcome from the audience as he took his place in the orchestra, and when the curtain drew up and Miss Henrietta Hodson stepped forward as the Spirit of the Past to speak the first words of the appropriate dramatic prologue which had been written for the occasion by Mr. G. F. Powell, she was greeted with tumultuous cheering, several bouquets being thrown on the stage. It was most appropriate that Miss Hodson should speak the first words in the new theatre, for it

MISS ELLEN TERRY.

was she who, as "The Little Rebel," spoke the last words on the boards of the old one. There were persistent calls for Mr. Chute, who presently stepped forward leading on Mr. Phipps, and both were received with enthusiasm, the cheering lasting some minutes. All the various members of the company, particularly old favourites, were most heartily welcomed. After the prologue came the National Anthem, in which Miss Hodson, Miss Cruise, and Mr. E. Rignold took the leading vocal parts, and then the orchestra played Rossini's overture to " Guillhaume Tell," this being followed by Mendelssohn's charming overture to " Midsummer Night's Dream." It will be interesting to reproduce the playbill for this night, from which it will best be gathered what an excellent company Mr. Chute had brought together at that time, the subsequent career and reputation of several of those who took part in that night's performance testifying to the foresight displayed by the lessee in the selection of his companies :—

NEW THEATRE ROYAL, BATH.

FIRST NIGHT.

Lessee and Manager ...   . JAMES HENRY CHUTE.

Prices.—The following scale of Prices has been adopted for the opening night :—Dress Circle, 5s. ; Upper Circle, 3s. ; Pit and Amphitheatre (entrance in Beauford Square), 2s. ; Gallery (entrance in St. John's Place), 1s.

No Second Price.

The prices of Admission, after the first night, will be as follows :—Dress Circle, 4s. ; Second price, 2s. 6d. ; Upper Boxes, 2s. ; Second price, 1s. 6d. ; Pit, 1s. 6d. ; Second price, 1s. Amphitheatre (entrance in St. John's Place), 1s. Gallery, 6d. Private Boxes, 20s., 25s., 30s.

Box Office.—The Box Office, under the direction of Mr. Gifford, for a few days, will be at Mr. H. N. King's Photographic Establishment, 42, Milsom Street, the Proprietor having kindly placed his View Room at the service of the Manager.

Leader of the Band   ...   ... Mr. T. H. SALMON.
Stage Manager   ...   ... Mr. MARSHALL.
Scenic Artist ...   . Mr. G. GORDON.

DRAMATIC PROLOGUE.

Written expressly for the occasion by G. F. POWELL, Esq.
The Spirit of the Past, by Miss HENRIETTA HODSON.
The Spirit of the Future, by Miss ELLEN TERRY (her first appearance here).
The Spirit of the Hour (Lord Dundreary), by Mr. W. RIGNOLD.
The Spirit of the Times (Sensation), by Mr. A. WOOD.
The Spirit of Fashion, by Miss DESBOROUGH (her first appearance here).
Fortune, by Miss ELIZABETH BURTON.
Comedy, by Mr. CHARLES COGHLAN (his first appearance).
Tragedy, by Mr. GEORGE YATES (his first appearance).
Mr. CHUTE (Lessee and Manager), by Himself.

"GOD SAVE THE QUEEN,"
Verse and Chorus by the Company.
To be followed by Shakespere's

MIDSUMMER NIGHT'S DREAM,

As arranged for representation by Mr. CHARLES KEAN, and performed 150 nights at the Royal Princess's Theatre.

With entirely New Scenery, Costumes, Decorations, Appointments, Mechanical Appliances, and Mendelssohn's Music.
The Scenery by Mr. W. GORDON, Mr. GEORGE GORDON, Mr. GEO. PHILIPS, Mr. HORNE, and Assistants. The Machinery by Mr. HARWELL. The Costumes by Miss JARRETT and Assistants. The Appointments by Mr. PRITCHARD. The Action and Dances by Miss POWELL. The Music arranged by Mr. J. L. HATTON and Mr. SALMON.

Theseus (Prince of Athens) ... ... Mr. GEORGE RIGNOLD
Egeus (Father to Hermia) ... ... Mr. ROBERTSON
Lysander } in love with Hermia { Mr. WILLIAM RIGNOLD
Demetrius } { Mr. CHARLES COGHLAN
Philostrate (Master of the Revels to Theseus) ... Mr. BRUNEL
Quince (the Carpenter) ... ... Mr. MARSHALL
    (his first appearance these two years)
Snug (the Joiner) ... Mr. DOUGLAS GRAY
Bottom (the Weaver) ... ... Mr. A. WOOD
Flute (the Bellows-Mender) ... ... Mr. H. ANDREWS
Snout (the Tinker) ... ... Mr. MARCHANT
Starveling (the Tailor)... ... ... Mr. GIBSON
Hippolyta (Queen of the Amazons, betrothed to Theseus)
    Miss LOUISA THORNE (her first appearance in Bath)
Hermia (Daughter to Egeus, in love with Lysander) Miss ELIZABETH BURTON
Helena (in love with Demetrius) ... ... Miss DESBOROUGH
Oberon (King of the Fairies) ... ... Miss HENRIETTA HODSON
Titania (Queen of the Fairies) ... Miss ELLEN TERRY
Puck, or Robin Goodfellow (a Fairy) ... Master EDMUND MARSHALL
First Singing Fairy .. ... Miss M. CRUSE
Second Singing Fairy ... ... Miss MADGE ROBERTSON
Third Singing Fairy ... ... Miss F. DOUGLAS
Fairies who join in a Shadow Dance, Miss POWELL and her Pupils
Peablossom ... ... Miss ELLEN SEYMOUR
Moth ... ... Miss E. FRAILLY
Cobwebb ... Master F. MARSHALL
Mustard-seed... ... ... Miss I. MARSHALL
    Fairies :
DEMOISELLES MARGARETS, MONTAGUE, OWEN, FANNY MARSHALL, BULLOCK, VAUGHAN, CLARKE, A. CLARKE, GIBSON, MARCHANT, HOLMES, WOOTTON, &c.
    Other Fairies attending their King and Queen :
Misses SEYMOUR, C. WOOTTON, GOODYER, FRAILLY, E. FRAILLY, C. MARCHANT, F. MARCHANT, WATTS, &c.
    Characters in the Interlude performed by the Clowns :
Pyræmus, by Bottom ; Wall, by Snout ; Thisbe, by Flute ; Moonshine, by Starveling ; Lion, by Snug.
Attendants on Theseus and Hippolyta, Huntsman, Esquire, &c.
    The New Act Drop by Messrs. GRIEVE and TELBIN.
To conclude with the New and Laughable Farce, by J. WOOLER, Esq., called

MARRIAGE AT ANY PRICE.

Brownjohn Brown (of the Laburnums) ...   . Mr. MARSHALL
  Simon Gushington   ...   . Mr. WILLIAM RIGNOLD
    Tubs, Mr. GIBSON | Alick, Mr. WILSON
      Peter Peppercorn ⎫
      Jemima Ann   ⎬ Mr. A. WOOD
      Charley Bitt   ⎭
      Kate Gushington   ⎫
      Bob, Tiger   ⎬ Miss HENRIETTA HODSON
      Jemima, a Housemaid ⎭
    Alice, Niece to Brown   ...   ... Miss MADGE ROBERTSON
      Matilda Peppercorn   ...   Miss LOUISA THORNE

This, it may be mentioned, was Miss Ellen Terry's first appearance
in Bath. Notwithstanding the difficulties of the production, the performance passed off very successfully, and lavish praises were
bestowed upon the scenery and the efforts of the company, though the
hurried manner in which the play was produced may be gathered
from the fact that a portion of the scenery was painted after the play
began. At the conclusion, the lessee and the architect were again
called before the curtain and rewarded with enthusiastic cheering.
And so the new theatre was started upon its career.

MISS ADA CAVENDISH.

CHAPTER XXV.

CONCLUSION.

GREAT CHANGES—LESSEES—WELL-KNOWN NAMES—THE LAST
STOCK COMPANY—"OUR BOYS"—RE-DECORATION—A PUBLIC-
SPIRITED LESSEE.

 HE fortunes of the present theatre being a matter of
purely modern history, we do not propose to deal
with them further than to briefly indicate some of the
principal names with which its annals are studded.
As was the case during the latter years of the old
Beauford Square Theatre, fortune has proved very
fickle, and though when the building was first opened
she seemed to smile upon the venture, she has since severely frowned.
Various causes have combined to produce these frowns, which cannot
be wholly attributed either to the management or to the public. There
have been shortcomings on both sides ; not all of those who have
undertaken the conduct of the theatre have consistently striven to
encourage the patronage of the public, but, on the other hand, they
have been greatly discouraged in the support which has been given
them. At one time, indeed, it almost appeared as if Bath would be
without a theatre, or, rather, what is worse, possessing one, but that one
closed. Fortunately all that is now changed, the theatre is open
practically all the year round, it has recovered much of its former
prestige, and seems to have a prospect of a brilliant and prosperous
future. That it should ever be to the English stage what the Bath
Theatre was a century ago is scarcely probable, or even possible, since
the circumstances of the drama have so greatly changed ; the death of
the old stock companies and the perfection of the touring system have
completely altered the position of the provincial theatre. No stock
company or management would be equal to the constant production of
the latest London successes which the public now demands. This can
only be accomplished by the combination of individual efforts which
goes to make up the touring system, and instead of certain provincial
theatres being in themselves centres of theatrical life, and the starting
point of many a theatrical career, their boards are trodden every week
by new companies and fresh actors of varying capabilities. There are
many advantages and also disadvantages in this change, but the new
system is firmly established.

The lesseeship of the present theatre has undergone no less than seven changes in the twenty-seven years of its existence. As we have seen, Mr. J. H. Chute was its first lessee, conducting the Bath and Bristol Theatres simultaneously, but in May, 1868, he terminated his lease of the Bath Theatre in order to devote his undivided attention to his larger venture. He was succeeded by Mr. Horatio Nelson King, who, in addition to conducting a photographic business, aspired to dramatic authorship and the honours of a musical composer, but his connection with the theatre was short and not very merry, for when he retired in March, 1869, he was forced to complain of a very heavy

loss. The late Mr. William Duck, of "Our Boys" fame, then undertook the management, and continued as lessee until the end of the season 1874-75, being succeeded by Messrs. Brandon Ellis and Frank Kenyon, whose joint reign lasted only for a season, Mr. Frank Kenyon alone being the lessee during the season 1876-77. In the following season Mr. Frederick Neebe, of the Exeter Theatre, assumed the management, retaining also his control of the ill-fated theatre in the Devonshire capital. His lesseeship commenced under favourable appearances, and for a while was fairly successful, but by the time he gave his farewell performances in Whit-week, 1884, he had become involved in considerable difficulties. A new lessee was found in Mr. Frank Emery, of the Prince of Wales's Theatre, Liverpool—who was not altogether a stranger to the city, having been acting manager to Captain Disney Roebuck's United Service Company, which played at the Bath Theatre in 1870—but he only occupied that position for one season, and the prospects of the house were then at a very low ebb indeed. At this point Mr. William Lewis, a private citizen who had always taken a great interest

From a Photo by]   *[London Stereoscopic Co.*
J. L. TOOLE.

in the theatre, and for many years was one of its directors, resigned
that office, and to relieve the board, who had no prospective tenant,
offered at his own risk to carry on the management till the end of the
financial year. This was attended with such conspicuous success that
at the end of the period he became the permanent lessee, and for the
result it is only necessary to point to the fact that, with the exception
of a vacation of five or
six weeks in the height of
summer, the house is open
all the year round, and
the public are favoured
with early productions of
all the principal London
successes.

In looking over the
names of those who have
visited Bath under the
touring system we come
across many well-known
in connection with the
modern drama, of which
the following are, perhaps,
the foremost. In the first
place, there is that gifted
actor, Henry Irving, who,
while he was yet ascending
the ladder to fame, twice
visited Bath, the first
occasion being for three
nights in September, 1867,
when he played with Miss
Herbert's St. James's
Company, appearing as
Joseph Surface, Capt.
Absolute and Young
Marlow, and the second
in August, 1871, when he
appeared as Digby Grant,
in the "Two Roses."
Ellen and Kate Terry

WM. FARREN, JUN.

visited Bath after they had left Mr. Chute's company, and so
did Marie Wilton (Mrs. Bancroft) ; Hermann Vezin, the well-known
Sothern, and Madame Ristori each made a first appearance in
Bath in the season of 1863-64, Sydney Bancroft appeared in
1865, as did Miss Bateman ; in 1866 67 we find the evergreen J. L.
Toole, Jefferson, Ada Cavendish, and Miss Siddons (Mrs. Scott

Siddons), great granddaughter of the renowned Siddons, and in
1867-68, Barry Sullivan and Madame Patey.   The great Vance was
here in May, 1870, and Edward Terry in the preceding November,
while in October, 1870, Wilson Barrett made his first appearance in
a company conducted by Miss Heath, appearing again in November,
1873 (in which year Lionel Brough also appeared), and in October,
1887, upon which occasion he was entertained at a luncheon at the
Grand Hotel by several gentlemen interested in the drama, and presented with a handsome silver salver.   The first visit of the Carl
Rosa Company was on the 15th November, 1873, and in the following
year we find the names of John Coleman and Miss Helen Barry.
Among other names we find Charles Collette, Shiel Barry, Lytton
Sothern, W. S. Penley, William Farren, jun., Kate Santley, Minnie
Palmer, Kate Vaughan, Laura Villiers, Lady Monckton, Miss Fortescue;
and of those who appeared in the former theatre, Charles Kean, Charles
Dillon, Charles J. Mathews and Sims Reeves.   Of course this does
not pretend to be a complete list, but it mentions the principal names,
most of whom have paid the city more than one visit, some very many.
     The last stock company was under Mr. Neebe's management, the
nearest approach subsequently being the companies which have been
brought together for the purposes of pantomime productions.   It will
not be without interest to recall a few names of those who were
included in these companies.   Going back to Mr. Chute's lesseeship,
in addition to those given in the preceding chapter, there were Messrs.
Arthur Wood, G. Yates, Barker, Rouse, Arnott, Peel, F. Buckstone,
G. Temple, and W. Elliott ; the Misses Fanny and Carlotta Addison,
Jane and Susan Rignold, Kate Terry and Jenny Lemoine.   At later
dates the Bath Theatre had the services of Messrs. Chas. Dornton,
Leonard Boyne, Mark Moss Mellor, Walter Fisher, Henry Bracy, E.
J. Lonnen, E. W. Royce, Compton Coutts, T. C. Valentine, G. W.
Harris (subsequently lessee of the Shakespeare Theatre, Liverpool),
and Alfred Nelson (at present connected with the Guildhall School
of Music) ; the Misses Lottie Venne, Elise Holt, Millie De Vere,
Chippendale, &c.
     Naturally the twenty-seven years' existence of the theatre has
yielded a variety of interesting incidents, to one of which a reference
must be made, as it stands out very prominently among the note-
worthy performances in the present building—namely, the production
of " Our Boys." The extraordinary success attained by Mr. H. J.
Byron's comedy is phenomenal in the history of the drama, and it was
at Bath that the first performance out of London was given on Easter
Monday, the 29th March, 1875, after the provincial rights had been
purchased by the then lessee, Mr. William Duck.   The reception
given to the piece was sufficient to cheer the heart of any manager,
and " Our Boys " was launched on its eventful career amid abundant
enthusiasm and good wishes.   Four years later (it had been played in

Bath more than once in the meantime), on the 5th February, 1879, there was again a crowded house, very similar to those which witnessed the first performances, only this was commemorative of the 1,000th night. After the performance an address, written for the occasion by Mr. H. J. Byron, was delivered by Mr. E. W. Garden, and subsequently Mr. Duck entertained the company and some friends at the Grand Hotel, when all the members of "Our Boys" were presented by him with a handsome gold locket, those presented to Mrs. Egan and Miss Vernon, who had been members of the company continuously from the first, being set with diamonds. But the piece was far from being near the end of its career, and the 2,000th night was also celebrated at the Bath theatre, a thing unprecedented in the annals of the stage.

While this volume has been in the press an extensive work of re-decoration, alterations and additions has been in progress at the Theatre, under the direction of its architect, Mr. C. J. Phipps, F.S.A. Some seventeen

W. S. PENLEY (The Private Secretary).

years had elapsed since a similar work was carried out, and even then it was not on such a large and liberal scale as that disclosed to view when the house re-opened on August 29th, 1892. The lessee, Mr. William Lewis, whose energy and public spirit have been the means of raising the Theatre from the low level to which it had sunk after the failures of successive lessees, to the rank of a first

N

class provincial theatre, has borne himself the large expense incurred
in the work that has been so successfully carried out, at the same
time practically illustrating his interest in the Theatre, and his faith
in its establishment as the principal amusement of the city, by taking
it on a long lease at an increased rental. A brief description of the
scheme of redecoration designed by Mr. Phipps, will not be out of
place. The ceiling is a design of light Louis Seize, consisting of
panels of cream, light blue and gold, with ovals containing cupids,
floral and other ornaments, the four large spandrils having trophies of
musical instruments boldly painted on them. The large proscenium
soffit is also panelled in the prevailing tones of colour, cream white,
pale blue, yellow, crimson and gold. In the same manner the fronts
of the upper tier of boxes and the gallery are painted, enriched with
gilding, the front of the lower tier being treated in rather a heavier
style of colouring to give a base for the whole scheme, while
the proscenium columns are covered with a raised material and
gilded solid. The private boxes are decorated in a neutral blue
tint, and the walls forming the back of the circles with a rose
red, which throws up the delicate shades of the fronts and other
portions of the auditorium, producing a very rich and artistic effect.
The private boxes, too, are hung with curtains in rose-coloured satin
in keeping with the decorations, which, taken altogether, are of a
character calculated to satisfy the most fastidious taste, while impart-
ing to the house that attractiveness and brightness so essential in
a building devoted to the purposes of public amusement. The Pit seats
have also been comfortably upholstered. The work is carried beyond
the auditorium, all the corridors, the stairs, and the entrance hall
having been entirely redecorated in a simple but tasteful manner, the
walls being salmon colour, with a rich red dado and border, the entrance
Vestibule being also stencilled and ornamented in warm tones, while
a great improvement has been effected by the floor being laid in
Mosaic, which is also carried through the corridor to the stairs leading
to the Dress Circle. The heavy, and by no means ornamental, entrance
doors have been replaced by polished teak doors with plate-glass
panels, and similar swing doors in the corridor beyond have been
hung in place of the old-fashioned red baize doors formerly existing.
The work of redecoration has been extended behind the curtain,
where all the dressing-rooms have been tastefully painted, and
both behind and before the curtain the sanitary appliances
have been entirely replaced by new apparatus of the latest and
most approved pattern — particularly in the dressing-rooms, thus
setting a worthy example to very many theatres, both metropolitan
and provincial. While the house may now be reckoned among
the handsomest in the provinces, it is also one of the safest and most
complete from a structural point of view. We have already alluded to
alterations which have recently been effected with the object of

increasing the safety of the building in the event of an emergency, additional means of exit being provided, in particular, a new and convenient staircase leading from the gallery to the street, so that the emptying of the house, even when it is crowded, is a matter of only two or three minutes.

WILLIAM LEWIS.

Our task is now at an end, and, having chronicled the varying fortunes of the Bath stage down to the present day, it is a matter of great satisfaction to know that, after all its vicissitudes, we have to take leave of it while it is enjoying a condition of renewed prosperity, and with every prospect of a successful career in the future. There is no city apart from the Metropolis which has so much cause to be proud of its theatre; and, in conclusion, we can but express the hope that the public of Bath will be ever mindful of its brilliant history attaching to this institution, and will never let it sink into insignificance or decay.

THE END.

TURNER BROS.,

33, Milsom Street, BATH,

NAVAL, MILITARY & DIPLOMATIC UNIFORMS,

TAILORS, BREECHES MAKERS, AND SPORTING OUTFITTERS.

RIDING HABITS, GOWNS, &c.

LEATHER BREECHES, LEGGINGS, COATS, WAISTCOATS
AND LADIES' SKIRTS.

DRESS SUITS, Speciality.

TELEGRAMS: "TURNERS, BATH."

THE

OLD CURIOSITY SHOP,

1, WOOD STREET,

Corner of Queen Square, BATH,

And 42, *PARK STREET, BRISTOL.*

MRS. P. J. ELLIOTT

DEALER IN

Antique Silver & Jewellery,

OLD PAINTINGS,

BARTELOZZI & OTHER ENGRAVINGS,

ANTIQUE CHINA,   MINIATURES ON IVORY,

OLD FANS AND LACE,

CARVED OAK AND CHIPPENDALE FURNITURE,

RARE OLD BOOKS.

Any of the above Bought or Taken in Exchange.

Lansdown Grove Hotel, Bath.

THIS Hotel stands at an elevation of 400 feet above sea level in its own beautifully wooded grounds, replete with the advantages of a Town and Country Residence combined.

Air dry and bracing. Sheltered from north and east. Splendid views of the surrounding country. Royal Victoria Park, Assembly Rooms, Pump Room, and Roman Baths within easy distance.

Tennis Lawns and Billiards.

Omnibus to and from the City and Hot Mineral Baths, Free of Charge to Visitors staying at Hotel. Good Stabling.

CO-OPERATIVE
CASH SYSTEM,
46. Milsom Street, BATH.

For the distribution of High-Class GROCERIES,
WINES, SPIRITS, ALES, PATENT MEDICINES,
GRAPES, MELONS, TOMATOES, BANANAS, &c.,
at Prices arranged for the benefit cf Cash Purchasers.

---

*Cheques should be crossed "National Bank of Wales,"
and made payable to Wm. Peach.*

WILLIAM PEACH,
46, *MILSOM STREET*,
BATH.

CITY.

Special arrangements are made for the Daily Collection
and Delivery of Orders, and in such cases Accounts are
rendered Weekly.

COUNTRY.

Orders Collected Fortnightly and Delivered Free
by Own Vans.

Sole Agents for the ALES of
WORTHINGTON & COMPY., Burton-on-Trent.
DEVENISH & COMPY., Weymouth.

WILLIAM HILL,

UMBRELLA & PARASOL MANUFACTURER,

Walking-Stick and Cane Merchant.

---

*Patentee of the Celebrated " Lock-rib"
Umbrellas.*

18, NEW BOND STREET, BATH.

THE BATH BREWERY
LIMITED.

EXHIBITION
ALES.

These beautiful Ales, so light and elegant, so agreeable to the palate and so nutritious to the system, are now in fine condition.

In Casks of all Sizes, from 10d. to 1|8 per Gallon.

WINE AND SPIRIT MERCHANTS.

DAVIES & JOHN'S
COCA WINE,
Tonic and Restorative.

Relieves Depression, Stimulates Appetite, and Gives Tone to the whole System.

COCA ERYTHROXYLON.—The medical properties of this plant are known as being Tonic and highly restorative. In South America at the present time the annual consumption of leaves cannot fall short of a hundred million pounds (vide *Canadian Pharm. Journal*, Aug., 1887); a fact in itself sufficiently suggestive and conclusive : " Coca has for ages been to the Indian Tribes an incalculable blessing." Sir R. Christison, writes : "Coca removes extreme fatigue and prevents it, hunger and thirst are suspended, but eventually appetite and digestion are unaffected. It has no effect on the mental faculties, as far as my own trials and other observations go, except liberating them from the dullness and drowsiness which follow great bodily fatigue."

This Wine contains the entire medicinal virtues of the plant, and presents them in a palatable and agreeable form.

To Persons of sedentary occupations it is invaluable as its recuperative properties are unique.

DOSE—ONE WINE-GLASSFUL TWICE OR THREE TIMES A DAY.

PREPARED AT

The Bath Pharmacy and Laboratory,
15, OLD BOND STREET, BATH.
ESTABLISHED 1786.

Sold in Imperial Pint Bottles, 3/6 ; per Dozen, 36/-
SUPPLIED IN PORT, SHERRY, BURGUNDY AND MARSALA

MISS PHILLPUT,
Ladies' & Children's Outfitter
8½, BARTLETT STREET, BATH.

THE

Newmarket Corset.

Dresses will fit to perfection if worn over these Corsets, which afford moreover a degree of comfort and support most grateful to the wearer.

DRESSING GOWNS
in large variety.

BABY LAYETTES.

Wedding and India Trousseau receive personal and prompt attention

ORDERS BY POST RECEIVE CAREFUL ATTENTION.

The Dress Making Department is under competent Management.

THE BATH
AND
Somersetshire Dairy Co.
LIMITED.

DAIRIES:

Bladud, Brock Street, Quiet Street,
Oldfield Park, Weston & Batheaston.

VISITORS to BATH are Invited to DAILY INSPECTION of MODEL WORKING DAIRY on BLADUD BUILDINGS, 10 a.m. to 1 p.m.

OPERATIONS—Mechanical Separation of Cream.
Butter Churning by Steam Power.
Original Bath Cream Cheese.
Old-Fashioned Bath Cheese, &c.

EACH FARM UNDER MEDICAL SUPERVISION.
All Milk Tested before Delivery.
Special ALDERNEY and JERSEY COWS for INFANTS and INVALIDS.
ALL THE LATEST MILK SPECIALITIES.
WHEY, Sweet BUTTER-MILK DAILY.
BUTTER without Salt where required, or supplied in the Grain direct from the Churns.

WHOLESALE MILK AND BUTTER MERCHANTS.

BATH CITY HOUSE.

FAMILY AND

Furnishing Drapers

Silk Mercers, Costumiers, Milliners,
Hosiers & Carpet Warehousemen,

𝕷𝖆𝖉𝖎𝖊𝖘' 𝖆𝖓𝖉 𝕮𝖍𝖎𝖑𝖉𝖗𝖊𝖓'𝖘 𝕺𝖚𝖙𝖋𝖎𝖙𝖙𝖊𝖗𝖘.

F. EALAND & Co.

**Large Showrooms replete with all the Latest
Novelties in**

Mantles, Capes and Jackets,

FRENCH & ENGLISH MILLINERY,

Costumes, Jerseys, &c., &c.

The Dress and Mantle-making Departments are under competent
and skilful Costumiers, and everything possible is done to
ensure good style and perfect fit, at moderate charges.

1, 2, 3, 4, New Bond Street
and 2, Northgate Street, } **BATH.**

CATER, STOFFELL & FORTT

The Grocers.

DEPARTMENTS:

GROCERIES of the Finest Description.

PROVISIONS from the most Celebrated Curers of England, Germany and France.

STATIONERY direct from the Manufacturers at First Cost.

IRONMONGERY — Spacious Showrooms contain an immense variety of Cutlery, Electro, Silver, Domestic Machines, Baths, &c., from the most noted Manufacturers.

DRUG AND DISPENSING—-

This Department is entirely under the care of Mr. A. J. WHITE, A.P.S., from the Army and Navy Stores.

Customers may rely upon getting their PRESCRIPTIONS Dispensed with Accuracy at half the USUAL CHARGES.

All the above are being Offered at CASH PRICES, which means a saving of from 20 to 30 PER CENT.

20 & 27, High Street,
And 8, Margaret's Bdgs.,
BATH.